THE ONLY ONE

MELODY GRACE

MELODY GRACE BOOKS

Thank you for reading!
Sweetbriar Cove is a new series for me, set in a charming small town on Cape Cod.
I have tons of happy memories of New England, and it was so much fun inventing the town - and all its inhabitants. Brooke, the heroine of The Only One, winds up in Sweetbriar by accident, but soon fall for its small-town charm - and the handsome bartender, Riley.

I hope you enjoy reading The Only One as much as I've enjoyed writing it. So pack your sunscreen, take a mini-vacation, and enjoy a taste of summer, wherever you are.
xo Melody

~

ALSO BY MELODY GRACE:

The Dirty Dancing Series

The Promise

Welcome to Sweetbriar Cove: the small town where happily-ever-after is guaranteed.

Book Three
The Only One

Brooke Delancey is looking for a fresh start. She's packed up her heartbreak and traded her old life for a new beginning, managing the prettiest hotel on Cape Cod. She swears this time will be different: no drama, no distractions, and definitely no heart-stopping kisses with a handsome stranger. Which is exactly what she finds the night she meets Riley Ford.

Riley is gorgeous, charming... and intrigued by the buttoned-up blonde whose kisses are anything but restrained. He knows a thing or two about starting over, and he's convinced a little fun is exactly what Brooke needs to put the past behind her. And he knows exactly the man for the job...

With a tempting offer like that, Brooke can't help but try another kiss - or two, or three. But as the chemistry gets hotter, and their connection deepens, Brooke and Riley will discover that building a new future means reckoning with the past.

Can two unlikely hearts take a chance on a new tomorrow? Or will their sparks burn out with the end of summer in Sweetbriar Cove? Find out in the sweet and sexy new read from New York Times bestselling author Melody Grace!

The Sweetbriar Cove Series:
1. Meant to Be

*B*rooke Delancey needed to trust her instincts.

She knew that plan hadn't exactly worked out for her so far—the wreckage of her romantic life was plenty evidence of that—but her luck had to change sometime, right? Intuition, sixth sense: it was supposed to be wired into her DNA, a gift from her ancestors to avoid getting snapped up by a grizzly at the watering hole, or picking a fight with a caveman who had a bigger club.

Or, in this case, agreeing to a blind date she knew from the start was doomed.

"He's perfectly nice," her new friend Eliza had promised. "He dated my sister for a while, until it fizzled out. No crazy exes, no secret My Little Pony fetish, no baggage at all."

That made one of them, at least.

"Who knows?" Eliza had urged. "You might feel a spark."

So even though Brooke's gut was telling her that blind dates—dates of any kind—were a bad idea, she decided to give it a try. After all, she'd moved to Cape Cod over four months ago, and her life still consisted of her work managing the hotel, running errands, and evenings alone watching *The Great British Bake Off* on TV.

Who knew? Maybe perfectly-nice-Doug was really the man of her dreams, and tonight was the start of a beautiful love affair. But now, sitting across the table, listening to him explain —in *great* detail—about the mating habits of spider crabs, Brooke thought longingly of her comfy little sofa and that solitary glass of wine.

At least Netflix occasionally asked if you were still watching, instead of talking for an hour without a break.

"Did you know there are Japanese spider crabs that can span over fifteen feet?" Doug pushed his glasses up his nose, fixing Brooke with an earnest expression. "They're known to live up to a hundred years."

"Wow." Brooke nodded. "That's . . . an interesting job you have there."

"Job? Oh no, I work with *fresh*water crustaceans!" Doug exclaimed, chortling. "This research into saltwater species is just for fun."

Crabs, fun? Brooke tried not to laugh.

At least they were the edible kind.

As Doug launched into another monologue, Brooke tried to stay positive. He was clearly passionate about his hobbies, that was something, and he'd been punctual—already waiting at a table in the corner when she'd arrived. Sure, it was because he liked to clean everything down with the antiseptic wipes he carried in a little plastic pouch, but hygiene was always a good thing.

Right?

Brooke stifled a sigh. Who was she kidding? This date was a

disaster. Which was probably a good thing, since she had no business getting involved with anyone right now. Her broken heart was mending, but she was still a long way from peeling off the Band-Aid just yet.

She sipped her drink and let him talk, her attention wandering around the bar. It was one of the casual waterfront places in Provincetown, the largest community on the Cape, and tonight it was packed with a crowd of tourists and summer people, fresh from a day on the beach. They were well into the summer season now, and people came from all over, drawn to the gorgeous beaches, laid-back pace, and small-town New England charm. Brooke had spent her life as a city girl, with the hum of traffic and electric pace, but even she could see the appeal of waking up to those wide-open blue skies, and the expanse of sparkling ocean, and—

Him.

Her eyes stopped wandering, drawn to the guy waiting by the bar. He was tall and broad-shouldered, with messy blonde hair, his skin tanned to a golden bronze against his casual white T-shirt and jeans. He looked like he'd just stepped off the beach, giving an easy-going grin to the bartender as he took a sip of his beer and turned to scan the room.

His eyes locked onto Brooke's, catching her gaze. He flashed her a smile, and just like that, Brooke's stomach did a slow pirouette.

She looked away, her cheeks flushing. She knew she shouldn't stare, it was too obvious in a place like this, but she couldn't resist: she had to glance back.

He was still watching her. And still just as gorgeous as five seconds ago. This time, he gave her a wink, and one of those nods that almost seemed to beckon her over.

"What about you?"

Brooke snapped her head around. "Hmm?"

"I asked, what about you?" Doug asked. "What brought you to the Cape?"

Brooke cleared her throat. What was she playing at, drooling over some other guy in the middle of a date? "I moved here for work," she said quickly. "I manage a small boutique hotel just outside of town. The Sandy Lane Hotel."

Doug furrowed his brow. "I think I know that one. A friend of mine got married there, a couple of years ago. Great views."

"Yes, it's right on the water." Brooke nodded. "I'm hoping to expand that side of things, and make it a real venue for ceremonies and events."

Most hotels steered clear of weddings; they were just too much trouble. Tensions ran too high, tempers frayed, and invariably someone wound up crying over the party favors because the roses were blush pink instead of apricot. But with a little work, they could also mean big business, especially now that every bride-to-be plastered photos of her special day online. Even a small venue out of town could be booked solid for months with the right strategy—which was exactly what Brooke was hoping to achieve in her new position.

"Eliza mentioned you just moved from Chicago," Doug said. "What brought you all this way?"

"Oh, you know, time for a change," she said lightly, and took a quick sip of her wine. "I wanted a different pace. New challenges."

And to put as much distance between her and her old life as possible. A thousand miles, to be exact.

"I totally relate." Doug smiled. "I just got accepted for a research fellowship. I'll be studying the mating habits of the *grapsus grapsus* crab. We should try some!" he declared suddenly. "Not grapsus, of course, but they have some excellent Dungeness on the menu."

"I can't," Brooke said apologetically. "I'm allergic."

Doug froze. "To shellfish?"

"Yes. Can't even go near them. I break out in hives all over, not a pretty sight."

Doug frowned. "Oh. Well. That changes everything."

"It does?" Brooke tried not to laugh.

"Shellfish is very important to me." Doug looked stricken. "I'm not sure I could have a relationship with someone who didn't support my passion."

Brooke couldn't keep it together any longer. She quickly pushed back her chair.

"Excuse me. I'll be right back."

She ducked through the busy crowd to the restrooms. Once the door swung shut behind her, she could finally let out the snort of laughter she'd been holding in all night.

"Crabs," she said aloud in disbelief, just as the bathroom stall swung open. Another woman emerged and caught her laughing.

"Sorry," Brooke explained. "My date . . ."

The woman winced. "I know a good doctor," she said, helpful, but that just made Brooke giggle harder.

"No, not that kind of crabs. But thanks!"

The woman gave her a weird look and exited the bathroom, and Brooke tried to pull herself together.

Poor Doug. It wasn't his fault. This was clearly the universe's way of reminding her that when it came to love, she was still radioactive.

Steer clear: cleanup could take another hundred years.

But glancing at her reflection in the mirror, Brooke had to admit, she hadn't exactly stacked the deck in her favor. She'd come straight from work, so she was still wearing a crisp button-down shirt and pencil skirt; her hair pulled back in its usual neat French braid. It was a look that said, "Where are the quarterly projections?" not, "Ravish me, darling." Still, at least she hadn't spent all afternoon primping for Doug's sake. She would finish up her drink, close up the tab, and be home in time to see if bread week got the better of the bakers on TV.

Brooke was heading for the door when her phone buzzed in her purse. Just like that, her stomach dropped. She couldn't help it. She'd changed her number—even tossed her SIM card ceremoniously out of the car window, somewhere between Toledo and Cleveland—but still she flinched with every call, expecting to see that familiar number on the caller ID. Her ex could charm anyone; getting hold of her new number would be no problem at all.

She braced herself and checked the message. To her relief, was just Eliza, checking in on the date.

Well?!

You owe me a drink, Brooke texted back.

That was an understatement. After learning everything there was to know about crabs, she deserved a bottle, but back outside, she found their table empty. She could see Doug on the patio, talking on his phone, so she made her way to the bar instead. It was even more packed than when she'd arrived, and she spent a couple of minutes trying in vain to flag down the bartender—who seemed oblivious to anyone who wasn't tall, ripped, and handsome.

"Let me."

A voice came from behind her, and then the Adonis from before was leaning in beside her at the bar.

Brooke caught her breath. Up close, he was just as

gorgeous; those tanned biceps straining at the fabric of his frayed white T-shirt, and three-day stubble rough on his jaw.

She tried not to stare. Usually, the scruffy, rumpled thing didn't do it for her—she preferred a man in a suit, or crisp button-down—but there was no denying this guy's appeal. Or the fact he was looking at Brooke with a tempting gleam in his blue eyes.

"I wondered when you'd come say hello," he teased. "Couldn't resist, huh?"

Brooke didn't have a chance to protest before the bartender came rushing over.

"What can I get you?" he asked, all eyes on the man beside her.

"Another beer for me, and . . . ?" The Adonis raised his eyebrows at Brooke.

"Just my check, thanks. The table in the corner."

"Leaving already?" Adonis asked, arching an eyebrow. "The fun's just getting started."

"Not for me," Brooke replied.

He grinned. "Blind date?"

"How did you guess?"

"He doesn't look like your type."

"Looks aren't everything," she said, feeling strangely defensive. It wasn't poor Doug's fault that he hadn't been born with the genes of a Hemsworth brother, and a smile like James Dean. "He's fascinating."

"I'm sure." The Adonis just grinned, like he didn't believe her for a moment. "I'm Riley, by the way."

A woman appeared, snaking through the crowd to rest a hand on his arm. She was slim and gorgeous, with a mane of dark hair and at least five inches of flat, tanned stomach bared between the waist of her gauzy skirt and the hem of her cropped bandeau top. "Hey babe," she cooed, ignoring Brooke completely. "The girls are meeting at this new raw food bar down the street. Did you want to come with? It's supposed to be *so* healthful."

"Nah, I'm good," Riley drawled, his hand resting on her hip. "You go have fun, and call me after. Leave some room for dessert," he added with a wink.

"Only if it's gluten-free," the woman frowned, his innuendo flying way over her glossy head. "You know I'm detoxing right now." She kissed him lightly on the cheek and sashayed away.

Brooke arched an eyebrow. "Looks aren't everything, huh?"

Riley smirked. "She's fascinating," he quipped, and Brooke had to laugh at that.

"So, do you want to tell him or should I?" he asked, nodding to where Doug was pacing on the terrace, still talking on his cellphone.

Brooke paused. "Tell him what?"

"That you're coming home with me."

Brooke snorted in surprise. From any other man, maybe a line like that would have come across as creepy, but this guy had such a cheerful attitude that it seemed charming instead.

Charming, and arrogant, and infuriatingly sexy.

"What about your dessert date?" she asked, amused.

"She'll live. Besides, I'm in the mood for ice cream. Too many calories for her."

"But not for me?" Brooke teased.

"You look like a woman who knows how to enjoy herself," he said. "And I'm exactly the man to help with that."

Brooke laughed. "You're pretty full of yourself, you know that?"

"I'm told. Frequently." He grinned. "Luckily, I've got the goods to back it up."

"Sure you do."

"So, how about it?" Riley gave her a lazy look from head to toe that somehow did something wicked to Brooke's insides. "My place is nearby."

She blinked. "Wait. You're serious?"

"Rarely." He grinned. "But about this? Absolutely."

"But . . . that's ridiculous!" she spluttered, suddenly feeling flushed. "You don't even know me!"

"And this would be an excellent chance to work on that."

He was still watching her with that molten smile. Brooke shivered, feeling her skin prickle with anticipation. That was a dangerous smile. Smooth as whiskey, with twice the kick.

And she already wanted a taste.

Brooke caught herself. "Thanks for the offer, but no."

"Too bad." Riley didn't seem heartbroken by her rejection. In fact, his smile hadn't slipped at all. "Can I ask why not?"

"Let's just say I'm on a diet," she replied.

Abstaining from sexy men for the foreseeable future.

"Now that's a shame," he drawled. "Sometimes you just need a little . . . indulgence in your life."

Brooke flushed. He was looking at her like she was covered in whipped cream with a cherry on top. She couldn't remember the last time a man had looked at her like that, so blatant and sexual. Not since—

Archer.

She stopped. The memory of the man she'd left back in Chicago was like a bucket of ice water, jolting her back to reality. "Thanks, but no," she said shortly. The bartender brought her credit card, and she scribbled her signature on the slip. "Enjoy your night," she said, avoiding Riley's gaze, and quickly crossed the room back to her date.

Doug was still pacing on the patio. "Sorry, it's work," he

said, cupping his hand over the phone. "The salinity levels are haywire at the lab."

"That's OK, I'm going to head home," Brooke said, pulling on her jacket. The sooner she got a safe distance from Riley and his molten smile, the better. "Good luck with your crabs!"

2

rooke slipped through the crowd and exited into the cool twilight breeze. The bar was set down an alleyway, right on the waterfront, and she took a moment to breathe in the salty tang. She still felt flushed, her heartbeat racing from that odd encounter at the bar, and she couldn't help but think of Riley's brazen invitation—and the suggestion gleaming in his eyes.

What would it be like to say yes?

Brooke shook her head. Going home with a complete stranger was madness—and the last thing she needed in her life right now. She'd uprooted her life and moved cross-country to leave all her romantic drama behind, not dive headfirst into something new.

She heard the door swing open behind her, and a rush of music and laughter coming from inside.

"Having second thoughts?"

She recognized the voice before she even turned. It was Riley again, just stepping outside.

"Are you following me?" Brooke narrowed her eyes.

"Nope, just heading out for the night." He held up his hands in innocence. "I've got plans, remember?"

"Right." Brooke relaxed. "Gluten-free dessert."

He chuckled. "You don't approve."

"It's none of my business." Brooke shrugged, trying to seem nonchalant even as her pulse kicked, having him near again. "You can eat whatever you like."

The words were out before she realized just how dirty they could be. Riley grinned wider. Brooke flushed. "You know what I mean!"

"Oh, I do."

She bet he did.

Brooke looked away. "I'm just going . . ." She gestured towards the street, her face still burning. He nodded, but for some reason, she didn't take a single step.

What was it about this guy that kept drawing her in? He was just another handsome player, she knew his type, but still, he was igniting something in her bloodstream that Brooke had almost forgotten how it felt.

Hot and restless, wanting more.

"It's OK, you know." Almost as if he was reading her mind, the man took a step closer.

"What is?" Brooke asked, her heart beating faster as he approached.

"That you want me."

She tried to roll her eyes, but Brooke knew she wasn't fooling anyone. Especially not the man who was now standing just inches away, close enough for her to feel the heat from his body, and see the wicked gleam in his gaze.

"It's not rational," he said softly, his voice a low, sexy drawl.

"There's no pro/con list, or reasons why. It's elemental. Just simple chemistry in the end."

"You're saying we have no control?" Brooke managed to reply, even as her own grip on it felt very far away—and getting further with every second.

"Sure we do," he replied, his lips curving in a tempting grin. "But why do you want control so bad? You know what your body needs. Don't you want to know how it would feel to just . . . give in?"

Brooke shivered. Even though she knew it was just another line from a guy who'd probably told it to a million girls before, she couldn't help the way her pulse kicked at his seductive words —or the surge of heat that flooded through her as he reached out and gently brushed a stray lock of hair from her cheek.

His touch burned through her, and Brooke felt every nerve in her body spark to life again.

God, she wanted him.

The realization made her stomach twist with shame. She knew how dangerous this desire could be. She should have learned her lesson by now, but still, here she was, ready to make the same mistakes all over again.

Leaping first, head-long into passion, not thinking she would ever hit the ground.

"I should go," she said, but still, her feet didn't move.

"OK," he replied, his gaze not wavering.

"Right." Brooke swallowed. She'd thought his eyes were blue, but out here in the shadows, they were more a flinty grey. Watching her, unwavering, like he could see the struggle whirling in her mind.

Riley took another step closer. Now he was touching her, his torso just barely grazing hers, hot and solid. Brooke felt herself sway closer, drawn by some invisible force. She hated to admit it, but he was right.

This didn't make any sense, but God, it felt like the most natural thing in the world for him to close the distance between them, take her face in his hands, and kiss her like she'd been wanting ever since the moment she first laid eyes on him across that crowded bar.

Hot, and slow, and achingly sensual. He teased her lips, easing them open as his tongue roved deeper, sliding into her mouth. The sensation shuddered through her, a jolt of desire that set her blood alight.

Damn, this man could *kiss*.

In an instant, Brooke gave up the fight. There was no use pretending she didn't want this too, not with her heart racing in her chest, and desire snaking through every inch of her, a sweet ache clawing between her thighs.

One kiss, she told herself. One kiss, and then she'd stay away from temptation. She'd learned her lesson.

What harm could one little kiss do?

She pulled him closer, her arms going up around his neck, her lips parting wider, kissing him deeper. She licked into his mouth, and felt him tense against her, the lean muscle of his stomach clenching at her boldness. Brooke felt a shiver of satisfaction. She was surprising him.

Good.

He wrapped his arms around her waist, and then before she knew what was happening, they were up against the wall, his body hot and hard, his lips demanding, teasing her, tasting her, the sensual slide making her moan out loud. Brooke's head spun with the heat of it all. She didn't recognize herself, but she didn't care; all that mattered was the feel of him against her, and the wicked things he was doing to her mouth.

He slid his hands over her body, possessive: the small of her back, the curve of her hips. Brooke found herself pressing closer, wishing they weren't separated by layers of clothing, so that she could explore the muscular planes of his body and feel his hands on her bare skin. Deeper and deeper, the kiss became an inferno. The world faded away, until Brooke forgot the past year of heartache, and the ball of guilt and shame that stayed knotted in her stomach; she forgot her inhibitions, and her solemn vow to keep her heart protected this time around.

She only wanted him.

More. *Now.*

Riley finally tore his mouth away with a ragged groan, kissing a blazing trail down the bare arch of her neck. Brooke shuddered to his touch, trapped deliciously between the solid planes of his body and the wall behind her. She could feel him, hard against her, and it just made her hotter, gasping for breath as his hands, and mouth, and wicked tongue roved across her body, taking her to heaven and back.

This was madness. This was bad news. This was—

"*Oh,*" Brooke moaned aloud as his hand skimmed across the swell of her breast. She pressed into his palm, already aching for more, but he teased her, gently skimming over her blouse until Brooke could hardly stand it. Those promises of self-control she'd made herself just a few moments before seemed like a distant dream.

Why settle for one kiss, when she could have a dozen?

And why stop there when this man seemed more than willing to make the pleasure last all night long?

Brooke opened her mouth, ready to give in to temptation, when the bar door swung open again and the sound of laughter and voices flooded out.

"You should have stopped me at that second margarita," a

woman exclaimed, her high-pitched voice piercing Brooke's haze of desire.

"Or third, or fourth," her friend giggled, their heels clattering on the sidewalk.

Brooke snapped back to reality.

What was she *doing*? Besides almost stripping naked in the back alley of some beachside bar.

Oh God. Brooke gulped. So much for making better choices!

The man with his mouth currently doing incredible things to her earlobe hadn't noticed they had company—or maybe he just didn't care. But Brooke did. She pulled away just in time, putting a precious few feet of space between them by the time the women stumbled past.

They disappeared out onto the street, and Brooke took an unsteady breath. Her heart was racing, and her knees felt weak. She didn't understand it. Since when could a kiss undo her like this?

"Where are you going?" Riley gave a lazy smile and reached for her again, but Brooke skittered back.

"I . . ." she started, her mind still scrambled. "I don't . . ."

Speak!

"I have to go." Brooke finally managed to get the words out. "This was . . . something."

She turned on her heel and started walking swiftly, before she did something really stupid, like invite him back to her place to ravish her until dawn. Part of her almost hoped he would come after her, but she made it to the street alone, no footsteps sounding behind her on the sidewalk.

Her car was parked right there by the curb. She quickly tumbled in behind the wheel and started the engine, driving away so fast her tires let out a squeal of protest. She managed to make it through the winding town streets and back onto the highway, the shoreline blurring into twilight strips of blue and hazy gold as she drove back down the coast.

She took a deep breath, and then another. The intoxicating mix of adrenaline and desire was fading with every mile, leaving a hollow feeling instead. The thought of the empty apartment waiting for her was no comfort, and for a moment she felt truly rootless, the distance between her and her old life stretching further than just the miles of empty roads.

She suddenly pulled off the highway, following a dirt road down to a deserted strip of beach. It was a beautiful spot, but they all were out here at this time, the last of the sunset fading over the horizon. She sat there in the driver's seat, watching the water turn from blue to grey to glinting midnight in the dark.

What was she doing?

The question echoed in her mind again, but this time, it wasn't about a hot stranger, or a kiss—however epic that kiss might have been. It was about everything. Her career, her life; Brooke couldn't believe that it was only a few months ago that she'd been back in Chicago, feeling like she finally had it all figured out. A job she loved at one of the most exclusive hotels in the city, and a man she was crazy about: it had all seemed so perfect.

Seemed being the right word.

Brooke sighed. She could still feel the echo of heartache, lingering there behind her ribcage.

God, what a fool she'd been.

She'd met Archer at work. He was technically her boss, brought in to audit and reorganize the hotel, but their late nights poring over occupancy rates had led to even later nights in the hotel bar, talking about everything under the sun.

Brooke had been smitten, the kind of butterflies-in-her-stomach crush she hadn't felt since high school. He was charismatic, smart, and well-traveled, but even so, she'd been cautious at first, not wanting to complicate her career. Archer didn't have any such reservations.

He pursued her with thrilling determination, showering her with flowers and steamy texts and sweet little gifts, until she happily believed every word he said. That this was the real thing. She was the one he'd been looking for. His divorce was almost final, just some paperwork to get squared away, but he promised that wasn't going to hold them back. They signed a lease together on a gorgeous apartment downtown, and Brooke even splurged with her savings, picking out furniture to make it their perfect home.

Even now, she cringed to think of it. Of course she should have seen it coming. Of course, it was the oldest story in the book.

Of course a strange woman showed up on her doorstep one cold March morning to inform her that yes, she was Archer's wife, and no, they weren't separated—at least, they hadn't been, until she'd found a strange credit-card bill full of charges for the days that Archer was supposed to be traveling, out of town.

He'd been lying to Brooke all along.

She felt the hot sting of shame all over again. How could she have believed him so easily? She was a smart woman, she had a college degree and great references, she could program her universal remote and tell when her friends started dating low-life, no-good cheaters. But it turned out, when a low-life, no-good cheater came along to sweep her off her feet, Brooke was swept right up in all his pretty lies.

Whatever the signs, she'd been blind to them at the time.

She'd been so caught up in the thrill of it: first the sneaking around, to stay under the radar at work, and then the pure rush of being with someone so handsome and powerful. Hearing him tell her she was the most important thing in the world, making those plans together, a life she could imagine as if it was already real.

She'd fallen for him, in the worst possible way. Free fall, no grip on solid truth—and nothing to save her from the pain of impact when she finally hit the ground.

Heartbreak and humiliation, all in one sickening moment. After learning the truth that night, Brooke couldn't even bring herself to confront him. She'd packed up her things and crashed on a friend's couch, handed in her resignation at work, and burned up the phone lines all weekend calling every professional contact and acquaintance she could think of, searching for any available position until finally, she had a lucky break.

The Sandy Lane hotel, Cape Cod, Massachusetts.

They needed a new manager; she needed to put as much distance between her and Archer's treacherous smile as possible. Immediate start? No problem. She drove for two days with a car full of boxes, hoping desperately that she could leave her mistakes behind.

But of course, it didn't work that way. She'd thrown herself into work, made friends, and tried to build a new life for herself here, but four months later, she could still feel that sickening lurch of guilt and shame like it was yesterday.

Would it ever get any easier, knowing what a fool she'd been?

The last of twilight disappeared into the dark of the ocean. Brooke watched it go, then turned her key in the ignition. Tonight had been a mistake from start to finish. She had no business dating anyone right now—not when she couldn't see a liar when the truth was right in front of her.

Or when she let desire do the talking, up against the wall of that alleyway.

She felt a shiver, remembering Riley's mouth on hers, then pushed the thought away. From now on, the only man she needed in her life was the British guy on TV, telling her how her cake should rise.

She didn't trust herself with anything more than that.

3

*R*iley Ford woke up alone.

That wasn't so unusual; he preferred to end the night on his own. It was hard to sleep with someone else tossing and turning in bed with him, and besides, while the cabin on his sailboat was sized just right for one, most women's idea of comfort was a little more than a ten-foot-square room bobbing on the ocean tide.

No, what was unusual that morning was that he hadn't just crawled out of someone else's bed just a few hours before.

Riley sauntered into the tiny galley kitchen and set his espresso machine on to boil. It took up half the counter space in the slim room, but there were some things from his former life he wasn't set to compromise.

His phone buzzed on the bench. A message from Layla.

I missed you last night. Hang later?

Riley winced.

He shouldn't feel guilty for blowing her off. They weren't serious, just a handful of dates while she was in town for a yoga retreat, but still it would have felt wrong to fall into bed with one woman, when his body still ached for someone else.

The blonde in the bar.

She'd struck him as a curiosity at first: so buttoned up and restrained in the middle of the bar. But her flirty quips had sparked a challenge Riley couldn't resist—and that was before she turned him down and left him hanging. Talk about waving a red flag at a bull. He couldn't remember the last time a woman had done that. Hell, had it ever happened before? Not back when he wore designer suits, that's for sure, dropping cash on expensive dinners and bottle service at the latest clubs. Even here, rolling out of bed in jeans and two-day stubble, Riley had never had a problem finding an appreciative audience for his charms.

But this woman? She hadn't bought his lines for a second. In fact, she'd seemed almost amused, which only made him want her more. Still, he wasn't about to go out of his way chasing someone who wasn't interested in having a little fun; not when he had plenty of girls on call who knew exactly how the game was played. This one had turned him down flat, and he knew how to take a hint. But when he'd stepped out of the bar and seen her there in the alleyway, her hair falling out of that prim braid, and the heat in her gaze enough to ignite his blood at twenty paces . . .

Well, like he said, he knew how to take a hint.

Riley's blood ran hot just remembering it. The feel of her body, pressing against his. How she'd teased him, her tongue sliding over his, and her teeth grazing his lower lip in a wicked nip. That kiss had been wild, and passionate, and sexy as hell.

And he didn't even know her name.

She wasn't a tourist, that was for sure—unless tourists came equipped with a leather briefcase and crisp button-down shirts. No, she must be from around here, but a newcomer, otherwise he would have run into her by now. And he definitely would remember a woman like that.

Still, Riley wasn't concerned. He took his coffee up onto the deck and admired the morning view. Calm blue ocean, golden sands, and a collection of colorful sailboats, bobbing gently beside his on the morning tide. The listing for his last home boasted of a million-dollar view, but as far as Riley was concerned, his little sailboat had it beat. Plus, zero maintenance, and these days, Riley was all about keeping things stress-free and easy.

The harbormaster, Pete, gave him a wave from the pier, and Riley waved back.

"You're up early," Pete called.

"A mistake I won't repeat," Riley yelled back. It was almost nine a.m., which was unheard of for him. When you roll into bed at dawn, it usually takes a little while to recover the next day, but luckily, Riley's job at the local pub left him plenty of time for that. He pulled on a clean shirt, poured another coffee into his Thermos, and hopped off the deck onto the jetty. It was a short walk up from the harbor into Sweetbriar Cove, so he didn't bother driving, enjoying the quiet leafy lanes and the chirp of morning birdsong.

So this was what the world looked like before noon.

He detoured via the bakery on Blackberry Lane, and was surprised to find a crowd already filling the small shop, eating muffins and croissants, and Summer's famous sticky morning buns.

"Riley?" The baker herself did an exaggerated double take when she saw him by the counter. "Are you feeling OK?" Summer leaned over the register and pressed her hand to his forehead. "You don't seem to have a fever—"

"Hey!" He batted her away, laughing. "Can't a guy get a morning pastry without it being a big deal?"

"Not when the guy in question never shows his face before noon." Summer grinned, her eyes sparkling. "Let me guess, you've been up all night."

"Does it look like I slept in these clothes?" Riley protested, only half-joking.

She grinned. "Knowing you, there wasn't any sleeping involved."

Riley gave her a smug look. "I'll have you know, I slept all night through—alone."

"Are you sure about that fever?" Summer reached her hand up again, and he ducked away.

"Hey, I'm not that bad," Riley protested again. "You're talking like I'm a total man-whore." There was silence. "This is where you say no, of course not," Riley prompted her, but Summer just smiled.

"What can I get you?" she asked instead.

He took in the spread of delicious-looking treats. "I don't even know. Usually there's nothing left by the time I come by."

"Early bird catches the pastries." Summer grabbed a paper bag and slipped a couple of sticky buns inside. "Here, I'm experimenting with a cherry glaze. Let me know what you think."

"Feel free to test your recipes on me anytime." Riley pulled a few bills from his back pocket to pay. "I'm surprised Grayson hasn't put on ten pounds since you arrived in town."

Summer laughed. "I'm working on it!"

Riley exited the bakery, his mouth already watering from the scent of sugar and cinnamon. Maybe there were perks to this whole morning thing, although he didn't see it becoming a regular routine. He'd had enough dawn alarms to last a lifetime, stumbling out of bed and into his car for the morning commute, then staying so late at his computer it was dark by the time he even came up for air. Eighty-hour workweeks vs. a leisurely stroll to open up the bar. He knew which got his vote.

His phone buzzed as he made his way into town, and he answered with a mouth full of sticky bun. "Mhmum?"

"Good, you're picking up."

Riley sighed. "And there I was, having a delightful morning."

"I wouldn't need to call if you'd reply to my emails," his brother pointed out dryly.

"I'm detoxing," Riley said. "No screens. This girl I dated said the rays were damaging our free radicals, or something like that."

"You're avoiding me," Max said. "Correction, you're avoiding everyone. Mom says you aren't calling her back, and I have a stack of mail piling up for you here. Why did you set it to forward to my office?"

"Because I knew you'd take good care of it for me. Come on, Max, you know that stuff's all junk now. It's over, I'm done."

"Not until you sign the final settlement, it isn't."

Riley sighed. Even out here on an empty country lane, the real world had a way of muscling in. "I'll sign when I'm ready."

"They're not happy, you know," Max warned him. "The lawyers are calling every week. They don't understand why this isn't wrapped up already—and neither do I. We came to an agreement almost a year ago now."

"So a few more months won't hurt. Let them wait," Riley said. "Patience is a virtue."

Max didn't sound happy. "You ever think you'd be better off just putting it all behind you and moving on?" he asked.

"I have moved on," Riley said firmly. "Doesn't mean I have to make it easy for them. Tell Mom I'll call her on the weekend."

He hung up, feeling a grim satisfaction. Tate was getting antsy? Good. Maybe it was petty, but Riley thought he deserved it after the damn mess he'd been through. Losing his best friend, business partner, and the project he'd worked seven years on was bad enough, but having the whole thing drag through half a dozen lawsuits was even worse. They'd finally reached an agreement Riley could just about live with, but that didn't mean he was just going to roll over and thank the guy for screwing him over like that. He had more important things to do.

Like the woman from the bar . . .

Riley's mood lifted, just at the thought of her. He'd see her again. The Cape was full of small towns, and his was smaller than most. Someone in Sweetbriar Cove would know about his mysterious blonde, and when he found her, well, they could pick up right where they'd left off.

Preferably with fewer clothes. And more ice cream.

Riley smiled to himself and polished off the last pastry. She was out there, somewhere. And he had nothing but time.

BROOKE WAS RUNNING LATE.

It was only five minutes, but with her schedule, that five minutes could prove disastrous: setting off a domino effect that would throw the whole morning out of sync. She'd been awake most of the night, tossing and turning, and had only drifted off a few minutes before her alarm rang, leaving her sleepy and disoriented. She would have given anything for another couple of hours of sleep, but there was no time to spare, and she raced to get to work. Her cell phone rang just as she was pulling up at the hotel, and she stabbed the call button, trapping the handset between her ear and her shoulder as she scrambled out of the car.

"Can't talk!" she yelped, struggling to tuck her blouse in and make sure her underwear wasn't showing.

"Sorry, just checking in on your date last night," Eliza's voice came. "Did it turn around at all?"

"Nope." Brooke flew through the back doors and down the polished hallway towards her office. "I'm taking a break from men for the foreseeable future."

"Now, don't be rash," Eliza laughed. "There are plenty more fish in the sea."

"Or crabs," Brooke quipped, remembering Doug's lifelong passion.

"What?"

"Nothing." Brooke paused, noticing a vase of wilting hydrangeas on the table. She'd have to talk to someone about that. "Thanks for trying, but I think I'm safer staying out of the dating pool."

And away from hot men in dark alleyways.

"Sorry to hear it. Are we still on for drinks this weekend?" Eliza asked. "It's karaoke at this bar I know, it should be fun."

"I'm in," Brooke said. "Just as long as I don't have to sing!"

She hung up, stashing her phone in her purse and grabbing the massive vase with both hands so she could hoist it out of sight. Better a polished table than a vase of dead flowers; she prided herself on attention to detail, and she knew it was the little things that mattered in a boutique hotel like this. They may not have the flashy budgets of the larger, luxurious resorts, but their guests went away raving about the small, elegant touches—and rebooked for next year.

She shoved her office door open with her shoulder and backed into the room, only to find her boss waiting inside. "Ash!" she exclaimed, surprised to see him there, every inch the meticulous businessman in a smart shirt and jacket. "I didn't know you were in town."

"I had some business in the city, so I thought I'd drop by and see how things were going." Ash Callahan looked at the flowers questioningly, and Brooke hurried to set them down and check her schedule for the day.

"Of course, I have a staff meeting now, but we could sit down at noon? I've been looking over the occupancy rates, and I already have some proposals I'd love to discuss."

Ash gave an approving nod. "That sounds fine. I'll see you then."

To Brooke's relief, the rest of her day ran smoothly. She breezed through her meetings—with the help of three cups of coffee—and even had time to pull her notes together so that by the time she joined Ash on the terrace, she had a neat file for him laying out her efficiency savings and future goals.

"Weddings have always been a consistent business for the hotel," she explained, taking him through the plans. "I propose we really grow that opportunity. I've already reached out to local vendors about partnerships, so we can offer a full-service package to brides."

"A kind of one-stop shop for their wedding?" Ash looked interested.

"Exactly. These days, most of them are juggling florists, catering, décor, and hiring an expensive wedding planner on top of that," Brooke said, feeling nervous. She shouldn't be worried; in the few months since she'd taken the reins, she'd already overseen several successful events, and had a summer schedule booked solid. Still, Brooke wanted to impress him. "By providing a package that connects them directly with the best vendors, we save them time and stress. And those local relationships mean we can jump to the head of the line for bookings. In summer season, you can't find a free linen rental in a hundred-mile radius," she added with a rueful grin.

Ash flipped through the rest of her folder, then smiled. "I have to say, I'm impressed. This could be the niche the hotel has been looking for." He looked around at the terrace, full of guests enjoying their lunch, and the magnificent sea views. "Just between us, I've been thinking about selling this property."

Brooke's stomach dropped.

"My wife, Noelle, is pregnant," he continued, "and so much of my business is further south in Beachwood Bay, I want to spend more time close to home. But it seems like you have some great ideas here. Plus, you won't be needing me around for any of it," he added. "Which is just fine in my book."

Brooke let out a breath of relief. "Well, congratulations," she said. "And thank you for your vote of confidence. I know this place is small compared to some of your other resorts," she continued, "but I think there's a great opportunity. I mean, who wouldn't want to get married here?"

Ash grinned. "Noelle and I did it barefoot on the beach," he said, with clear affection. "Just family, a few friends; we couldn't have asked for anything more."

"Don't say that too loud," Brooke joked, glancing around. "We want them ordering five hundred white roses and a flock of doves."

"We offer that?" Ash asked.

"Just as soon as I find an aviary with some quiet, well-trained birds." Brooke grinned.

"If anyone can, it's you," Ash laughed. "I'm looking forward to seeing what you do with the place. Let me know if there's anything you need."

Brooke smiled, already imagining the booked events calendar and parade of social media posts—all tagged with the Sandy Lane location. With some work and careful planning, she could make the hotel the wedding destination of choice on the Cape, and prove to Ash that it was worth hanging onto the property for a while longer.

And if all her grand plans kept her working overtime, distracted from the heartache and shame she was still trying to outrun? Even better.

Some people would call it denial; Brooke preferred to call it being productive. Archer had already thrown her career plans off track back in the city, and she was determined not to let that ever happen again. And maybe, just maybe, her work could tip the karmic scales a little closer to even again. She'd been the reason for a marriage falling apart, so it only seemed fitting that she help as many other unions get off on the right foot, and provide the wedding of their dreams.

From now on, she would have a one-track mind: weddings and work, yes. Men, no!

4

———

*B*rooke spent the rest of the week finalizing her plans for New England wedding domination, but she remembered to drag herself away from her laptop in time to meet Eliza for their drink on Friday night.

Her new apartment was set above her landlord's garage, in the back of the property. She locked up and descended the rickety staircase, meeting Eliza just inside the gate. "This place is so cute!" Eliza sounded surprised. "The front yard is so overgrown, you would never guess there's a whole property back here."

Thanks to her landlord's green thumb, the small courtyard was crammed with old glazed pots and plants: bright golden marigolds and nasturtiums in one corner, lavender spilling from the other. Small magnolia trees vied for sunlight against a wall of blooming roses, and honeysuckle and hydrangeas billowed up the trellis all the way to her balcony.

"I'd invite you up," Brooke apologized, "but I haven't unpacked yet, it's just boxes everywhere. I keep hoping I'll wake up one morning and it'll all be magically put in its place," she admitted.

Eliza laughed. "Where are some cartoon forest animals when you need them?"

They headed out front to Eliza's car, a vintage Mustang. Her friend slid behind the wheel and checked her lipstick in the mirror.

"You said it was casual, right?" Brooke asked. She'd thrown on some jeans and a navy tank top, but Eliza was wearing a cute red sundress, her brunette hair pulled up in a fancy twist, and looked ready for a cocktail party, not a night at the local bar.

"Oh, don't worry, I came from work," Eliza explained. "I was interviewing a new fashion designer, so I didn't want to show up looking like a complete slob. Like usual," she grinned.

Eliza was a freelance journalist, based up in Boston, but her family had a house on the Cape, so she traded her subway pass and studio apartment for beaches and a hammock every summer—at least that's what she told Brooke the day they'd met, contorting themselves into pretzel shapes in the back of a beginner's yoga class. Brooke had been there to try to relax and Eliza was researching a story, but they barely made it through the opening vinyasa before calling it quits and retiring to the nearest ice cream shop for a double scoop of chocolate chunk and some good old-fashioned girl-talk. Now, Eliza was her closest friend in town, and Brooke was glad to have someone to drag her away from work—and Netflix.

"So Doug was a bust, huh?" Eliza asked, pulling out of the drive.

"To put it mildly. Turns out, he's more interested in crustaceans than women. I can't believe your sister dated him," Brooke said.

"For six months!"

"No!" Brooke laughed. "Does she have a fetish for seafood or something?"

Eliza rolled her eyes affectionately. "Jane's too nice for her own good. She was probably too polite to ever break up with him."

"Still, it was probably for the best," Brooke said. "It's too soon to be dating, I guess it turns out I'm not ready."

Eliza gave her a sympathetic look. "Aww, I'm sorry. Breakups are the worst. You think you're fine and then BAM, you see a guy who looks like him on the street or hear a song on the radio, and it's like they stomped on your heart all over again. I had this one boyfriend in college," she added. "It went down in flames, totally wrecked me. I thought I saw him everywhere—in the library, by the dorms—I had to brace myself just to leave my room. Months later, I find out he wasn't even in the country. He went on a study abroad program! All that stress was for nothing. You did the right thing, moving away," she added. "At least here you know you won't run into him on the way to the gym with no makeup on."

"There's a simple fix for that, you know," Brooke quipped lightly. "Don't ever go to the gym!"

Eliza snorted with laughter, but Brooke felt a small pang of guilt. She hadn't told Eliza all the messy details about what happened with Archer. Maybe it was selfish, but she didn't want to see the judgment when she admitted she'd been the Other Woman, breaking a family apart.

"So where is this bar, anyway?" she asked, looking curiously out the window. They were driving down the main highway, Old King's Road, with the shore along one side and lush green woods on the other. It was still light out, the sun sinking over the water, and she could taste the salt in the air.

"Sweetbriar Cove," Eliza replied. "It's just a few miles away. You must have been."

"No, I don't think so. I haven't really done any exploring," Brooke admitted. "I just head straight to the hotel, and then pick up groceries in Provincetown."

"You've been here months!" Eliza exclaimed. "What have you been doing with your time?"

"Working," Brooke protested. "Some of us don't get to do it in a hammock."

"All day and night, and weekends too?" Eliza shot back.

"OK, OK," Brooke admitted with a sigh. "So *maybe* I'm a workaholic. But I'm changing that. See, look at me: out with you instead of running revenue projections."

"On a Friday night, wild." Eliza grinned.

Brooke laughed. "So, Sweetbriar, why does that name sound familiar?"

"They have an annual Christmas festival, it's a big tourist draw," Eliza explained. "And in summer there are all kinds of street fairs and outdoor movie screenings. Last year, they did a harvest hay-bale maze right in the middle of the town square."

"No," Brooke laughed. "You're making that up."

"Cross my heart." Eliza beamed. "I got lost twice."

They turned off the highway and down a winding road before reaching the Sweetbriar town square. Brooke had to admit it looked idyllic: set around an open green park with cute stores, cafes, and even a picture-perfect gazebo overlooking the bay. "This would be a great spot for wedding photos," she mused, already adding it to her mental list of package options.

Eliza grinned. "Do you ever stop working?"

"Sorry," Brooke sighed. "I promise, no more work—or wedding—talk for the rest of the night."

They parked and made their way across the square to the pub on the corner. It was an old, charming building with exposed beams, an open fireplace, and walls crammed with nautical souvenirs, and it was busy with Friday night locals. "You guys definitely have a thing for ships," Brooke said, looking around. "You can't move for anchors and oars on the Cape."

"We're big on history," Eliza agreed. "Ooh, look, there's a free table." She darted across the room and slid into a seat, almost before the other party had even stood up. A group of women were caught off guard, drinks in hand, halfway to the table. "Sorry!" Eliza beamed at them with an innocent look. "Were you waiting on this one?" They slunk away as Brooke joined her.

"You snooze, you lose," Eliza crowed under her breath. She caught Brooke's surprise. "Sorry, it's a journalist thing. Too many years spent loitering in coffee shops, fighting over a free outlet."

Brooke smiled. "I'll get the drinks, you guard our territory."

"White wine for me, thanks," Eliza said. "And fries. There should always be fries."

Brooke headed to the bar. She could see a karaoke machine set up on the other side of the room, but she was guessing they would all need a few drinks before anyone was brave enough to give it a try.

"Well, look who it is."

She turned and promptly lost her breath.

It was him, Riley, the guy from the other night, leaning casually against the bar just a few inches away.

What was he doing here, of all places? Her pulse leapt, but she fought to keep her cool. This was why it was safer to stay home, working, on a Friday night: she didn't stumble over the one guy she thought she wouldn't see again.

"Oh. Hi." Brooke managed to speak.

"I was just thinking about the other night, and then here you are," he said, looking pleased. "The universe delivered you right to me."

He smiled at her, and damn it, but he was just as gorgeous as she'd remembered; blonde hair falling over those stormy blue eyes, his jaw dusted with tawny stubble.

"What can I get you?" he asked, and she had to remind herself of why she'd turned and fled from their amazing kiss.

Dating kryptonite. Swearing off men. Past mistakes.

OK then.

"Thanks, but I don't need you to buy me a drink," Brooke said, trying to sound polite.

"I wasn't offering." Riley smirked. "I was taking your order. This is my bar."

Brooke flushed. "Oh. Good for you. It's very . . . nautical."

He chuckled. "It came with the decoration, I didn't have the heart to take it all down. Half the people in town have a relative up on the walls, so I didn't think it would make the best first impression to go trashing their ancestors."

He grinned, and Brooke felt lightheaded. How could this man ever make a bad impression?

"You know, I never got your name," Riley said, rounding to the other side of the bar. "Granted, we were busy with . . . other things." He shot her a wickedly suggestive look that had Brooke flushing all over again.

"It's Brooke," she blurted quickly. "Brooke Delancey."

"Pleasure to meet you, Brooke Delancey." Riley held out his hand.

Brooke hesitated, but it would have been rude to ignore it, so she reached across and shook it firmly.

"Excellent handshake you've got there," Riley teased. "Very professional."

Brooke didn't know what to say. She dealt with high-stress, unexpected incidents all the time at work, but she didn't know where to start when it came to making friendly conversation with the guy she'd been wantonly kissing in a dark alleyway.

The guy who was looking at her like he wanted to do it all over again.

Brooke gulped. "Two white wines, please. And some fries."

Riley looked amused. "Coming right up. Another blind date?"

"No!" Brooke exclaimed quickly. "I'm with a friend."

"Glad to hear it. Maybe we could meet up later?" he asked smoothly. "I get off around midnight."

Brooke swallowed. "Sorry," she said carefully. "But what happened the other night, it wasn't . . . I mean, I'm not . . . I'm taking a break from all of that."

"That?"

"Dating. Men. Drama."

"I can promise you, I'm about as easy as they come," Riley promised, and Brooke couldn't help but laugh.

"I'm sure you are, but I mean it. I'm swearing off men."

"Are you now?" Riley quirked an eyebrow at her. "Nothing I did, I hope."

She snorted. "Not everything's about you, you know."

"Most things are." He grinned, too irresistible for his own good. "You staying for karaoke?" She nodded. "Good. You'll change your mind once you see me do Sinatra. It brings grown men to tears."

"That's not always a good thing," she pointed out, but Riley was unruffled.

"Ye of little faith. Just you wait." He winked and then sauntered away, over to serve another customer.

Brooke should have been relieved to see him go. After all, she didn't want him flirting, promising a repeat of the other night.

Did she?

AN HOUR, two glasses of wine, and a bucketful of fries later, Brooke wasn't so sure. Riley's performance of "The Best is Yet to Come" wasn't exactly tuneful, but what he lacked in musicality, he more than made up for with charisma.

"Baby you're gonna fly." He sent Brooke a wink from across the room. She glanced away, but not quickly enough.

Eliza gave her a look. *"Hello.* Who's that guy?"

"Just . . . someone." Brooke took another sip of wine. "We met the other night."

"When you were on your date?" Eliza arched an eyebrow. "Multi-tasking, huh?"

"It's not like that," Brooke protested, then she stopped. "Who am I kidding? It's exactly like that," she admitted. "I don't know what came over me. One minute I'm heading home, and the next . . . we're making out in the alleyway," she said, in a whisper.

Eliza choked on her wine.

"As my editor would say, way to bury the lede!" She grinned. "I guess we know who's taking you home tonight."

Brooke shook her head quickly. "No! You don't understand. I shouldn't be doing *anything* with *anyone* right now. I can't trust my instincts. Especially not with a guy like that." She watched as Riley flirted up a storm with some coeds in the front row. They wore cut-off jeans with tiny cropped tank tops, looking young and toned and annoyingly hot.

She dragged her gaze away. Riley could flirt with whoever he wanted—as long as it wasn't her. "I'm going to get another drink!" She bounced up. "Want anything?"

"I'm good. But please, take these fries away," Eliza begged, even as she grabbed another handful. "I swore, I was going to try that whole detox thing for the summer."

Brooke laughed. "Good luck with that."

She took the basket out of harm's way, heading to the bar to get some water. Not that she was getting heated with Riley so close. Not at all.

"Well?"

There he was again, too close for comfort. Riley leaned against the bar and gave her a rascal grin, "Admit it, you're ready to throw your panties onstage."

"You don't take a hint, do you?"

Brooke hadn't meant her words to come out so harshly, but as soon as they left her mouth, Riley's smile slipped.

"Hey, I'm sorry." He frowned. "If you're serious about backing off, I will, I promise. But you've given me some pretty mixed messages," he pointed out.

"I know, I'm sorry." Brooke winced. "I'm just in a weird place right now. I'm still getting over a bad breakup," she found herself admitting. "And I guess I'm just . . . off balance. I didn't mean to lead you on," she said. "I mean, you seem nice—"

"Ouch." Riley clutched his chest. "Just what every guy longs to hear. Nice."

"You know what I mean." Brooke found herself smiling again. She was relieved Riley was taking it so well, but she guessed a guy like him didn't need to pine over the occasional rejection. "But I am serious. What happened the other night was . . ."

Hot. Delicious. Impossibly sexy.

" . . . a mistake," she said.

"A damn good one," Riley grinned. "Which I'm happy to repeat, any time you like."

Brooke shook her head. "Not going to happen. Really, I'm doing you a favor. I should carry a warning sign. Keep away, hazardous ground."

"Don't be so hard on yourself." Riley gave her a quizzical look. "You don't seem too bad to me."

"That's because you don't know me." Brooke shrugged, embarrassed now. She'd said too much, and now Riley probably thought she was a basket case. "Anyway, I'll let you get back to your adoring fans." She nodded to the coeds, who were busy taking selfies. "See you around, maybe."

She left before she made even more of a fool of herself. Blurting her romantic history to a complete stranger? This was why she needed to stay away from temptation. Everything that happened with Archer had short-circuited her self-control, and she needed to pull it back together before she went making the same mistakes all over again.

Eliza was happy to call it a night, so she drove Brooke back to her place. "What are you up to Sunday?" Eliza asked, as Brooke climbed out. "Want to pretend to get some health shakes, but go get waffles instead?"

Brooke laughed. "Sounds good. I might have some work, but I'll give you a call."

"Work, or a hot bartender?" Eliza winked, then drove away before Brooke could protest.

Definitely work.

She opened the gate, maneuvered up the rickety stairs over

the garage, and unlocked her apartment door. Inside, she let out a guilty sigh. The space sat almost exactly as she'd found it: small and empty, with the bare floorboards gleaming under the bare light bulb. She hadn't been exaggerating before when she'd told Eliza it wasn't ready for company. There was a card table in one corner with a folding chair, an old crushed blue velvet couch she'd found at a garage sale, and a mattress and box spring in the next room, but her life still sat packed in boxes, stacked in corners and spilling clothing and toiletries into piles on the floor.

Brooke thought about the spotless penthouse she'd left behind and winced. She'd spent hours poring over paint samples and fabric swatches, so excited to be building a home with Archer that every little detail had taken on big significance. *These* were the coffee mugs they'd be drinking out of every morning, *that* was the throw blanket they would snuggle beneath together watching a movie late at night. She spent her evenings browsing Pinterest and her weekends shopping, but in the end, it had been for nothing.

Brooke sighed. She could have used some of that new furniture right about now—but no, she corrected herself. She wouldn't have been able to look at it without thinking of Archer, and he still occupied way too much of her brain. Better to start fresh, with a massive dent in her savings account, than bring all that stuff with her to pollute her new life.

New possibilities. The freedom of a blank slate. If she said it often enough, maybe she would believe it would come true.

Brooke dumped her purse on the counter and set the tea kettle on to boil. It was late, but she was still wide awake, so she went to the windows and flung them wide, leaning out over the small courtyard. Even though it was dark out, the moon was bright, and the lamps dotting the space cast a warm glow through the dark.

Brooke took in a deep breath, savoring the sweetness of the night-flowering jasmine. It was the scent that had seduced her, from the start. When she'd come to view the apartment, Brooke had been exhausted from days on the road—and the other listings she'd already seen: bland, boxy studios off the highway that had made her want to break down in tears all over again. Then she'd stepped through the peeling, blue-painted gate and found a corner of paradise. A secret garden, just for her. In the middle of her heartbreak, she'd needed a ray of sunlight, and waking up that first morning to a glorious riot of color—the blue ocean glinting in the distance outside her windows—she finally felt like something close to herself again.

Now, Brooke turned and looked around at the small, empty rooms, and tried to feel determined.

She could do this. Her heart still ached to think of everything she'd left back in Chicago, all her foolish hopes and wasted dreams, but she could do this. It was a second chance to build a life. Something true this time around.

She took a deep breath and reached for the first box.

She had some unpacking to do.

5

Brooke Delancey...

Riley couldn't get her out of his mind. All weekend, he tried to focus on his usual routine of relaxation and fun, but no matter what he did, his thoughts somehow seemed to drift back to her. Leaning by the bar in those figure-hugging jeans, with a smart retort on her gorgeous lips and that look of sad hesitation in her eyes.

She shouldn't have been wearing one of those things, and for once, Riley wasn't voting for her clothes.

It was a damn shame, that's what it was. For a woman like her to swear off men? Talk about the crime of the century. She seemed to think that one bad breakup was game over, not the start of a whole new quarter, and Riley would have loved to prove her wrong. But he'd been raised to listen when a lady said no, so Riley tried to block out the thought of bringing a smile to those sweet lips of hers—and a few moans too, for good measure. After all, it wasn't like he didn't have plenty of other options for some no-strings fun. Every night in the bar brought a fresh crop of possibilities, and judging by the number of digits scribbled on napkins, there were plenty of volunteers for the job.

Like the girl currently blowing up his phone, one of those sexy coeds from Friday night. Riley felt the buzz in his pocket, and checked to see the text.

What u up2 l8er?

He winced. "Since when did people stop using full sentences?" he asked, stepping into his friend Mackenzie's studio. She had a gallery just off the town square, selling pottery and sculptures, and could usually be found in the studio in back, covered in dust and paint. Sure enough, today she was up to her elbows in wet clay, with her wild red curls caught back in a bright blue bandana.

"Since 2010," she said, looking up from the potter's wheel. "That's what you get for dating freshmen."

"She graduated last year," Riley protested.

"And you're, what, pushing thirty?" Mac laughed. "What do you even talk about with these girls?"

"Who says we're doing any talking?" Riley grinned.

Mac rolled her eyes good-naturedly. "You know, one of these days, you're going to fall for a real woman. A grown adult with a personality and decent grammar, and I'm going to be here to watch you fall flat on your face."

"So supportive," Riley teased. "You really want the best for me."

"It's what friends are for." Mac pumped the potter's wheel again, effortlessly smoothing the lump of clay as a bowl took shape beneath her fingers. Riley watched, fascinated. He was always impressed by her skills.

"What is it this time, whales and lobsters?" he asked,

picking up one of the fired bowls that was waiting for a decorative glaze.

"Try Old Glory," Mac said. "I'm going red, white, and blue for the new line."

"Smart."

"Plus if I have to hand-paint another sea creature, I'm going to kill someone," Mac said cheerfully. "A girl can only stick an octopus on so many coffee mugs before those tentacles start choking some tiny sailors."

Riley laughed. "Now, I'd buy that."

Mac paused, getting a gleam in her eye. "You know, that's not a bad idea, actually. I could do a whole series of nautical disasters. Sinking ships and sirens luring men to their doom and massive flesh-eating squid. Thanks!"

"Anytime." Riley idled in the studio, picking up and putting down her unfinished work. "You know everyone on the Cape, right?" he asked, changing the subject.

"Pretty much." Mac finished off the bowl and set it in line to fire in the kiln. "I've spent most of my life here. Why?"

"Just wondering. I met someone the other night, but I don't know how to find them again."

"Them?" Mac arched an eyebrow. "Or *her*?"

"It's not like that." Riley shook his head. "She just moved here, and I figured I could be a good neighbor. Make her feel welcome and all."

"Mmmhmmm." Mac smirked. "Naked and welcome."

Riley gave her a look. "Her name is Brooke, Brooke Delancey."

Mac paused, furrowing her brow. "Blonde, yea high, scarily professional?"

"That's her." Riley tried to hide his triumph. "You know her?"

"Not really." Mac stripped off her clay-splattered apron. "I've seen her at the bakery a couple of times. She works at a hotel up the coast, I think."

"Which one?" Riley asked.

Mac looked amused. "Sand something? Sandcastle. Sandy road . . ."

"Sandy Lane." Riley remembered the name. It was right on the water, a classy boutique place, which suited Brooke down to her tiny pearl earrings. "Thanks. I might just drop by and say hello."

"Good luck," Mac said. "Something tells me she's out of your league."

"No way. I'm in a league of my own," Riley drawled. Mac paused, then gave him a mischievous look.

"You know, you should invite her to Summer's party tonight. You said you wanted her to feel at home, right?"

"Right." Riley narrowed his eyes. Mac was up to something, he could tell.

"So I'd love to meet her." She gave him an innocent smile. "It'll be a fun event. A great way for a newcomer to make friends."

"Hmmm." Riley studied her, but he couldn't figure out what she was doing. Besides, it was actually a good idea. It would be a totally innocent invitation, asking Brooke to join a big, friendly event. Not romantic at all. "Maybe I will."

"Great, see you there tonight." Mac rolled up her sleeves. "Now, time for some drowned sailors!"

RILEY LEFT Mac to her pottery and drove up the coast to the hotel. He'd been there for some event last year, and it was just as elegant as he remembered, set on perfect manicured lawns with sweeping views of the ocean. He strolled inside and looked around the polished lobby. "Hey, do you know where I can find Brooke?" he asked the guy on the front desk.

"She's in the salon, I think."

Riley followed his directions to a bright, sunny room in the back of the hotel. Brooke was talking to some staff members, and he paused in the doorway, watching her at work. She seemed focused and animated, explaining something with gestures and a smile. She was still as buttoned up as the first night he'd seen her, but she was definitely more at ease here than in the crowded bar.

At least she was, until she glanced over and saw him.

She froze.

"Hey." Riley lifted his hand. "Sorry, I don't want to interrupt."

"No." Brooke blinked. "I . . . uh, we're all done here. Thanks, everyone." She dismissed the other staff members and turned back to Riley, looking cautious. "What are you doing here? I told you—"

"That you've sworn off men and you're joining a convent, I know." Riley gave her a reassuring grin. He'd have liked a warmer welcome, but hey, one step at a time. "Don't worry, I won't try and change your mind. A friend of mine is having a party tonight, and I thought you might like to come."

"On a date?" Brooke was still looking at him suspiciously.

"The opposite of a date," Riley said. "No flowers, no dinner, no fooling around in the backseat of my car, I promise."

Brooke cracked a grin. "You sure know how to show a girl a good time."

"I do, but I won't be showing it to you. Scout's honor." Riley crossed his heart. "What do you say? It's my friend Summer's birthday, I think you'd hit it off. She makes a mean chocolate cake."

Brooke's expression changed. "Summer Bloom, the baker? I know her! She made the most incredible cake for a wedding here. It had a peach frosting; I still dream about that cake." Brooke looked longing for a moment, and Riley was struck with jealousy.

He wanted to be the one to put a smile like that on her face.

And the one to lick it off.

"Well, drop by tonight, and you might get another taste," he said, pulling himself together. "Eight o'clock." He took a pad of hotel paper from the table and found a stub of pencil in his pocket, scribbling Summer's address on the letterhead page.

Brooke took the paper, looking torn. "I don't know, I'm so busy here . . ."

Riley wanted to stay and convince her, ask about her job and what brought her out to the Cape, and a million other questions that had crossed his mind since the other night, but he knew to tread gently. He was playing it cool, remember? Platonic.

"No problem, just thought I'd give you the invite. I better get going, but see you tonight. Maybe."

He gave her a wink and then strolled away like he had someplace better to be, even though it felt wrong to be walking away from her. This is what happened when a woman turned him down for once, he thought ruefully. It scrambled his whole damn system. Still, the party tonight should be fun. Either Brooke showed and he'd get to know her a little better, or he'd take on that cake table alone.

Now that sounded like a win-win situation. His favorite kind.

~

BROOKE WATCHED RILEY WALK AWAY, still feeling thrown. She'd thought she was imagining him at first, strolling into the spotless formal sitting room in worn-out jeans and an old band T-shirt, but he'd been all too real.

And so was Brooke's temptation.

She tucked the paper away and quickly straightened up some stray cushions. She didn't have time to drool over off-limits men, she was due to meet a potential client right now. And as for his casual invitation . . . ?

It was a bad idea. A very bad idea. Never mind the promise of making friends and sampling cake; Brooke knew a guy like that didn't make an offer like that without an agenda, and she'd already had a preview up against the wall of that alleyway.

The memory hit her in a rush. His mouth easing her lips wider, his tongue teasing her with wicked heat. And his body, *God, his body*, crushing her to him with hard muscle and coiled, devastating power . . .

"Brooke Delancey?"

A voice cut through her X-rated visions. Brooke startled.

"Yes!" she yelped, spinning around. A polished-looking woman was standing there, sizing up the room. She was clutching a thick binder, with her phone in one hand.

"Meredith Porter?" Brooke extended her hand quickly, still feeling flushed. "It's great to meet you. Thank you so much for considering us for your wedding."

"My . . . ?" Meredith repeated, then smirked. "Oh, no, I'm sorry I was so cryptic in my email. It's all pretty hush-hush, you understand."

Brooke didn't just yet, but she gestured to the couch. "Why don't we sit down, and you can tell me all about it?"

Meredith took a seat, perching on the very edge of the couch. "Before we get started, I'm going to need you to sign this." She produced a sheaf of papers from her file and handed it to Brooke. "Standard non-disclosure contract, guaranteeing confidentiality for everything we discuss."

Brooke blinked. "Umm . . ." She scanned the page, and the dense legal writing. "I can assure you, I treat all our events with discretion—"

"I'm sure you do." Meredith produced a pen. "But I'm under orders."

Brooke paused another moment. What was this about? She was too curious to resist. She scribbled her name, and passed the pages back.

Meredith seemed to relax. "Now we can get down to business. I work for a client out in Los Angeles," she explained. "We're scouting for the perfect Cape Cod location to use for her upcoming wedding."

"Great." Brooke flipped open her planner. "When were you thinking?"

"We're looking at the weekend after Labor Day."

"Next year?"

"No. This summer."

Brooke burst out laughing. "You're kidding, right?" she spluttered.

Meredith stared back, totally serious.

"But . . . that's four weeks away!" Brooke tried to stop her giggles. Was she serious? "I'm sorry," she said, trying to collect herself. "But that's impossible. Summer weddings on the Cape are booked years in advance. I could do my best to try to squeeze you in around . . ." She flipped through her calendar. "February, at the earliest, but even then, that's just the venue rental here. We'd still need to find the decorations, catering staff, flowers . . ." Brooke trailed off. "I hate to break it to you, but four weeks to arrange a wedding from scratch is a tall ask at the best of times, let alone during summer season here."

"Very well." Meredith snapped her folder shut. "I'm sorry to have wasted your time. I'll move on to my next appointment."

She got to her feet, and Brooke followed, but something was still pricking at her. "Just out of curiosity, who's the client?" she asked. "Since I've signed the forms already."

Meredith glanced around, checking the room. They were alone. She leaned in, and dropped her voice. "Lila Moore."

Brooke froze. "Lila Moore, the actress?"

The it-girl, famous reformed partier, style icon, heading-for-her-first-Oscar-nomination actress. She had broken out in a big trilogy, adapted from a bestselling young adult series, and gone on to deliver star-making performances in big-budget blockbusters and small indie movies alike.

Meredith nodded. "She's marrying Justin Cartwright. You know, the Cartwright heir," she said, naming a political dynasty that rivaled the Kennedys for their ambition and style.

"I didn't even know they were dating!" Brooke gasped. She hadn't kept up with her guilty-pleasure gossip magazines since her move, but even she wouldn't have missed that.

"It's all highly confidential." Meredith fixed her with a warning look. "That's why we're on such a tight schedule. We want to have the whole event planned and executed before anything leaks."

"Good luck with that. If I were them, I'd just elope," Brooke said wryly. Hollywood royalty plus political prestige? "It'll be a circus once the press gets hold of it."

"I agree." For the first time, Meredith looked tired. "But the Cartwrights are insisting on a traditional ceremony, here in

Massachusetts. So, we're going to need something small and intimate, but without cutting corners on style."

Brooke felt torn. Lila Moore? This was the opportunity of a lifetime. Sure, the happy couple was keeping things under wraps for now, but once the news was out, then there would be magazine spreads and photos everywhere. Front page news around the world. A single social media post from Lila would get a million likes—and hundreds of copy-cat brides wanting exactly the same royal treatment.

It would be foolish to turn this down.

She opened her calendar again, looking over the schedule. Luckily things were a little quieter after Labor Day, when the bulk of the summer tourists started dropping off. "I guess I could move some things around . . ." she said, already thinking of the champagne and discounts she'd have to send everyone as an apology.

"Perfect. You can pitch next week."

"Pitch?" Brooke repeated, confused.

Meredith looked at her. "This is just the first round," she explained. "You and the other venues will all present your plans, and then Lila and Justin will pick. The winner gets the contract."

"And three weeks to host the biggest wedding of the season," Brooke finished slowly.

Meredith smiled. "It'll be worth your while, believe me. There's an unlimited budget for the event, and me and my team will use our contacts to help get whatever you need." She pulled a card from her folder and offered it to Brooke. "Here are my details, I'll be in touch to confirm the pitch. We can't wait to see what you come up with!"

Brooke studied the card as Meredith whisked away. Hollywood plus Washington plus an impossible deadline? Something told her she was signing up for a world of trouble—but Brooke didn't mind. She loved a challenge, and this was about as big as they came. If she could win the pitch and actually pull this off . . .

She looked around, just imagining the event. It was her chance to put the hotel on the map—and prove to everyone back in Chicago that she hadn't just fled in shame.

She tucked the card away into her organizer and a slip of loose paper fell to the ground. She reached to pick it up. It was the party details that Riley had left, an address scribbled in confident cursive.

Brooke paused. She needed to give Summer a call anyway now, and line up some cake samples for the pitch to Lila. After all, what better way to entice them to pick the hotel than with a plate of delicious treats? She could drop by tonight to talk about it in person, and meet some of the other locals in Sweetbriar Cove.

It was only polite, as a new neighbor. And good business sense too. Nothing to do with Riley and that tempting smile of his, or the memories of his mouth pressed hungrily against hers.

Nothing at all.

---

6

*B*rooke drove over to the party that night with butterflies dancing in her stomach. She'd left work on time for once, and she'd agonized over half a dozen outfits, standing in front of the thrift-store mirror she'd found in a little store outside town. Would a dress be too dressy? Would Riley think she was trying too hard—for him? Brooke tore through her newly unpacked closet of clothing and despaired. It was easy for someone like Riley; he probably rolled out of bed and threw on a pair of jeans whether he was heading to the beach or a five-star restaurant, but Brooke didn't have it so easy.

What outfit said, *I can't kiss you again, but I want you to want me anyway?*

Eventually, she settled on a pair of blue linen shorts, with her favorite red off-the-shoulder top, and pulled her hair back in a simple French braid. She was being ridiculous, she knew —she was a grown woman, not a high schooler trying to impress her crush—but as she followed her GPS's directions off the main coastal highway, Brooke felt sixteen all over again.

Snap out of it, she told herself, driving past open fields and woodland until she saw the turn. He'd said it himself, this wasn't a date. No dinner, no flirting, and no kissing in the shadows at the end of the night. She had no reason to feel that lurch of anticipation in her stomach, or to check her makeup in the rearview mirror as she parked alongside the other cars and trucks strewn haphazardly down the long driveway.

She got out of her car and took a deep breath, trying to calm her nerves. It was a warm summer night, still bright out with the last of twilight, and she could hear birdsong chirping and the distant sound of music coming from further up the track.

Her phone buzzed in her pocket as she started the walk. It was a message from Eliza.

Want to come to a party tonight? 52 Willow Drive.

Brooke laughed. It was the same address Riley had scribbled for her, but in a small town like this, she shouldn't be surprised.

I just got here.

She rounded the corner and found a sprawling old farmhouse, lit up with Chinese lanterns hanging in the trees. People and laughter spilled out onto the porch, and music came, louder, echoing out across the fields. Brooke climbed the front steps and stepped inside. To her relief, everyone looked as casual as her, drinking beer and wine and eating some delicious-looking pastries.

"How do you know Summer?" Eliza appeared from the crowd to hug her hello.

"Cake," Brooke explained, and Eliza laughed.

"Same goes for the rest of us. Come on, let me introduce

you to some people." She led Brooke into the house, stopping every few paces to introduce Brooke until her head was spinning trying to keep up with the names.

"And here's the birthday girl!" Eliza announced, as Summer emerged from the kitchen with a tray of cupcakes. "What are you doing baking at your own party?" she scolded her playfully. "Relax, you should be having a good time."

"Baking is a good time," Summer grinned. She had her dark hair tumbling in natural curls, wearing a cute print sundress and bare feet. "Brooke, hey!" she sounded surprised. "Great to see you again."

"Riley invited me," Brooke explained quickly. "I hope that's OK."

"The more the merrier." Summer beamed. "How are things at the hotel?"

"Good. Hectic," Brooke added. "But I like it that way."

"You're probably the only person who moved out here to work *more*," Summer said with a rueful look. "The rest of us are all chasing a break."

"You work around the clock at the bakery," Eliza pointed out.

"True, but it doesn't feel like work," Summer replied. "I mean, I would bake all day long even if it wasn't my job."

"Lucky you," Eliza groaned. "I was up until midnight finishing my latest article. And let me tell you, a thousand words on redistricting regulations isn't my passion."

Summer patted her shoulder sympathetically. "Have some cake, you'll feel better."

Eliza brightened. "You're right. Thanks." She took two of the mini-cupcakes and devoured them in five seconds flat.

"What was that you said about a detox?" Brooke teased her.

"Frosting doesn't count," Eliza protested. She waved at

somebody across the room. "Be right back." Eliza ducked away, and Brooke took a cupcake.

"These are delicious," she exclaimed, tasting the tart frosting.

"Thanks." Summer smiled. "I'm going crazy with the summer harvest right now, all these fresh blackberries around."

"Do you have some time this week?" Brooke asked, seeing her opening. "I'd love to chat to you about some more wedding opportunities."

"Sure, just swing by the bakery anytime," Summer offered. "I'd love to pick up any extra gigs you have going."

"Perfect." Brooke smiled, relieved. Finding a master baker worthy of a Hollywood wedding was no short order, and having Summer as her secret weapon for the pitch might push her over the top.

The crowd shifted, and Brooke caught a glimpse of a familiar face. Her stomach turned a slow pirouette. Riley was making his way towards them, wearing a crisp button-down shirt, white against his tanned skin, and was that . . . ?

"You shaved?" she said as he reached them.

Riley rubbed his smooth jaw. "Don't get used to it. What do you think, I scrub up good?"

Try *amazing*.

"Sure, I guess." Brooke shrugged and glanced away, hoping that her jolt of lust wasn't written all over her face.

"So what did I miss?" Riley looked between them. "If you were singing my praises, please, don't let me interrupt. Go right ahead."

Summer snorted. "Find one of your coeds if you want constant adoration. Us grown women have better things to do."

"Grown?" Riley teased. "I just saw a funfetti cake with milk shooters out back."

Summer just laughed. "You're never too old for funfetti." She looked past them and winced. "I better go save Grayson from my mom. Here, have fun!"

She thrust her tray of cupcakes at Riley and took off, leaving Brooke alone with him.

"You made it, then," Riley said, depositing the tray on a table before turning back to Brooke.

Was it just her, or did his voice drop, intimate? Suddenly, the alcove they were standing in felt like a separate room; away from the crowd, and close enough to touch.

"I made it," she agreed, searching for something to say. "How's the bar?"

Dumb.

"Fine," Riley said, clearly amused at her terrible excuse for small talk. "How's the hotel?"

"Fine."

Brooke wracked her brain, feeling awkward as hell. What happened to the casual, flirty Brooke that she'd been earlier, bantering with him at the bar the first night they'd met?

That woman was long gone, and she knew exactly the moment for the switch. One kiss, all-out, and she waved goodbye to poise for good.

"It's a great party," she said eventually. "Thanks for inviting me."

"No problem." Riley reached out his hand to her face, and Brooke flinched back, startled. "Sorry." Riley grinned. "But you've got some frosting . . . there."

He touched his thumb to the corner of her mouth, then brought it to his lips. He licked it slowly, his eyes not leaving hers, and damn, if the heat there didn't melt Brooke from the inside out.

How was this man so sexy?

"Bathroom?" she blurted, flushing hotly.

"Down the hall." Riley nodded in the right direction.

"OK!"

Brooke turned and fled before she could do anything stupid, like yank that irresistible mouth down to hers for another kiss.

BROOKE STAYED at the party another hour, meeting Sweetbriar locals—and giving Riley a wide berth. As long as there was a crowd of people between them, she was fine, so she threw herself into having a good time, getting all the local recommendations, and even some invites too.

"She has to come to book club, doesn't she have to come to book club?" Summer's friend, Poppy, insisted, after they got talking about a shared love for beach reads.

Mackenzie—a local potter—grinned. "Definitely. We meet in a couple of weeks," she told Brooke. "Bring a bottle and something sweet."

"I don't know if I have time to read anything right now . . ." Brooke said regretfully.

Mackenzie laughed. "Neither do we. It's just an excuse to get together and gossip," she confided. "Poppy's going to read us the dirty bits from her next book."

"Am not!" Poppy protested. Her wine splashed. "Sorry, did I get you?"

"No, I'm good." Brooke checked her blouse. "And I'd love to come, thanks."

"I'll send you the info, or just get your number from Riley," Mackenzie said casually.

"He doesn't have it."

"Oh?" Mackenzie quirked an eyebrow. "OK."

Brooke caught a glance between her and Poppy. "We're not . . . I mean, we're not seeing each other. I don't really know him," she hurried to explain.

Aside from the whole "life-changing kiss" thing, that was.

"Sorry, my mistake." Mac smiled. "I can't keep up with him these days."

"That's not to say he's some kind of playboy," Poppy added quickly, giving Mac a nudge. "Riley's great. A really good guy."

Mac nodded. "He's just . . . friendly, is all."

Brooke was amused. "It's OK, I know his type. I mean, you don't look like *that* and live like a monk," she said, and they laughed, looking relieved.

"We love him, but yes, he's pretty popular," Poppy said.

"And by popular, she means the hottest bachelor on the cape," Mac agreed.

They all turned to look at Riley, who was currently surrounded by three gorgeous women. He caught them staring, and looked puzzled for a moment, before sending a wave and a wink.

They all laughed again.

Brooke relaxed. So Riley's charm was legendary—she should have guessed. Which meant there was nothing special about their little rendezvous, and she didn't need to tie herself up in knots speculating about it anymore.

She checked the time. It was getting late, and she wanted to be up early tomorrow to start planning her pitch. "I should get going," she said reluctantly. "I have work in the morning."

"Aww, well take some cake with you for the road," Mac suggested. "And drop by my studio sometime."

"I go there whenever I'm having a bad day," Poppy agreed. "Just smash some pottery, and everything feels better again. It's the perfect stress-reliever."

"I'll keep that in mind," Brooke smiled.

She said her goodbyes, then headed out, driving back up the coastline, now shadowed in the dark. She rolled the windows down and took a deep breath of the sea air, feeling happier and lighter than she had in a long time.

Moving all this way, starting fresh—she'd been so focused on her job and everything she was trying to leave behind, Brooke hadn't thought much about the life she could build to replace it. But tonight, for the first time, she saw all the good things that could come from life in Sweetbriar Cove, things that had nothing to do with putting space between her and her heartbreak. Friendship, a sense of community, the slower pace of life . . . Maybe she would even find some of that work-life balance she'd heard so much about, although, she wasn't betting on anything.

Brooke smiled, thinking of all the new people she'd met and invitations she'd received. Things were turning around for her, she could just feel it. But she wasn't even a mile outside Sweetbriar when she heard a splutter coming from the engine. She'd spoken too soon.

"No," Brooke groaned. Her trusty old Honda was pushing 200K on the speedometer, but it hadn't let her down yet. "Just a little further," she pleaded, listening to the rough grinding noise. "You can do it."

But it couldn't.

The engine gave one more cough of protest, then gave up the ghost. Brooke was just able to steer over to the side of the road before it cut out completely, and her car came to a lurching stop.

Brooke's heart sank. If she was back in the city, she would have just called triple-A and booked a cab to ride home, but she was pretty sure those options weren't around this late in Sweetbriar Cove.

She got out of the car, and used the light on her phone to try and peer under the hood. But who was she kidding? She could change a flat and refill her wiper fluid, but that was about the most of her auto skills. She checked her call list, wondering if she could get one of the assistant managers to come pick her up. Then she saw her cell reception.

Zero bars. No reception.

A cricket sounded in the woods nearby, and the road lay dark, not even another house in sight.

Brooke felt a shiver of unease, but before she could head into full-on panic mode, a pair of headlights came around the bend.

Relief flooded through her. Brooke leapt out into the road and started waving. "Hey!" she called, as the Jeep drew closer. "Hey, over here!"

The vehicle slowed and came to a stop beside her.

"What seems to be the problem, little missy?"

The familiar drawl stopped her in her tracks.

It was Riley. Of course it was.

$\mathcal{R}$iley leaned out the window and thanked the gods of welcome coincidence. He'd been wondering where Brooke had slipped off to at the party, and now here she was, waiting on the side of the road in those ridiculous strappy sandals. "Flat tire?" he asked.

"My engine died," she said, looking reluctant.

"I'm not surprised." Riley got out and strolled over. He took in the peeling blue paint and whistled. "This thing is a zombie, how is it even running?"

"Hey!" Brooke protested. "I've had this car since I was sixteen."

"And this is the universe's way of telling you it's time for an upgrade." Riley went around and looked under the hood.

"What's the problem?" Brooke trailed him. "Can you fix it?"

"Me?" Riley grinned as he slammed the hood shut. "You probably know more than I do about engines," he said, "but I do have the local repair shop's number, if you need."

"Thank you." Brooke looked relieved. "Can you please call? I don't have any reception on my phone."

"Sure. Tomorrow," Riley added. "I saw Bill back at the party, and he's in no state to drive. Come on," he said, beckoning. "I'll give you a ride."

Brooke took a look around at the dark and empty woods, then grabbed her bag and locked up. "Thank you," she said, climbing into the passenger side. "I don't know how long I would have been standing there if you hadn't come along."

Probably only a couple of minutes, until the rest of the party guests started heading home, but Riley wasn't about to wreck his white knight moment.

He started the engine. "Where are we heading?"

"Just up past Wellfleet."

"That's not far," he said, "you could have walked it."

"In these?" Brooke stretched her leg, displaying a wedge sandal with ribbons crisscrossing her calves.

Damn, they were some sexy shoes. "Don't you wriggle your toes at me," he teased. "A man could get the wrong idea."

Brooke snorted. "Sure, because my bunions are so sexy."

"I don't know about that." Riley smirked. "There are all kinds of internet groups just dying for some close-up shots."

"Eww!" Brooke laughed. "That's disgusting."

"I dated a girl once who had a thing about my ankles," Riley confided, glancing over. "I don't know what it was, but the girl went crazy when I wore flip-flops."

Brooke was still laughing. "This guy I knew in college was obsessed with knees. Not anything kinky, just, women's knees. I found him in the library once, hiding under a table to stare."

"Humankind is a rich tapestry," Riley proclaimed. "What about you? What's your fetish?" He glanced over and waggled his eyebrows, only half-teasing. He already knew Brooke wasn't half so buttoned up as she seemed, and he wondered what other wanton secrets she was hiding under her polished surface.

"Hmmm," Brooke mused. "There is one thing . . . But no, I can't tell you that."

"Go on!" he urged her. "I won't tell. Scout's honor, I swear."

"Something tells me the only merit badges you got were for flirting and teasing girls."

"And navigation," Riley said proudly. "I can find my way out of the woods with just a compass and a pencil. But don't change the subject. You can't tease a guy like that and leave him begging for more. What is it, hairy guys? Tattoos? Whips and chains? It's always the quiet ones," he added with a smirk.

"Well, OK . . ." Brooke seemed reluctant, and it only made his curiosity burn stronger. "It's weird, I know, but one thing just drives me crazy . . . I can't seem to control myself around . . ."

Riley leaned closer in anticipation.

" . . . Competence."

"What?" Riley blinked.

"Nothing sexier." Brooke fanned herself. "Someone with skills and efficiency? Ooh baby. Gets me hot under the collar every time."

Riley chuckled, and shook his head. "You're an odd one, Brooke Delancey."

"Why thank you." She grinned. "I'll take that as a compliment."

She glanced out the window and pointed to a gate up ahead. "This is me," she said, and Riley pulled over. "Thanks for the ride," Brooke said, getting out. "I really appreciate it."

"No problem." Riley got out too. He caught her look. "Hey, I'm a gentleman. I know to walk a lady to her door. You never know what's lurking in the bushes," he added, opening the gate for her.

"Probably just the neighbor's cat." Brooke climbed the stairs to her apartment ahead of him, while Riley thought fast for an excuse to stay. Not because he still held out any hopes of seduction, but because somehow, he'd had more fun just talking with her on the ride over than he had all night.

"Do you want to stay for a drink?" Brooke asked suddenly. "Just a drink," she added quickly, and Riley tried not to jump over himself to reply.

"Sure," he agreed casually, and he followed her inside. He stopped just inside the doorway and looked around the room. A table, a couch . . . and not much else. "Wow. Either you're big on the whole 'minimal design' thing, or you just got robbed."

"Don't." Brooke sighed. She flipped on the lights, and headed for the small kitchen area. "Believe it or not, this is me unpacked. I think there's some whiskey in a cabinet somewhere . . ."

"Actually, some tea would be great." Riley looked over. "I'm not much of a drinker."

"But you run a bar."

"And the profits stay in the register this way," Riley said.

"Coming right up." Brooke set the tea kettle on the stove, setting out two mugs and an array of herbal teas on the counter. "I've got chamomile, peppermint, rosehip, rooibos . . ."

"What are you, the neighborhood dealer?" Riley chuckled, coming closer.

"I have trouble sleeping sometimes," Brooke explained. "It's been better since I moved here, but some nights I just can't get settled. I usually give up around two a.m. and get some work done instead."

"That's rough," he said sympathetically. "I went through it a couple of years ago."

"What cured it?" Brooke asked.

"Three lawyers and a disappearing act," Riley answered wryly, then caught her curious look. "Long story. Don't worry, I'm not a fugitive or anything."

"I figured. You couldn't stay under the radar to save your life," Brooke teased. The kettle began to whistle, so she poured it into their mugs and looked around. "Let's sit outside," she proposed brightly. "It's so warm out."

Riley followed her back outside and down the stairs to the courtyard. There were a couple of patio chairs set up by a table, with a string of lanterns hanging nearby, casting them in a warm glow. Riley kicked back, relaxing, and took a sip of his tea. "Have you tried exercise?" he asked. "For the insomnia, I mean. I started running, could have trained for a marathon by the time I was through."

Brooke shook her head. "Not yet. It's only been a few months. I'm hoping it just goes away naturally now."

She let out a sigh, wistful and weary, and Riley wondered what it was keeping her up all night. Something had happened back in Chicago, that much was clear, and he was guessing it had something to do with the bad breakup that had her swearing off all mankind. Still, he didn't want to pry into anything painful, so he changed the subject. "How did you like the party?" he asked instead.

"It was fun." Brooke smiled again. "Everyone's so friendly."

"Let me guess, they recruited you to book group."

"And the carnival committee, and local restoration team, whatever that means." She laughed. "And Mackenzie says I need to come learn pottery, too."

"That sounds about right," he chuckled, remembering the

culture shock when he'd first moved to town. He was more used to flying solo, but he'd learned fast just to roll with the endless events and town spirit. "Granted, all the festivities can get kind of suffocating sometimes, but when that happens, I just pull anchor and dock a little further out in the bay."

Brooke looked delighted. "You live on a boat?"

"Most of the time. I have an apartment over the bar I use in winters," he explained, "but I prefer to stay out on the water. No nosy neighbors."

"No room for a woman to start leaving her stuff behind," Brooke added perceptively.

Riley shrugged, feeling oddly self-conscious. "I prefer it this way. No baggage."

"I wish it was so easy." Brooke's smile dimmed again. "I thought leaving everything behind would help, but sometimes baggage has a way of following you around."

She gripped her mug with both hands and paused a moment, as if weighing something. "The breakup, in Chicago . . ." she said slowly. "He was married."

He blinked. Whatever he'd been expecting, it wasn't that.

"This is the part where I say I didn't know," Brooke added, looking miserable. "I mean, he said they were getting a divorce, that the relationship had been dead for years . . ." She trailed off, and Riley could see it in her expression: the guilt and misery.

This was what she'd been beating herself up over? It was the oldest line in the book.

"It's not your fault," he told her gently, but she shook her head.

"No, it is. Because I did know. I knew enough, at least. He was married," she repeated sadly, "and I should never have gone anywhere near him, not until the ink was dried and the papers were filed. So everything that came after . . . ? I deserved it."

"Come on, you don't believe that." Riley frowned. "He's the lying, cheating asshole, not you."

Brooke gave him a weak smile. "I know. And I'm not making excuses for him, believe me. But I should have known better. I should been on my guard, or asked more questions, or *something*. But I was too in love with him to see the lie that was right in font of me."

"So you're human," Riley said, hating to see her like this. He didn't know her well yet; hell, he didn't really know her at all, but he could tell that she wasn't someone who took honesty lightly. Some people didn't think twice before breaking up a relationship, but here Brooke was, months later, still blaming herself for her part in it.

"You trusted someone, and you had that trust betrayed. We've all been there."

He paused. He hadn't spoken a word of his own bitter history to anyone, not since arriving on the Cape, but something made him want to confide in Brooke—if only to take that guilt out of her eyes. "For me, it was my business partner," he admitted to her. "My best friend. We built a company from the ground up, and then . . . he tried to take it all."

Brooke frowned. "That's terrible."

Riley found himself wishing he had a glass of that whiskey in his hands, after all. Somehow, tea didn't take the edge off that betrayal that still reared its ugly head whenever he thought about Tate, and everything that went down between them. He took a gulp. "It's a long time ago now, going on . . . four years. We had a tech company, over in Silicon Valley."

"Wait, what?" Brooke looked so surprised at that he laughed.

"I know, not a lot of streaming video apps in Sweetbriar Cove," Riley agreed. "I was always into programming, ever since I was a kid," he explained. "Tate was my roommate in college, and we landed on a way to compress video files—I won't bore you with the details. We found some investors, lived off ramen, built the thing ourselves, working eighty-hour weeks for years until we had something." Even now, he couldn't help but smile at the memory. It had been stressful and chaotic but there was nothing like it, that feeling when you'd been working all night but suddenly you found the fix that turned everything around.

"Anyway, things blew up, we got too successful, too fast," he continued. "Suddenly, we were being courted by the whole town: press, investors, the works. It's what we always wanted, but, well, be careful what you wish for, I guess," he said, rueful. Sure, they were on the VIP list for every hot event in town, getting flown on private jets, and giving talks to adoring crowds, but at the end of the day, that stuff was a poisoned chalice. "We started fighting more, the people we hired were picking sides . . . It got toxic. Then a big competitor came along, offered us stock options and all the perks to sell out. I said no, but Tate wanted to take the deal. We went round and round on it, God, it was ugly."

"So what happened?" Brooke asked, her eyes wide.

He shrugged. "He stabbed me in the back. Got some of the investors together and held a vote of no confidence, used some small-print buried in our partnership agreement to try and say I was jeopardizing the future of the company, and was unfit to have a say."

"No." Brooke looked outraged, but it wasn't even a fraction of the anger Riley had felt, the pain that had fueled his fight and stopped him from just rolling over and letting Tate take the whole damn thing. "What did you do?"

"I fought back. I sued him, he counter-sued, we dragged the whole mess through the courts. It took another couple of years," Riley said grimly. "But I didn't stick around to wait it out, I moved out here and let the lawyers duke it out. We settled last year," he said with a sigh. "They finally caved to a fifty-fifty split."

"That's great," Brooke said. "You must be relieved to have it all behind you."

"Not quite." Riley gave her a wry look. "We're not officially divorced just yet."

Brooke shook her head and sighed. "I don't understand people," she said, looking out into the dark. "How they can just lie and cheat and steal. How are you supposed to trust anyone when the people you love can just turn around and stab you in the back?"

Riley had wondered the same thing for a long time, but the worst of his bitterness was behind him now. "Not everyone," he told her gently. "The assholes are out there, sure, but there are good folks too. People with integrity. The trick is, you just take things as they come until you can figure out which one they are."

"It sounds like you've got it all figured out." Brooke looked over at him.

"I wouldn't say that," Riley said. "But I'm working on it."

They fell silent, and for a moment, he listened to the distant crashing of the waves and a couple of noisy crickets nearby. It was peaceful out here—with her. Some people couldn't sit still, they vibrated with restless energy, but Brooke was calm and totally at ease. She didn't say a word, she just seemed content to sit there in the stillness with him, under the dark, star-scattered sky.

"You can actually see the stars out here," he said, looking up. Back on the West Coast, there was so much light pollution, it had taken him by surprise those first nights out on the water on his boat, seeing the constellations lit up so clearly.

"Hmm?" Brooke yawned.

He looked over and saw her curl in her chair, sleepy. She wasn't just calm, she was almost out for the count. He smiled.

"Come on, you should get to bed while you're still tired."

She got up, yawning again. "Thanks again for the ride. And the conversation," she added, taking their empty mugs. "I'm glad we're going to be friends."

Friends.

Riley looked at her. Her blonde hair was falling out of that braid, and the sleepy smile on her face seemed so innocent and warm, it was like all her anxious defenses had melted away.

She was beautiful.

And just a friend.

Riley bit back a sigh. "Me too," he said instead, and he meant it.

Whatever Brooke wanted right now, that was just fine with him.

8

_____

With her car on life support over at the auto shop, Brooke spent the week begging rides from her delivery guys and rolling out of bed at dawn to catch the morning bus, which chugged slowly through every small village and dead-end stop on its way up the Cape. At least it gave her an extra hour in the mornings to plan her show-stopping wedding pitch—and think about Riley. He'd texted the morning after the party: nothing special, just a link to an article with insomnia tips, but she'd replied, and now, she felt a skip in her stomach whenever her phone lit up with a new message.

Instead of counting sheep, you could count puppies. There's a shelter in need of foster homes.

Brooke paused a moment then tapped out a response.

Because puppies are so restful and quiet.

She tucked her phone away with a smile. It was silly, she knew. The whole text thing had always passed her by, and she preferred speaking to people on the phone or in person, but still, there was something about seeing his name on her screen, along with a funny picture or message, that made her day seem a little brighter.

Friends, she reminded herself sternly, as the bus wound down the coastline—this time towards Sweetbriar Cove. He was just a friend.

A friend who looked too damn sexy in the moonlight.

Brooke sighed. The stretch of blue ocean blurred outside the window as she remembered the way he relaxed in that chair the other night, looking so at ease. Shadows cast along his jawline, lamplight gold against his hair. He was almost too gorgeous to resist, and she'd had to wrap her hands tight around her tea mug to make sure she didn't accidentally do anything stupid.

Like reach for him.

Kiss him.

Take his hand and lead him upstairs—

The bus suddenly stopped with a lurch, and a gaggle of older ladies got on with their wheeled shopping trolleys. Brooke blushed.

She shouldn't have asked him to stay. She regretted it almost as soon as the words left her mouth, but sitting there, talking and laughing like that, it was the most comfortable Brooke had felt in a long while. Riley had a way about him that was just so open and at ease. It's why she found herself spilling the whole story about Archer. She winced to think of it now, but instead of judging her, Riley had surprised her with his supportive words. And it turned out he had his own difficult past lurking beneath that easy smile, his own betrayals, and new beginning.

Maybe she'd underestimated him.

"Sweetbriar Cove."

Brooke glanced up at the driver's announcement, and found they were already in town. "Wait, this is me," she called, grabbing her bag and scrambling for the doors.

Outside, she got her bearings and headed for the auto shop. It was still early, and none of the stores were open yet, but she had Lila and the Hollywood team coming for the pitch at three, and she needed her hulk of a car back to get those last-minute preparations set. She crossed her fingers as she reached the garage and found Bill, the grizzled mechanic, who explained the long laundry list of things they'd had to fix.

"So what's the damage?" she asked, bracing herself.

He passed her the invoice. She winced. "Old cars like this, it keeps adding up," he said with a shrug. "Let me know if you want to upgrade. I have a lead on a couple of used models, fifty thousand miles on the clock."

"Maybe in a little while." Brooke sighed as she signed the check. Her car, the apartment, furniture . . . This move was costing her big-time—which was why it was even more important she land this wedding pitch, wow Lila Moore, and get the hotel schedule booked solid for years.

Then, maybe, she could ask her boss about a raise.

She climbed in the driver's seat and started the engine. This time, at least, it started with a purr. "Thanks again," she called out the window, and Keith waved as she drove away.

Next stop: the bakery.

Brooke found the leafy back lane with people lining up and enjoying their morning coffee and muffins at the bistro tables outside. Her stomach gave a rumble. She'd left the house too early to grab breakfast, and it would be a crime to look a gift pastry in the mouth . . .

"I'll try one of those sticky buns," Brooke said when she reached the counter. "And three wedding cake samples, please."

Summer was minding the register, wearing a bright-pink apron around her waist. She lit up. "Brooke! I've got them all boxed up for you in the back. Come on through."

Brooke followed her behind the counter and into the back kitchen, where every surface was covered with a tray of something delicious, and the scent of cinnamon and sugar wafted in the air. "This is heaven," she sighed, looking around.

"Yup." Summer grinned. "But hell on my waistline. Here," she said, pulling some confectioner's boxes from the refrigerator. "I know you said three, but I went a little crazy trying some new flavors. I hope that's OK."

"Uh, yes." Brooke laughed. "More is always a good thing."

She lifted one of the lids to peek and found a small, perfectly-formed cake nestled there, decorated with elaborate swirls of white and tiny rose petals. "This is beautiful!" she exclaimed.

Summer leaned over to check. "That's the white chocolate and guava," she said. "Most people do raspberry, but I wanted to try something exotic."

"You're a real artist," Brooke said admiringly. "Hopefully, these will help land me the pitch. I figure they can't turn me down with a mouthful of cake."

"Good plan." Summer grinned. "Here, let me help you take them out to the car."

They carefully stacked the boxes and made their way outside. "Thanks again for letting me crash your party," Brooke said, following her around the side of the building. "It was a really fun night."

"You're welcome any time," Summer replied, ducking past a thicket of blackberry bushes. "Any friend of Riley's is a friend of mine."

Brooke's stomach did an impromptu flip.

"Have you known him long?" she asked, trying to sound casual.

"A few months." Summer flashed her a smile. "I only moved here in the spring."

"Oh." Brooke blinked. "I didn't realize. You seem so . . . at home."

"I do, don't I?" Summer sounded pleased. "Don't get me wrong, there have been some bumps along the way, but that's the thing about this town: you can try to resist its charms, but it gets you in the end."

Brooke laughed. "I'm beginning to see that now."

They reached her car, and Brooke opened up the trunk. "Be sure to invoice the hotel," she said, as they placed the boxes gently down. "Fingers crossed we get the event, it could be a big job—and great exposure for you."

"You still won't tell me who it is?" Summer asked hopefully.

"Can't. I'm pretty sure I signed my soul away on that contract," Brooke said. "But let's just say, this wedding will make a splash. At least, if I do my job right."

"Good luck!" Summer told her. "Oh, wait right here."

She dashed into the bakery and re-emerged a moment later with a paper bag. "Your sticky bun," she said, handing it to Brooke. "On the house."

"Thanks!"

Brooke couldn't even wait until she'd started the engine before tearing into the soft, yeasty dough. *Mmmm.* There were definitely some perks to the job.

She turned back onto the main highway and headed for the hotel, running down her mental to-do list. Cake samples, check. Floral design, check. Sixteen-point plan how she would pull off the most elegant, understated, and drama-free wedding Lila Moore had ever seen? Check, and check!

She had just plugged in her headphones and was about to record a voice memo to herself, when her cellphone rang. It was her mom. Brooke answered, surprised. "Hey, everything OK?"

Her mom was notoriously flaky with phone calls—she preferred to stay in touch with long forwarded email chains and care packages full of newspaper articles about how chocolate gave you (or cured) cancer.

"Oh, fine, hon. I just had a moment here at the office, and thought I'd give you a call. It's all quiet here until Gladys Weathers comes in about her hip replacement. She says she put it out playing tennis with her trainer, but I bet that's not all they were doing—"

"Mom!" Brooke cut her off. Her mom still worked as a secretary in her dad's medical practice, and was liable to break all kinds of confidentiality rules gossiping about the patients if Brooke gave her half a chance. "I really don't need to know."

Her mom tutted. "I'm just saying. You never know with some people."

No, Brooke thought sadly, you didn't.

"So how are you settling in?" Her mom's voice took on a fretful edge. "I looked you up on Google Maps, and you're miles from anything. What if there's a storm and you get cut off from the mainland?"

"It's summertime," Brooke reassured her, trying not to giggle. "And the cape is fifteen miles wide. It's not getting washed out anytime soon."

"Oh, good." Janice took a breath. "Archer called."

Brooke almost slammed on the brakes. "What? When? What did you say?" She felt a chill all through her body. "You didn't tell him where I was, did you?"

"No, I just said what you told me to say. That you didn't

want to hear from him. But I still don't understand why." Janice turned plaintive. "You didn't have to take this job, and you could have tried long-distance. You two were just perfect together."

A perfect sham.

Brooke gulped. She still hadn't told her parents the whole sorry story. She felt too ashamed, so she'd just told everyone that she got this opportunity on the cape and broke up with Archer to start fresh. It was easier to field their confusion and disappointment than have to take their judgment, and putting a few thousand miles between her and the fallout hadn't hurt either. But her mom had loved Archer—what's not to love? He was handsome, successful, and charming, everything a parent would want for their daughter.

Everything, except that whole "secret wife" part.

"Thanks for not saying anything," Brooke said carefully. "Trust me, it's better this way."

"For who?" Janice countered. "You should have heard him, honey. He sounded so broken up. He misses you terribly."

Brooke's heart clenched. "He'll be fine," she said shortly.

Fine with his wife.

She saw the hotel driveway up ahead. "Look, Mom, I have to go. It's crazy here at work."

"There's more to life than work," Janice scolded. "You should think about calling Archer back. Talk to him," she added. "I'm sure he'd be willing to give you a second chance."

Brooke said her goodbyes and hung up. Maybe taking all the responsibility for the breakup wasn't the best strategy, but she hadn't been thinking straight through the tears and heartbreak. The only thing that mattered at the time was getting out of town as fast as possible, before her humiliation was revealed. She could take some misguided scolding from her mom if it meant her shameful secret affair stayed hidden a little longer, and right now, she didn't want Archer taking up any more of her heart—or her mind.

She strode into the front entrance of the hotel and called one of the desk clerks aside. "Can you please grab everyone for a staff meeting?" she said, checking the time. Just past nine a.m. Six hours to game time. "I need all hands on deck."

WHEN THE BLACK town car pulled up outside the hotel that afternoon and Meredith emerged with the happy couple in tow, Brooke was waiting on the front steps.

"Welcome to the Sandy Lane Hotel," she beamed, striding forward to greet them all. "It's a pleasure to meet you."

They all shook hands. Meredith was tapping on her cell-phone, already looking stressed, but Lila seemed every inch the off-duty starlet, in casual cut-offs and a pair of designer sunglasses that probably cost more than Brooke's entire wardrobe. Her fiancé Justin was clean-cut and had the trade-mark Cartwright smile—and a politician's handshake.

"Wow." Lila blinked, looking at the entrance, which was festooned with fresh lilacs and elegant ribbons. "Do you have an event here today? I'm sorry if we're interrupting."

"No, this is all for you," Brooke said, doing a mental fist-pump. She'd take that *Wow* and turn it into *Where do I sign?* before the afternoon was through. "I thought about showing you samples of our vendors and our vision for the wedding, but it's much better for you to see it for yourself. That way, you can imagine everything the way it will be on your special day."

Lila looked impressed. "That's a lot of trouble. Did Meredith explain we haven't committed to anywhere just yet?"

"She did." Brooke smiled. "That's why I'm going to do my

best to convince you it should be right here. Shall we go inside?" she said, gesturing to the doors. "I have champagne and cake samples waiting."

Lila brightened. "Now there's an offer we can't refuse."

Brooke led them inside, explaining about the hotel facilities and the different options for the big day. "I like to use the formal salon here for the bridal party," she said, showing them the space, which had been filled with more fresh flowers, candles, and décor in Lila's favorite shade.

"Lilacs," she gasped. "They're my favorite."

"I also read in an article that you love to read," Brooke continued. "So I took the liberty of finding some vintage books to use as decoration. We could use classic fairytales as themes for each table, and there's even a local artist who can sculpt the pages into centerpieces."

She opened the grand double doors out onto the back patio. "And here we are for the main event."

She stood aside, watching as Lila stepped out—and immediately reached to clutch her fiancé's hand. "Oh my God, look. It's perfect!" she breathed.

Brooke had to admit, she'd outdone herself. She'd set up rows of white chairs leading down the lawn and a wedding arch strewn with fresh flowers and ribbons. It stood, fluttering in the breeze, overlooking the most picture-perfect ocean scene she could imagine. There wasn't even a cloud in the sky—even the weather was on her side.

Lila turned back, her face lit up with excitement. "It's perfect. This is it."

"Are you sure?" Meredith interrupted. "We have two other appointments—"

"I'm certain." Lila cut her off. "This is where I want to get married." She looked happily at Justin. "What do you think, babe?"

"I think whatever you want is fine with me."

Brooke tried to keep her excitement in check. Wild celebration wasn't exactly professional, so she kept it to a smile. "And you haven't even tasted the cake yet," she joked. Lila laughed, but Meredith's head snapped up.

"About that. We're going to have to talk about the menus," she started, flipping open that file of hers as Lila and Justin drifted off to look at the view. "Gluten-free is a must, and we need vegan options as well. Also, I'm going to need three other décor proposals, as well as the floral samples and music."

Brooke paused. "But Lila said she loved this design—"

"Lila isn't the one planning this wedding." Meredith gave a brisk smile. "Justin's mother, Bitsy, is in charge, and she's a woman with very particular taste."

"Of course." Brooke wasn't deterred. She was used to mothers—and fathers—of the bride weighing in with their opinions. "I'll be happy to sit down with her any time."

"It'll have to be soon," Meredith reminded her. "We're on a deadline here. The wedding will be taking place in three weeks' time."

Brooke swallowed hard. Three weeks to plan the wedding of the year? That was asking a lot, even for her. "No problem!" she exclaimed brightly. "We've got it all under control."

Meredith and the happy couple departed, leaving Brooke alone. She looked around the lobby, realizing just what a massive job this was going to be. Never mind rebooking everyone who already had reservations for that weekend; she still had to source, select, and deliver a wedding fit for Hollywood—and Washington, DC—royalty, with zero time to spare.

Some people would spend a year planning for an event like this, but she had less than a month.

Stop. Brooke managed to get a grip before she could spiral into stress and panic. She would have it under control. She always did.

Her phone buzzed.

Want to grab a drink? I know the owner, I could hook you up.

Brooke smiled.

Maybe later, she texted back, wanting to play it cool, but as she checked her schedule for the rest of the day, her thoughts returned to Riley. A drink sounded like fun, and besides, she should toast the win while she still had a free moment in her day.

She deserved to celebrate.

aybe later ...

Riley stared at his cellphone, trying to read between the lines of Brooke's text. They'd been sending messages back and forth all week, just casual notes, but Riley would never admit just how much time and thought went into composing those brief messages.

Promises, promises, he typed back, then paused. What was the deal with these emojis, anyway? He'd spent years developing cutting edge apps and programs, but when it came to the finer points of technology, Riley came up blank. He was too old for this.

"Hot date?"

His head snapped up. His buddy Cooper was sitting at the bar, a quizzical eyebrow raised.

"None of your business," Riley replied good-naturedly, then shoved his phone deep in his pocket. "Isn't it kind of early for you?" he asked, strolling over. Cooper was usually on his construction sites until late, working to restore the historical homes on the cape.

"I'm on vacation," Cooper replied.

Riley snorted. "You?"

"I know." Cooper smiled. "I'm between projects right now, so Poppy suggested we both take some time to enjoy the summer. Right before her editor sent back notes on her new book," he added wryly. "So now she's chained to her laptop and sent me packing. Apparently, my mere presence is distracting."

"Well, you're welcome to seek refuge here." Riley poured him a pint of beer and slid it across the bar.

Cooper took a sip. It was peak season, so even in the afternoon, there were some tourists enjoying a late lunch, and a group of women in the corner taking advantage of the happy hour deal on local wines. "You ever think about doing something with this place?" Cooper asked.

"Like what?"

"I don't know," Cooper mused. "A restaurant, some theme nights . . . The crowds here in summer would jump for that stuff."

"I don't need any bells and whistles to get their business." Riley leaned back against the bar. "Is this your way of telling me you want karaoke nights to become a regular thing? Because that mic is yours anytime you want."

Cooper gave him a look. "No thanks. I guess I'm just wondering if you ever want to try something different," he asked thoughtfully. "I mean, you can run this place in your sleep."

"Which leaves me more time for extra-curricular activities," Riley pointed out. Cooper was still waiting, so he shrugged. "Why make life more complicated than it needs to be? Work so hard, I need two weeks in the summer to call vacation?" he asked. "Thanks, but I prefer my whole life to be a vacation."

"You don't get bored?"

Riley smirked. "Bored of waking up at noon and making my own schedule? Sure, I'm just dying to get back to my morning commute."

Cooper chuckled. "Fair enough." He checked his watch. "You think Poppy will be done with her chapter by now?"

"Look at you, itching to get back home." Riley was amused. He could remember the days when Cooper was a sworn a bachelor—before a certain romance author moved to town. "No more late nights and wild partying for you now."

Cooper gave him a look. "My partying days are long behind me. Thank God. I'd much rather spend the night at home, with a glass of wine and my woman."

"More fun left for me," Riley quipped, but he had to admit that sounded pretty good to him too. Especially if the woman in question was a certain blonde events manager . . .

A group of people came to the bar for drinks, and Riley went back to what passed as honest work for him these days. Pouring beers, chatting to his regulars, ringing up the sales—it was a long way from coding and software in Silicon Valley, that was for sure, but Riley had been out of the rat race so long now, his old life felt like a dream. Or a bad nightmare.

It had been a spur-of-the-moment decision to uproot and move out here. He was deep in the mess of the lawsuit when his brother insisted he get out of town. So, Riley flew to Boston on a whim and drove down the coast, trying to clear his head. A girl he'd met at the beach had invited him for drinks in Sweetbriar Cove one night, he'd seen the for-sale sign by the door, and—five whiskeys later—had written a check for the down payment. It made zero sense at all, but after the hammering he'd taken with lawyers and depositions, and the whole damn mess of his former company, Riley just knew that he needed a change. He'd spent ten years staring at computer screen; here, he picked up the phone to place orders and looked people in the eye to chat. He liked being a hub for the local community, seeing his friends every Friday night, and after a couple of years, Cooper was right: the place practically ran itself. He had a couple of assistant managers and a rotating parade of bartenders just passing through. He barely needed to think at all.

Which was probably why he had so much time on his hands to think about Brooke, and wonder if he was kidding himself with this whole "just friends" thing. He had plenty of female friends: Mackenzie, Summer, and Poppy, for starters. He certainly didn't want to do the kinds of things with them he was imagining doing to Brooke—

"Hi."

Brooke appeared in front of him so fast, Riley had to pause for a moment to check he wasn't still having an X-rated fantasy.

Beside her, Larry from the hardware store burped and scratched his bald spot as he read the local newspaper.

Nope. Definitely reality.

"Hey." Riley smiled at her, his day suddenly way better. "What's up?"

"Nothing much." Brooke smiled back, looking effortlessly beautiful in one of her buttoned-up blouses with a skirt that hugged all her curves. Riley tried to drag his gaze away from her body.

Friends don't check out friends' asses, he reminded himself sternly.

"So, this is what you do all day." Brooke looked around. "Holding court with all your buddies."

Even though Riley had just been boasting how easy he had it, he didn't want Brooke thinking he was a total slacker. "It's harder than it looks. Come on, you try it." He gestured for Brooke to join him on the other side of the bar.

She laughed. "For real?"

"Sure. Let's see how you handle the fast pace and high pressure of a job like this."

Brooke circled around, and came to stand beside him. "How was your day?" he asked, resisting the urge to tuck a stray piece of hair behind her ear.

"Great." She beamed wider. "I landed a massive pitch. It's going to be total chaos, working around the clock to get it done."

"And that's a good thing?" He was only half-kidding.

Brooke laughed. "To me, yes. It's a huge opportunity," she explained. "And I love a challenge."

"Them be fighting words," Riley cracked. He pulled down a fresh glass, and beckoned her closer. "Pete needs a pint of cider. Ready for your first lesson?"

"Yes, sir," Brooke said, a flirty edge in her voice.

She leaned in, close enough for him to catch a breath of her perfume, something light and floral.

Riley clenched his jaw. Damn, this was going to be an exercise in self-control.

"Tilt the glass," he instructed her, "and then pull the lever . . ."

Brooke poured a perfect pint on her first try. "Harder than it looks?" she asked, smiling.

"Beginner's luck," he replied. "Try doing that on a busy Friday night, with six people waiting on their drinks."

"I take it back," she said, placing the drink on the bar. "You're a regular hero."

Riley chuckled. "They should put up a monument in the town square."

Another lock of hair fell in her eyes, and he couldn't resist. His hand reached out of its own accord, and gently pushed it out of her face.

Brooke blinked, her eyes locked on his.

The world stilled.

What was it about this woman that sent him from zero to totally distracted in just one breath? Riley had to hold onto the bar to keep from reaching for her—pulling her close to his body, the way he already knew she fit just right. Kissing her, the way he'd done that night in the alleyway, before he even knew how good it would be—

The sound of smashing glass came from across the room. Brooke looked away, breaking the moment, and Riley felt a curious mix of relief and regret.

"Duty calls," he said, grabbing a dishcloth. "Don't go anywhere."

BROOKE LIKED the view from behind the bar, she decided as she leaned back to take in the room. She was separate from the crowd, but a part of it too: the first stop for anyone stepping through the doors. And seeing Riley up close at work, it was clear he was the most popular guy in town. And not just because of his generous pours. He had a word or a joke for everyone, asking about their family and work and even their pets.

"Mr. Freckles has a bad leg," he explained, straight-faced,

after an older woman spent ten minutes chatting about the vet visits before retreating to a table with her glass of lemonade. "We're hoping he hangs in there until Pooch Day."

"Pooch Day? Brooke felt a long way from Chicago. She didn't even know her neighbor's names, let alone their pets' medical problems. "Do I even want to ask?"

"Probably not." He grinned. "Just look for the dog show."

Brooke caught her breath. That man's smile should be illegal—or come with a warning, at the very least. *Danger: accelerated heart rate up ahead. May cause shortness of breath, dizziness, and public swooning.*

"You know everyone and everything about this town, huh?" She'd thought Riley was just a natural flirt, but now she could see his easy charm actually came in useful and made everyone feel at home.

"Pretty much. This town likes to gossip," he added, with a warning look. "And most of it passes through my doors."

"I imagine you give them plenty to talk about," Brooke teased.

"I'm a perfect gentleman," Riley protested, giving her a virtuous look.

She didn't buy it for a minute.

The doors opened and a group of women entered. It was the coeds; she remembered them from karaoke night, now looking fresh from the beach in bikinis and cover-ups. "Hi Riley!" they chorused, waving at him.

"Ladies." He flashed that same smile at them all, and Brooke's heart sank a little. Of course it wasn't just for her. "Another hard day tanning?"

They giggled. "We're on vacation."

"We're allowed to take it easy."

"Of course you are," Riley agreed. "Go, sit, take a load off. I'll come get your orders in a sec."

"You're the best." One of the girls, a tanned blonde who couldn't have been more than twenty, gave him a flirty wink. She sashayed away, her cut-off jeans riding high over her long, twenty-year-old thighs.

Brooke had never felt frumpier. Why hadn't she changed after work? She probably looked like that girl's maiden aunt, all buttoned up in her jacket and silk top.

"You OK hanging here?" Riley asked her, as he pulled out an order pad. "You want something to eat? I can have my guy rustle you up some killer tacos."

Brooke shook her head. "I'm good."

She watched him walk over to the group—and be greeted with adoring smiles. But who could blame them? They tossed their hair, flirting up a storm, and Riley . . . Well, Riley flirted right back.

Brooke felt a twist of disappointment.

She shouldn't be envious of some kids barely out of high school, but she couldn't help it. Watching him turn on the same easy charm he'd just been shining at her, it reminded her that her first impression had been right. Riley was still a player, through and through.

Brooke tried to shake off the little voice whispering in her mind. She had no right to be jealous, she was the one who'd told him she only wanted to be friends. Riley was free to flirt with whomever he wanted.

But she didn't have to stand around and watch.

She grabbed her purse and rounded the bar.

"Hey," Riley called after her as she headed for the door. He crossed the bar. "Heading out already?" He looked confused, and Brooke pasted on a smile.

"I need to get started on work," she said.

"On a Friday night?"

"Like I said, I'm on a deadline. Anyway, you don't need me getting in the way here," she added brightly. "I'll see you around."

BACK AT HER APARTMENT, Brooke turned on some music and spent the evening planning a day-by-day schedule leading up to the big day. Riley was right, she thought ruefully, she sure knew how to party, but with Meredith already filling her inbox with notes and instructions, there was no time to delay. Flowers, music . . . she made lists for her lists, color-coded and filed away under a dozen different tabs, until the plans were practically a work of art.

It was midnight before she finally set her laptop aside. She put on her PJs, drank her sleepy-time tea, and put on the soothing whale sound playlist that people online swore sent them straight to sleep. Then she lay in bed feeling wide awake, with her mind buzzing.

It happened almost every night now.

Brooke sighed, kicking off her sheets. She used to love sleeping, savor collapsing into bed and drifting off after a long day at the hotel. But now, sleep taunted her, always just out of reach. She'd tried everything: from herbal remedies to soothing baths to new-age meditation. Her doctor had even prescribed some sleeping pills, but they just left her feeling like a zombie the next day, and with so much depending on her at work, she preferred feeling exhausted to missing some crucial detail that would spoil a guest's important day.

Another sleepless night it was then.

Brooke was just thinking about grabbing her laptop again, when her phone lit up with a text.

You up?

It was Riley.

Afraid so, she texted back, and was surprised when her phone rang a moment later.

"It's all this work you're doing." Riley's voice was deep and soothing. "Your brain needs to rest, too, if you're going to sleep."

"Believe me, I've tried." Brooke smiled to hear him, like he was right there with her. "I tried leaving my laptop at the office, I tried making my bedroom a no-tech zone. I even tried a sleep seminar, where we all did deep breathing exercises and imagined floating off on a sea of wispy clouds."

Riley chuckled. "I'm trying to picture you relaxing. I bet you treated it like a competition."

"Hey!" Brooke protested. "I can relax. And yes, I was the best in class."

She threw off the covers and stretched, yawning. It was a warm night, and her windows were open, but even the distant sound of the waves hadn't sent her off to sleep.

"So what are you wearing?" Riley's tone turned cheeky.

"Excuse me?" Brooke faked offense, even as her stomach flipped over.

"Being too hot or cold can stop you sleeping," he explained, with laughter in his voice. "I'm just trying to help you out here."

"Of course you are." Brooke smiled. "For your information, I'm wearing a tank top and sleep shorts. Light and comfortable."

"Cute."

"Are you still at work?" she asked, thinking of those women at the bar.

"Just walking home now."

Alone.

For some reason, the thought made Brooke grin. "To your boat."

"Yes, ma'am."

"You don't ever get seasick?"

"Nah, the water's pretty calm. There was a storm last winter, kicked up some real waves, but I hung in there OK."

"Lucky you," Brooke said. "My old job, they took us all out on a cruise on the river. It was supposed to be a team-building thing, but I spent the whole trip hanging over the side, vomiting."

She stopped. Vomit wasn't exactly the most attractive mental image, but Riley didn't seem to mind. He chuckled. "Aww, don't worry. Those bigger boats are bad, but my girl is a smooth ride. I'll take you out sometime, and you'll see."

"Just bring a bucket," Brooke warned.

"It's a date."

Brooke caught her breath. Date, or . . . *Date?*

"So are you going to tell me about this big event of yours?" Riley continued, so smoothly Brooke felt silly for picking over the meaning of his words.

"I would, but I'm sworn to secrecy," she said. "Seriously, I think they'd sue."

"Well, I know a great lawyer if you need one," Riley replied.

"Don't even joke." Brooke yawned, loud enough for him to hear.

"How long has it been now since you had a decent night's sleep?"

"Ugh." Brooke didn't even want to think about it. "I got four hours last night . . . a couple the night before. I don't understand it," she sighed. "Some nights, I zone out the minute I hit the pillow, and others, I'm lying awake for hours counting the cracks on my bedroom ceiling."

"Has it been going on long?"

"Just a few months," Brooke replied. "Since I moved here."

"Maybe you're still adjusting to the change."

"Maybe."

Brooke didn't say, but she knew the real reason for her insomnia, and it didn't take a genius to figure out. She hadn't slept through the night since finding out the truth about Archer. It was the guilt still keeping her awake—the guilt, and shame, and whole tangle of heartache.

But she didn't want to dwell on it now, so she changed the subject. "Tell me about yourself," she said instead, getting out of bed.

"With pleasure," Riley replied. "It's my favorite subject. What do you want to know?"

"Hmm," Brooke padded barefoot out of her bedroom. "Siblings?"

"One. Brother. Max. He's the lawyer I was talking about," Riley replied. "You'd like him. He's a stickler for details. You?"

"Only child. I'm their sole source of disappointment."

"C'mon, I don't believe that. They've got to be proud of you."

"I guess . . ." Brooke grabbed a blanket from the couch and opened the front door. She sat on the steps, breathing in the sweet scent of the night-flowering jasmine, looking out at the pitch-black bay. "But my mom wants grandkids, so I'm failing her in that department so far. She was already married at my age. They're still together, going on forty years now."

"Mine are the same," Riley said. "High school sweethearts, if you can believe it."

"That's nice." Brooke leaned back against the stair post, snuggling deeper in her blanket. "You think they knew, what they were getting into? Or do you just make the leap and figure it out along the way?"

"You know," Riley said, his voice husky. "When it's real, you know."

"I love staging weddings at the hotel," Brooke found herself admitting. "I mean, I tell everyone it's good business, and it is, but there's more than that, too. I get to give them a day they'll remember for the rest of their lives. I mean, maybe they won't remember what color the napkins were, or if the balloons were pink or gold, but they remember how they felt, just starting out on the rest of their lives together. It's special, being a part of that. Seeing them say their vows and mean every word. It helps me remember that kind of love really exists out there."

Brooke stopped. What was she doing, going on about marriage and commitment with a guy who probably changed women as often as he changed his socks? "I'm keeping you up," she said.

"It's OK. I'm a night owl," Riley said. "Comes with the territory, at the pub."

Along with hoards of admiring cuties, Brooke silently added.

"I should try to get some sleep," she said reluctantly.

"Want me to come tuck you in?" he asked, teasing, but Brooke gulped at the thought.

Sleeping would be the last thing on the menu with Riley in her bed.

"That depends," she answered lightly, "Do you snore?"

"Not that I've heard," Riley replied. "But I steal all the covers."

"Then it's a no from me."

"Shame," Riley drawled, low enough for Brooke to shiver. "But good luck."

"I'll need it."

"And I mean it, you need to relax," Riley added. "Take some time off work, unwind. That brain of yours needs to switch off sometime."

"Maybe." Brooke headed back inside. "After this big wedding is done."

"And when's that?"

"A few weeks."

Riley groaned. "That's no good. You're going to be a zombie soon."

"Think I could win Pooch Day?" Brooke teased. She yawned, finally feeling tired now. "OK, I'm really going to try this time. I've got my sleep mask and earplugs and everything."

"Just lie back and imagine you're on vacation," Riley suggested. "Palm trees, white sand, me rubbing in your lotion."

Brooke laughed. He really was incorrigible. "Goodnight, Riley."

"Goodnight, Brooke."

She hung up and hid her phone in a drawer, far out of reach. Still, his voice lingered in her mind, that seductive whiskey drawl. She lay back and closed her eyes, just like he'd told her to. Tropical sands . . . a clear ocean . . . and him. His hands smoothing over her skin, slowly caressing . . .

Brooke groaned, her body suddenly wound tight and alert.

Now how was she supposed to sleep with an image like that in her mind?

10

---

*B*rooke finally got her wish. She slept the whole night through—but with dreams of Riley dancing temptingly in her mind. By the time she woke, early Saturday morning, she was a pent-up ball of frustration and desire, haunted by the sensual fantasies that still lingered, just out of reach.

Couldn't a sleep-deprived girl catch a break around here?

She pulled on a pair of workout shorts and her sports bra, and laced up her sneakers, feeling determined. Clearly, soothing herself into sleep wasn't working, so she would just have to try the opposite tactic: sheer exhaustion. If she pushed herself to the limit all day long, then her brain would have to shut down eventually. Right?

She took off along the coastal road, her feet pounding the concrete. It was a gorgeous summer's morning, with a clear blue sky and white-topped waves, and it felt good to be out, so she detoured down to the beach to run along the damp sand.

The wide, windswept shore was empty this early, just a couple of people out walking their dogs and some optimistic surfers bobbing out in the freezing waters. As the miles disappeared behind her, Brooke's mind finally cleared. She felt her body stretch, and her lungs burned as she gulped the salty breeze.

She needed to forget him.

Moving here had been the right step, but it was no good putting a thousand miles between her and Archer if she still carried him in her heart. Not tenderly, not anymore, but the hurt and betrayal still took up just as much space, burning with unanswered questions and blame.

She was never going to move on by holding so tightly to the past.

One of these days, she was going to have to forgive herself for believing him.

Brooke finally stopped, bending double as she gasped for air. Her heart was pounding so loud it thundered in her mind, but still it wasn't enough to push the whispers away.

She should have known better. She should have seen the signs.

Brooke let out a noise of frustration that was swallowed by the wind.

She was so used to getting it right. In school, she'd been a straight-A student, working long hours on her assignments until she got those perfect scores. In college, she'd planned her schedule and kept careful watch on her GPA, secured all the best internships so she could graduate with her career right on track. She planned and put the hours in, taking care with every last detail to earn those glowing reviews, because she wanted to do it right—not to be the best, but to be the best she could be.

She'd thought Archer was right. The perfect match. They'd

been so good together—right up until the moment her feet had been knocked out from under her.

What had she missed?

Brooke straightened up, her heart rate slowing now. She stood, looking out at the bay and the wide expanse of blue.

Maybe she'd never know. Maybe she could go back over every last memory and see nothing out of place. No hints she should have registered, no red flags to send her running for the hills. She'd been careful, she'd taken it slow, and still, his lies had slipped past her with all the ring of the truth.

Maybe he was just that good.

After all, she wasn't the only one who'd fallen for his lines. His wife had believed them, too. Every night he was working late, every business trip out of town. Brooke's heart ached remembering the look on Julia's face as she'd stood there on the doorstep—her anger giving way to misery when she'd realized that Brooke wasn't some ruthless temptress, but a dupe, just like her.

"How did I not see this happening, right under my nose?" she'd despaired, and now Brooke felt the same way. They'd been blinded by love and hope for the future that Archer had promised them. Dazzled by the illusion, until the spell was broken and the mirage faded away.

Brooke took a deep breath, and then another.

She couldn't keep doing this to herself. Looking for answers, when the truth was there was nothing Archer could ever offer to explain. What could he say to her now? *I'm sorry. I never meant to hurt you.*

Or, worse still, *You made it easy, you were such a fool.*

None of it would change a thing. No, that part was down to her now. She had to start letting it go.

She took another breath and started running again. This time, towards home.

BY THE TIME Brooke arrived back at those blue gates marking home, she was a sweaty, exhausted mess. But something felt lighter, that knot in her chest unraveled a little more loosely. She could do this, moving on. No more dwelling on a past she couldn't change now. She was going to face forward and let herself off the hook, with—

"Riley?" Brooke stopped short. He was sitting on her steps, golden and easy in the morning sun. "What are you . . . ?" She fumbled for words, her mind suddenly flooded with all the hot, illicit dreams she'd been having. Her face burned. "I didn't expect . . . I mean . . ." Brooke grasped for a simple greeting. "Hi."

"Hey there." Riley slowly unfolded his limbs and got to his feet, that irresistible smile taking her in. "Good run?"

"Yes. Hard." Brooke gulped. She pushed back her sweaty mess of hair, wishing she didn't look such a wreck. "I'm following your advice, trying to wear myself out."

Riley chuckled. "Yeah, that's not what I said. My advice was to relax and have a good time. So, it's a good thing I'm here to teach you my tricks."

"You have tricks?" Brooke repeated, smiling.

"You bet, baby." Riley grinned back, and God, that smile should be illegal. "Come sailing. We can drop anchor by a beach, lie out in the sun . . . It's impossible to stay stressed out on the water."

Brooke paused, torn. It did sound incredibly relaxing, and the thought of spending the day with Riley was more tempting than she'd like to admit. "I was going to work," she said, reluctant.

"It's the weekend, c'mon," Riley urged her. "This is probably the last chance you'll get to switch off before that top-secret project of yours gets rolling. You need to have some fun."

Brooke paused, but there was really no contest. Spend her day at the hotel, solving every crisis in sight, or out on the water with this fine specimen of a man?

"OK, I'm in."

"Damn right you are." Riley looked pleased. "Go grab your things, I already stopped by the bakery, so I've got a basket full of goodies."

"That's what all the guys say." Brooke found herself winking as she skipped past him and up the stairs. Riley's surprised laughter followed her inside. Then she shut the door and caught a glimpse of herself in the mirror.

Oh God! No wonder he was laughing, she looked like she'd just run a marathon—in no makeup and her oldest sweats.

Brooke barreled for the bathroom, taking the quickest shower in the history of mankind. In ten minutes, she was back out on her porch, dressed in her bikini and some cut-offs, with a cool linen shirt tied up around her stomach. "All set," she said, trying to ignore the flip of excitement she felt, bouncing down to meet him.

This wasn't a date.

This wasn't anything at all.

Liar.

RILEY DROVE them the short distance to Sweetbriar Cove, chatting easily about his conversion to a life off solid land. "It was an impulse buy," he said, glancing over to Brooke. "But the best things always are."

"Wait, you bought a boat without even knowing how to sail?" She blinked. "That's crazy! Don't you plan anything in your life at all?"

Riley shrugged. "What's there to plan? You just trust your instincts, and everything will work out OK in the end."

There it was again: the same question Brooke had been grappling with for months now. "I don't know about that," she replied. "My instincts don't have the best record lately."

"Ah. Yeah." Riley made a face. "But that wasn't the end, was it?" He shot her an encouraging look. "You're still standing, aren't you?"

"Just about."

"Then there you go. As my friend Poppy would say, there's plenty of pages in your story yet. Actually, she'd never say that," he added. "I'm the one cracking bad novelist puns."

Brooke smiled again. There was just something about his upbeat personality that was infectious: bulletproof optimism, even after he'd had his own share of betrayals. She could learn a thing or two from him, she decided as they wound along the coastal road. Starting with how to actually unwind for a change, and leave all her stress and worry behind.

He was right. She deserved a little fun.

They arrived at the small harbor, where the seafood shack already had a morning crowd and a couple of guys sat fishing off the pier. Brooke looked around eagerly, trying to figure out which boat was his.

"Now, she's not the sleekest schooner on the water," Riley warned her as he retrieved a cooler and picnic basket from the trunk. "But she gets the job done."

"I have zero experience with boats," Brooke laughed,

hoisting up her tote bag of summer essentials. "As long as we don't sink, I'm good."

"That, I can do." Riley led her down the jetty, to where an old, charming sailboat sat bobbing on the tide. "Here she is, my one and only."

"She looks great." Brooke took in the blue paint and sleek white cabin. The sails were white with a blue trim, and the old wood looked weathered—but sturdy. *Week of Sundays,*" she read the script painted in red on the bow.

"My philosophy on life." Riley loaded the bags onto the deck. "Now, you've got your sunscreen?"

"Check."

"Shades?"

Brooke rifled through her bag. "Check."

"Cellphone?"

She nodded. "Never let it out of my sight."

"Wrong answer. This is a work-free zone," Riley informed her, mock-stern. "No phones allowed."

Brooke laughed, and made to move past him, but he held out his hand, waiting for her phone. "I'm not kidding. How are you going to switch off and relax if you're checking messages all day long?"

"But what if something happens?" Brooke blinked. She felt anxious just at the thought. "I always say they can reach me 24/7 in an emergency."

"They'll live. It's just a few hours," he reassured her. "Come on, live a little."

Brooke wavered, still clutching her phone tightly. But the invitation in Riley's eyes was too good to resist. She reluctantly handed it to him. "Be careful with that thing," she warned him, watching as he stashed it in a small lockbox on the dock along with his keys. "My whole life is in there."

"Then we need to get you a new one." Riley climbed on board and held out his hand to help her. Brooke stepped cautiously onto the deck, feeling the gentle shift and roll of the waves. She was worried about her less-than-stellar history on the ocean, but this seemed calm enough.

"Let me give you the tour," Riley said, a proud note to his voice. He led Brooke down to the tiny cabin, where a galley kitchen sat snugly beside a built-in bench and small fold-out table. There was a door to a tiny bathroom, and then the main cabin bedroom, which contained a bed . . . and not much else.

"Cozy," Brooke said, looking around. And it was. Despite the compact size, the space was warm and inviting. "How do you fit everything?" she asked. She'd been half-expecting a bachelor pad—complete with bachelor levels of messiness and grime—but Riley's bedroom was immaculate, with soft-looking grey sheets and a pile of pillows tempting her to lay back and . . .

She dragged her gaze away from the bed and tried to shut that train of thought down in a hurry. "I can't imagine cramming all my stuff in here."

"I keep it simple," Riley replied, stowing things from the cooler in the small fridge. "No mess, no fuss, that's how I like to live."

"And nobody outstaying their welcome," she teased.

He flashed a grin. "Ask nicely, and you can stay as long as you like."

The cabin was so small, she was standing dangerously close to him. Close enough to remember just how good his arms had felt around her. And as for his mouth . . .

"You won't say that when I'm vomiting all over you!" Brooke exclaimed loudly, before she realized what she'd just blurted.

Vomit. Sexy.

She stifled a groan. "I'll be up on deck," she said brightly, and scrambled up the stairs before she could see his reaction. Fun and relaxation were one thing, but if she wasn't careful, these close quarters might go giving her ideas.

Recklessly tempting ideas.

But would that really be so bad?

11

---

*R*iley watched Brooke bolt out of the cabin like she'd been burned, but he couldn't blame her. The chemistry between them was getting dangerously hot, and that molten smile of hers was almost enough to make Riley forget that pledge about staying platonic.

Almost.

Still, as he went about casting off and steering them out of the harbor, he couldn't stop from stealing glances at where Brooke stood on the bow of the boat, leaning out over the railing with her blonde hair tangling on the breeze.

She looked like a natural. Like she belonged out there—or, better yet, downstairs in his bed, with that hair getting tangled up for a whole other reason . . .

Riley gripped the steering wheel harder.

That was a topic for another day. Or, another night, after the hot, wild dreams he'd been haunted by. The universe sure had a way of taunting him. No sooner did he blow off those hot college girls slipping him their numbers than he wound up dreaming about the one woman who was most definitely out of reach.

Brooke turned and saw him watching her. "This is fun!" she called. "You were right, the water's really calm."

"There's a little cove, a couple of knots up the coast," he called back. "We can drop anchor there, hang out a while."

"Sounds good to me!"

When they were out of the harbor, Riley cut the engine, and set about hoisting the sails. Brooke approached, looking curious.

"Here," he told her, passing a rope. "Hold this."

"What are you doing?"

"Trimming the jib."

Brooke laughed. "What?"

Riley grinned. "I know. All the sailing lingo takes some getting used to. Basically, it means we pull this sail tight, until we get a pocket of air. See?" The rope ran taut, and he fastened it in place. "Now that wind will keep us moving, as long as we stay on the right side of it."

"It seems like a lot of work." Brooke looked up, shielding her eyes from the sun. "Wouldn't it be easier to just motor along?"

"Now, where's the fun in that?" Riley protested. "I mean, feel how smoothly she's running. The wind at our backs, the sun in the sky . . . What could beat this?"

Brooke smiled at him, looking relaxed and carefree for the first time in, well, forever.

"Nothing," she said, and everything was right with the world.

"Come here," he beckoned. "You can take the wheel."

Brooke looked nervous. "I don't want to steer us into anything."

"Don't worry, there aren't any icebergs out here. It's easy." He beckoned again, and Brooke came closer. "Just plant your feet," he told her. "And take it in both hands."

Brooke quirked an eyebrow at him, and Riley snorted.

"I didn't say a word!" she protested, flushing.

She moved in front of him, and carefully took hold of the old-fashioned ship's wheel. She gripped the spokes. "Like this?"

"Mmhmm." Riley was momentarily distracted by the way her hair was dancing on the breeze, brushing softly against him. "You want to keep us heading north, north-east," he said, standing behind her. He guided her hands on the wheel, turning it slightly. "Just keep parallel to the shoreline, with the wind to the port side. That's left," he translated.

"Are you sure about those icebergs?" Brooke turned to smile up at him, and Riley felt like he was the one sailing straight for impact.

He stepped back. "You want a beer?" he asked, saying the first thing that came into his mind.

"It's ten in the morning," she said.

"Exactly. Time for a beer."

Riley disappeared below deck, wondering what the hell had gotten into him. This was his patented move: the lazy day out on the water. Brooke certainly wasn't the first woman he'd shown how to sail, and she definitely wouldn't be the last. So why was he tripping over himself around her?

Because she was hotter than the rest of them combined, and he already knew how explosive they would be, given half a chance . . .

Dammit. Riley stifled a groan of frustration. This was what you got for late night calls that didn't involve phone sex, and hours spent talking, just getting to know each other. She was getting under his skin, and worst of all?

He liked it.

WITH BROOKE'S HELP, Riley steered them up the coast, to the peaceful little cove that was sheltered from the main sea winds. He dropped anchor, and the two of them lay out on the bow of the boat, lounging in the sun as the water dipped and rolled.

"God, this feels good," Brooke sighed from under the brim of her massive sunhat. She turned her head and gave him a lazy smile. "Thank you. This is exactly what I needed."

"My pleasure," Riley replied, and with her stretched beside him, it was. He was lucky he was wearing shades to hide his roving gaze, but damn, those cut-off shorts of hers weren't hiding anything. "We'll have you blowing off work to catch some rays in no time."

Brooke giggled. "I don't know about that. But you're right, I can't remember the last time I took a whole day doing nothing. Or even a few hours. It feels so . . . indulgent."

"We're just getting started, baby," Riley teased. "Stick with me, and you'll be taking afternoon naps and sleeping in until noon."

She laughed. "You live life on the edge, huh?"

"Damn straight."

"I better watch out, or you'll lead me astray."

Riley had to fight to keep from taking her up on that invitation. The things he would do with this woman . . .

Brooke stretched her long legs and yawned. She tilted her hat back over her face and fell silent, her chest rising and falling steadily in that demure bikini top.

Riley's pulse drummed faster.

He shut his eyes, trying to ignore the temptation right beside him, but it was no use. The sight of her gorgeous body was burned into his brain, and every shift and satisfied sigh just wound him tighter.

"Riley?"

He lifted his head. Brooke was looking at him with a bashful expression. "Would you mind . . . ?" She held out a bottle of sunscreen. "Sorry, my back . . ."

"Oh. Sure."

Riley took the bottle and steeled himself. Brooke turned so her back was facing him and swept her hair aside. "I burn like crazy," she said over her shoulder. "I never had to worry in Chicago, but here I have to slather it on with my moisturizer in the morning, otherwise I get so many freckles."

Riley squeezed a dollop of lotion, then gently smoothed it onto her shoulder.

Brooke flinched.

"Cold. Sorry." Riley's voice came out gruff.

Pull it together, man.

He spread another dollop on her other shoulder, exercising more self-control than he ever had in his life before. Her skin was soft and warm from the sun, and all he wanted to do was trail his fingertips over every inch of her, straying under that bikini top, and over her—

"Thanks!" Brooke pulled away. "I should be good now."

Riley cleared his throat. "Great. OK."

He took a breath. She was rubbing lotion into the rest of her body now, her skin glistening in the sun . . .

He stifled a groan. Whose bright idea was it to trap himself on a boat in the middle of the ocean with a woman who could drive him wild with a single look? If he spent one more second with her, he'd do something he'd live to regret—like kiss her until she forgot the meaning of the word "friendship."

There was only one way out of this.

Riley got up, tore off his shirt, and cannonballed over the side of the boat.

SPLASH.

∼

BROOKE SAW Riley hit the water, and let out the breath she'd been holding ever since she stepped onto the boat.

Good God, that man was too sexy for her own good.

She shivered, just remembering the feel of his hands, sliding over her back. His warm, sensual touch . . . The soft whisper of his breath on the back of her neck . . . She'd had to bite her lip to keep from moaning out loud at his touch, practically melting in a pool right there on the deck.

If this was what he could do with an innocent sunscreen application, she didn't want to think about what would happen with fewer clothes, and more hands, and maybe his mouth, too—

Brooke caught herself, skin flushing. She was playing with fire, just thinking about it. She was the one who put the brakes on, remember? Which made the situation even more dangerous. Because something told her that despite Riley's happy agreement that they would be friends, all it would take was one word from her to send that platonic business flying out the window.

A word like *yes*, or *more*, or *please*.

She watched him in the water below, splashing and swimming in the gentle waves. It looked good down there. Refreshing. She could certainly use some cooling off.

And the half-naked man had nothing to do with it.

Not at all.

Brooke shimmied out of her shorts and stepped to the edge

of the bow. It looked like a long way down, but she took a deep breath, sent a silent prayer, and leapt off the boat, arcing in a dive so she cut through the water with a ripple.

The water hit, ice-cold, and she surfaced, gasping.

"Nice moves!" Riley called, treading water nearby.

"Thanks." Brooke pushed wet hair from her eyes. She flipped onto her back, and floated, enjoying the gently-rolling waves. "I swam a little in college."

"Which, in Brooke-speak, that means you were at the pool by six every morning until you blew the competition away." Riley's voice was teasing, so Brooke didn't even care that he was right.

She laughed. "Five-thirty, actually, but yes."

"That sounds like a challenge." He had a wicked twinkle in his eye, his biceps rippling with every stroke. "Race you to the buoy and back?"

Brooke checked the distance. Not far. And racing Riley would definitely keep her from reaching for him.

"Sure, I'm in."

"What do you say we make it interesting?" Riley added. "Loser pays a forfeit. I'll even give you a head start," he offered chivalrously.

Brooke grinned. "Take all the time you need."

She took off, swimming for the buoy with strong, steady strokes. She heard Riley laugh behind her, and then he was splashing through the water nearby. Soon, her lungs were burning, and her arms ached, but Brooke kept driving forward, eyes on the prize. Maybe if she pushed herself hard enough, she could out-swim the desire coursing, hot in her system.

But when she returned to the boat, exhausted and gasping for air, and she looked back at Riley cutting through the water like some kind of tanned god—muscles rippling, drenched by the waves—Brooke had to admit defeat.

Exhausted or not, she still wanted him. Wanted those hands on her body, wanted that mouth wreaking its gorgeous havoc on hers. She'd been fighting it since the moment they met, but nothing was going to put out the heat between them.

So why should she even try?

"Damn, you're fast." Riley smiled, reaching the boat just a few seconds behind her. She climbed up the ladder onto the deck, and he followed, water running in rivulets over his toned chest and chiseled abs. "You were really killing it back there."

"Uh huh," Brooke answered vaguely. Her heart was beating faster now—and she knew it had nothing to do with the swim. She could feel the anticipation crackle in her veins, even before she'd made up her mind.

Her body knew. Her body always knew, half a heartbeat before her mind caught up.

"Guess this means I have to pay a forfeit." Riley grinned. "What's your price?"

She took a deep breath. "A kiss."

If Brooke had any lingering doubts, they disappeared the moment she saw Riley's gaze darken with lust. Her stomach turned a slow flip, every nerve in her body sparking to life.

Still, Riley paused, assessing her with that molten look. "You sure about that?"

Brooke nodded slowly, her eyes never leaving his. She was sure now, sure that whatever was about to happen was exactly what she needed. "You're the one who said, I should have some fun," she said, trying to stay light.

"I did, didn't I?" Riley took a couple of steps closer. "So you've decided to follow my advice?"

She nodded again.

His gaze slipped over her body, and Brooke realized too late that she was practically naked in her wet bikini. She shivered under his gaze, but instead of shrinking away, she found herself standing taller, loving the desire written so clearly on his face.

He wanted her.

And God, she wanted him too.

"So what makes you think I'm the man for the job?" Riley gave a smirk even as he moved closer still.

"You seem qualified," Brooke said, her heart racing. "And I'm sure your references would be excellent if I checked."

"Yes, ma'am." Riley gave an irresistible smile, coming to a stop in front of her.

He reached out and slowly trailed a fingertip over her shoulder, and up to her jaw. The feeling was electric, and Brooke marveled how her body could respond to such a small touch. Riley's eyes searched hers, dark and hot. "Last chance," he murmured, his voice low. "Because once you say the word . . ."

He didn't finish, but he didn't have to. Brooke felt like she was humming with desire, and she knew once they crossed this line again, there would be no going back.

But she didn't want to.

She only wanted him.

Brooke reached up and pressed her palm against his wet, naked chest. She smiled. "I'll have my prize now," she said softly, and that was all it took. Riley's eyes flashed with lust, and then he pulled her to him, and kissed her so hard, Brooke forgot her own name.

Oh my God . . .

Riley's lips roved over hers, demanding, easing her open and stroking his tongue deep into her mouth. Brooke shuddered at the intimacy, pressing closer, needing more. Riley answered with a low growl, reaching to tangle his hands in her hair, then slide them over her body. Caressing, exploring, molding her curves to his taut, chiseled muscles . . . Brooke clung on for dear life. She was dizzy with lust, and she could feel him, hard against her, nothing but the damp fabric of their swimsuits masking the heat.

Riley stroked lower, over the swell of her breast, and Brooke moaned into his mouth.

He tore his mouth from hers, panting. "God, you've been driving me crazy." Riley dropped a line of searing kisses down the curve of her neck. "You don't even know what you do to me. But I'm going to show you, baby. Just you wait."

Brooke shuddered at his words. Her blood was already burning, and she didn't think she'd been so turned on in her life before. "So show me," she murmured playfully. She didn't know what was happening to her, why she was suddenly so reckless and bold, but it felt too good to question why.

He felt too good.

She pulled his head up and kissed him again, feeling drunk on the taste of him, the salty tang from his lips. "Show me," she whispered again, and Riley's lips curved in a tempting smile.

"Yes, ma'am."

He lifted her suddenly, wrapping her legs around his waist and carrying her to the bow of the boat. He laid her down, right there on the deck where they'd been sunbathing just a few moments before.

"Don't hold back," he murmured, his smile turning downright wicked as he leaned over her. "Nobody's around to hear."

"Hear what—?" Brooke's question was lost in a moan as he bent his head and nipped lightly at her breast, toying with her nipple through the damp fabric of her bikini top. She flushed, shocked by his boldness, but then his hands joined his mouth, pushing her swimsuit aside, and it was all she could do to just lie back and revel in the incredible sensations flooding through her body. He caressed her, teased her, made her writhe and moan; his hands skimming lower as his mouth brought her to stiff peaks of pleasure.

What was this man *doing* to her? And please, could it never end?

Brooke felt his fingertips graze over her bikini bottoms. She tensed with anticipation. Oh God. This was really happening, out here in the sunlight, with the waves rolling gently, and the boat shifting on the tide.

She squeezed her eyes shut, already flushing with the thought of it, but Riley paused. "Oh no, sweetheart, you're not hiding from this." She felt him move back up her body, his body skimming hers, blazing with heat. "Look at me," he ordered softly, and she shivered, feeling exposed.

He stroked her gently through her bikini and a moan slipped from her mouth again.

She heard him chuckle, whiskey sweet. "I don't want you to miss a minute of this, baby. Open your eyes."

Brooke slowly obeyed, and looked up to find he was braced above her, that gorgeous, teasing smile on his lips. "See," he whispered, and stroked her again. "It's much more fun this way."

He pushed the fabric aside and skimmed a fingertip over her, and Brooke gasped at the touch. Riley was poised above her, those dark eyes just inches away, and there was nowhere to hide as he delved deeper, touching her just right.

She shuddered around him, her blood thick and hot. God, he was too sexy, and he knew just how to wind her tighter, watching as she tried in vain to keep from losing control.

"You're so beautiful," he murmured, dipping to lick her lips as his fingers curled higher. Brooke whimpered, pressing into his hand, needing more somehow. "Don't hold back now, baby." He kissed her softly, teasing. "I've got you now."

He did. Brooke couldn't deny the pleasure sweeping through her, or how wild and reckless it felt to come undone in his arms. She kissed him eagerly, their tongues dancing together as his fingers worked their magic, unraveling her inch by inch until she was moaning, pressing wantonly against him, her voice lost on the breeze. Higher, higher he drove her, until she was dazzled with the heat, out on the edge of something so strong, it was like she'd taken leave of her senses.

"Let go," he ordered her, his voice gruff. "Let go for me, sweetheart."

Brooke wanted to, she was so close, but still, something held her back. This chemistry between them was dangerous—burning too bright to give into, too hot to keep from the scars.

If she fell off the edge, could she trust him to break her fall?

Riley kissed his way down her body, his touch roving deeper, faster now, and then it was too much to keep at bay. He was everywhere, undeniable, and Brooke couldn't fight the pleasure anymore. She broke apart, crying out against him as the waves of bliss shuddered through her, leaving her gasping in his arms.

Wow.

Riley was right: he was exactly the man for the job.

Brooke couldn't help but smile. She felt so light, she might just float away. "Want a rematch?" she asked, her eyes closed. "Double or nothing?"

Riley laughed, rolling to one side. When Brooke opened her eyes, he was propped on one elbow, watching her with a satisfied smile.

"That good, huh?" he said, smirking.

"It's a start." Brooke grinned back.

Suddenly, she didn't know what she'd been so afraid of. This was Riley: king of the no-drama good time. She didn't need him to catch her, she told herself, pleasure still sweet in her bloodstream. This was just a little fun.

12

They spent the morning sunbathing, out there on the boat. Brooke felt all her stress and anxiety melt clean away, soothed by the gentle roll of the ocean—and Riley's lazy kisses.

"I'm beginning to see why you like this thing," she said, yawning. "It must be nice being able to just pull up the anchor and sail on whenever you please."

"I keep it close to home most days," Riley replied. He was lying beside her, one hand intertwined with hers. "My adventuring days are behind me. I like my creature comforts, a hot meal and a good glass of whiskey."

"Speaking of . . ." Brooke sat up. "I remember you saying something about a picnic?"

He grinned. "Worked up an appetite, have you?"

"Maybe." She smiled back. "And I could use some fuel for another round."

Riley's eyebrow arched.

"Another swim," she added, getting to her feet.

"Sure, that's what you meant."

She laughed and headed down into the cabin, where she found a picnic basket and a couple of glasses. She emerged back on deck and paused, just watching Riley. He was fixing something with the sail, looking sexier than any man had a right to; tanned skin golden in the sun, his muscles rippling.

She felt a delicious shiver spiral through her. She'd been joking before, but it was true—this was just the start of their fun.

Riley looked up and caught her staring. "Come here," he beckoned, and she moved closer. He kissed her softly, but even the gentle brush of his lips ignited something hot and craving deep inside.

A sudden chill whipped around them, and Brooke shivered. Riley broke the kiss. "You're cold." He frowned, gently rubbing Brooke's shoulders. He glanced back out at the water and paused. "When did the weather turn?"

Brooke looked too. The blue skies were now clouding over fast with an ominous grey, and the calm waters were getting choppy, the boat shifting and rolling on the tide.

"Come on," he said, looking concerned. "We better get back to harbor before this storm blows up."

Brooke grabbed a sweater and pulled her clothes back on over her swimsuit as Riley set about pulling up the anchor and setting their course back to Sweetbriar Cove. By the time they arrived back at the harbor, it had started to rain. The wind was whipping hard around them, and the waves were roiling high. Brooke held on tight to the railing, glad to see the dock right up ahead. She was already feeling queasy, and if she spent longer on this rollercoaster of a ride, she wasn't sure she could keep from doing something incredibly un-romantic.

The harbormaster met them to help Riley secure the boat

up tight to the mooring. "I was wondering where you were," he said, reaching out to help Brooke ashore. She staggered inelegantly off the boat and caught her breath, relieved to be on solid ground again.

"It was a race, but we made it." Riley grabbed her things and hopped onto the dock. "The storm sure picked up fast."

"Shouldn't last long." The harbormaster checked the horizon. "But I'd spend the night on dry land if I were you."

"That's the plan." Riley met her eyes with a secret smile, and Brooke grinned back. Now that she wasn't hanging on for dear life, she remembered exactly where they left off—and his tempting promises for where they would pick up again.

Riley opened the lockbox and retrieved his keys and her phone. "Four hours and counting," he said, passing it over. "I'm impressed. The way you were talking about that thing, I figured you'd be in a cold sweat by now."

"I'm not that bad!" Brooke protested, laughing. "I can go a few hours without—"

She stopped, seeing the screen. Fifteen missed calls?

"Come on," Riley said, starting out ahead of her. "Let's get out of this rain—and into a hot shower. Your place or mine?"

Brooke ignored him, frantically dialing the front desk at the hotel. They answered right away. "Kevin? It's Brooke," she said. "What's going on?"

"Only total meltdown!" he exclaimed, sounding panicked. "Where have you been? We're been calling everywhere trying to reach you."

"I left my phone for a few hours," Brooke gulped. "Calm down, tell me what's wrong. Did the drains clog in the Marigold suite again?"

"Worse," he whispered. "The computers are all screwed. Something happened, some kind of virus or something? I don't know, but the system's wiped. I called in tech support, but they don't know what to do either. Everything's gone!"

Brooke's stomach dropped.

"What do you mean, gone?!"

"Hey, put that away." Riley suddenly took the phone from her hand, grinning. "Your day off isn't over yet."

"Riley!" Brooke snatched it back impatiently and pressed it to her ear again. "Hello, Kevin? I'm on my way. Don't touch anything until I get there!" She hung up, her mind racing. The whole system? That was everything: reservations, orders, all the internal guides and training and—

"Everything OK?" Riley asked.

Brooke turned on him. "No! No, it's not OK!" she exclaimed, full of dread. "Nobody's been able to reach me for hours! What did I tell you about my phone? I can't just clock off and disappear like you. I have people counting on me!"

"Whoa, easy there." Riley placed his hands on her shoulders. "Take a breath."

"I don't need to breathe!" Brooke cried. "I need to get to work." She pushed past him and started for the parking lot before she remembered he'd driven. Crap. "Can you please drop me at my place?" she asked through a clenched jaw. "I have to get back right now."

Riley blinked. "Sure, we can head straight to the hotel."

Brooke shook her head. "It's out of your way."

"It's no trouble." Riley nodded to the car. "And whatever the problem is at work, I'm sure you can figure it out."

She'd always liked Riley's eternal optimism, but for once, it was no comfort. Brooke sat tense in the passenger seat as they sped up the coast to the hotel. What had she been thinking taking off like that today? Going AWOL wasn't a part of her job description, and who knew what mess Kevin had made blindly clicking about after the system went down? It was her job to be around for these disasters, on call so someone could minimize the damage and keep everyone from making a bad situation even worse.

What if they couldn't restore the files? What if the whole system was erased? Brooke's stomach churned just thinking of the information they'd never get back. And with the big wedding coming up in just a few weeks, she needed those contacts!

"It'll be OK." Riley reached over and squeezed her hand. He flashed her a reassuring smile. "Whatever it is, I'm sure you can fix it."

"You don't know that," Brooke snapped back, tense and guilty. She'd been sunning herself out on the ocean while everything was falling apart. "I never should have let you take my phone. They've been trying to reach me for hours."

"These things happen." Riley sounded supportive, but Brooke wasn't in the mood for his "easy come, easy go" approach to life.

"Not on my watch, they don't," she said tightly. "I'm supposed to be in charge, so I'm the one who has to answer to the boss for any mistakes. Not all of us have the luxury of running our own thing however we please."

Riley opened his mouth to reply, but they were pulling up outside the hotel. Brooke reached for the car door and opened it almost before they came to a stop. She dashed inside without a backwards glance.

"Kevin?" she called, hurrying into the lobby. She found the weekend manager huddled around the computer with her IT guy and a group of staff—all of them wearing the same panicked expressions on their faces.

"Brooke, thank God!" Kevin exhaled, looking relieved to see her. "We've tried everything. Nothing's working."

She strode forward. "Guys?" She looked to her bartender and bellhops. "Let's get back to work now, OK? I'll let you know if there's anything we need."

The crowd dispersed. Brooke turned to Kevin. "Tell me what happened," she said, trying to sound calm and totally in control of the situation. "Start at the beginning."

"I was, umm, working the morning shift," Kevin started, evading her gaze. "Things were quiet, the Newton wedding haven't checked in yet, they called and said their flights were delayed, so they won't be in until this afternoon, and—"

"The computer, Kevin," Brooke interrupted him.

He flushed. "So, it was quiet. And I already double-checked the rooms and the reservation schedule, and there was really nothing I needed to be taking care of, so I thought I would play some Bixy, just until anyone arrived."

Brooke frowned. "Bixy?"

"It's this new game." Kevin was the color of a tomato now, flushed all the way to the tips of his ears. "You can download it from the server and log in to access your old games. So I . . . ummm . . . I . . ."

"He downloaded a bootleg copy." Her IT guy, Jose, put Kevin out of his misery. "Packed with viruses, I'd say."

"The screens all froze, then they went black, and this logo flashed up." Kevin tilted the screen so Brooke could see the icon, a maniacally laughing cartoon frog.

"We checked the office computers and tried rebooting, but it's a system-wide shutdown," Jose said, looking grim. "I'm sorry, but this is way above my pay-grade. I've never seen anything like it."

Brooke stared at the screen in disbelief. The entire hotel ran off specialized software—everything from linen delivery to the restaurant orders to her entire reservations schedule. If it was all lost . . . She couldn't even imagine it. There was no replacing the information, they would be completely paralyzed.

"What about the back-ups?" she asked hopefully. "We back up the system, every night, so we don't lose anything."

Jose shook his head. "The back-ups are still a part of the main system. Right now, we're locked out. We can't get in to anything."

"Is there anyone we can call?" she asked desperately. "There has to be someone."

He shook his head. "Like I said, this is some messed up shit. Sorry, language." He looked panicked. "There are some specialized security places we can try, but it's the weekend, and they can be pretty pricy."

"How pricy?"

"Like, ten, twenty thousand." Jose looked grim.

Brooke felt faint. "Dollars?" she gulped.

She felt tears well up in her throat, and she fought to keep them back. She couldn't fall apart now. They had three weddings, two anniversary parties, and a whole host of other events—just this week! These guests had trusted Brooke with their most special occasions, and this was the thanks they got: slacker staff, technical nightmares, and a manager who was too busy playing hooky to keep them in line. She wanted to prove herself so badly, but she'd just plunged the hotel into total chaos.

This was it. She was getting fired for sure.

～

RILEY HUNG BACK, watching Brooke try to keep it together. To anyone else, she seemed in control, but he knew her now. She was in meltdown, and if the most drama-free, collected woman he knew was panicking, then this had to be bad.

Damn. He shouldn't have made her give up her phone, even as a joke. He may be able to go off the grid whenever he wanted, but she had responsibilities here that mattered to her, and he hated the thought that he'd moved this stressful situation from bad to worse.

He moved closer in time to catch some of what her IT guy was saying. It was some kind of hack, infected malware or a virus an unsuspecting staff member had downloaded.

Riley brightened. There wasn't much in the hotel trade he could help with, but this? This he could do.

"This is just a satellite unit, right?" he interrupted.

Jose, the IT guy, nodded. "The main hub is back in the office."

"Alright," Riley said. "Lead the way."

Brooke looked surprised. "Look, I appreciate the offer," she said slowly. "But I really think we should wait for the professionals."

Riley couldn't blame her hesitance. She'd only seen him hanging out behind the bar, serving beers, but then again, there weren't many coding emergencies in Sweetbriar Cove that required his expert technical skills. "Look, I know computers," he assured her. "We saw this all the time. Let me help. I promise, I won't make it worse."

It wasn't the most reassuring vow he could make, but Brooke was clearly desperate. "I guess it can't hurt," she said, and led him to the IT room in the basement. Riley looked around, checking the setup.

He glanced up and found Brooke hovering anxiously

nearby. "You go take care of things upstairs," he told her. "I've got this."

She looked like she was about to protest, but then her phone buzzed. "The wedding party's here," she exclaimed. "And now I don't know what rooms to put them in!"

"Go," Riley said again. "I promise, I'll find you if I need you."

"OK. Thanks."

Brooke bolted for the stairs again, leaving Riley alone. He settled at the computer and cracked his knuckles. God, it had been months since he'd even looked under the hood of a system like this. But he found a clean laptop to connect, and soon he was deep in the file directory, absorbed in the lines of code. It reminded him of the all-nighters he pulled in college, fueled by energy drinks and sheer determination. He and Tate would stay up for hours, pushing to get the software just right. He always loved it, getting absorbed in the challenge. Some people thought computers and code were just boring lines of data, but Riley saw the beauty in it—just how much you could make that data do, and how wrong it could go with one tiny flaw.

But this time, the stakes were higher than just the challenge. Brooke had too much riding on this for him to take a half-hearted look around; it was personal. He wanted to be the one to fix this for her and put that carefree smile back on her face.

He wanted to show her he wasn't just a pretty face—and damn fine kisser.

And then maybe they could pick up where they left off earlier, before bad weather and even worse computer mishaps got in the way.

Riley paused, hit with the memory of Brooke gasping against him on the boat and the look in her eyes as she came undone. It was the sexiest thing he'd ever seen . . . and he needed more. Something about her had taken hold of him, and now he would do just about anything to get another glimpse of that wild, passionate woman she kept hidden inside.

Like fixing this mess of a virus, before it did any more damage.

Riley got back to work, finding the source of the damage, and—luckily—the failsafe built into the code. Once he found the weakness, he was able to scrub it from the system and restore from the back-ups. In just a couple of hours, he had everything working again—and when he heard the shriek of delight from down the hallway, he could tell Brooke knew it too.

There was a rush of footsteps, then she came bursting into the room. "Thank you!" Brooke threw her arms around his neck, hugging him tightly. "How did you even do it?"

"I won't bore you with the details. I'm just that good," Riley teased.

"Yes, you are." Brooke beamed. She pulled him down and kissed him hard, and the heat surged between them, taking Riley by surprise all over again.

Damn, he couldn't get enough of this woman.

Brooke pulled back. "I'm sorry I snapped at you before," she said, looking guilty. "It wasn't your fault I went off the clock."

"No, I'm sorry," Riley insisted. "You were right. I forget not everyone is on permanent vacation. Your empire takes time, I know."

Brooke cracked a glimmer of a smile. "It's just one hotel."

"For now." Riley grinned back, relieved to see her smiling again. He gave her hand a squeeze. "But I can tell this is only the beginning."

Brooke laughed. "Well, thank you. I really appreciate it."

"How much?" Riley teased, pulling her closer. She smiled. "A *lot*. I'm going to be working late tonight, but why don't I show you, tomorrow? Dinner, my treat. And . . . dessert." Brooke gave him a mischievous smile, and Riley would have gladly spent all week chained to that computer for the chance to discover just what was on the menu tonight.

"I'm in."

13

"What's the best restaurant around?" Brooke asked Eliza when she met her the next morning in Provincetown for some last-minute date-prep shopping. "I want to take Riley somewhere nice tonight."

"Nice, like fancy silver and linen tablecloths nice?" Eliza asked, slurping on an extra-large iced coffee as they browsed the boutique rails.

Brooke paused. "Maybe not. Riley doesn't seem the six-course tasting menu kind of guy. But I want it to be someplace special. He really saved my ass at work."

"So you're giving it to him gift-wrapped as a reward?" Eliza held up a lacy lingerie set from the hanger.

Brooke laughed. "Umm, nope. Red definitely isn't my color. And who wears this stuff, anyway?" she asked, examining the thong. "It's like having cheese-wire riding up all night."

"Nothing like a wedgie to get you in the mood." Eliza grinned. The polished-looking shop assistant glared at them, and Brooke tried to hide her giggles.

"Come on, I'm not going to find anything here."

"Wait." Eliza flipped through the hangers, and pulled down another set. "I knew they carried Jane's stuff. See, what about this one? It's sexy, but really cute, too."

Brooke looked over. It was a bra and panty set in pale lilac lace, with silk panels and delicate purple embroidery at the edges. "That *is* cute," she said, surprised. "I thought your sister designed children's clothes."

"Officially, but this is her naughty little secret. She won't even put her name on it. Look, it says *Aphrodite Designs*."

"They're beautiful." Brooke paused. Buying lingerie to wear for Riley tonight seemed almost brazen, and even indulgent when she had drawers of underwear back at home.

Underwear that Archer had bought for her.

"You're right, I'll take it." Brooke grabbed the hanger. Fresh start, fresh man, fresh lingerie.

"They have it in peach, too . . ." Eliza added, tempting.

Brooke laughed, and took the second set as well. "She should pay you a commission."

"Great idea." Eliza followed her to the register. "But really, I'm doing this for you. I mean, if only one of us is going to be having wild sex with a hot guy tonight, then you need to do it right."

The clerk arched an eyebrow, and Brooke blushed. "Sorry," she apologized. But Eliza just smirked.

"She knows what I'm talking about. We buy this stuff for one reason, and it's not to sit at home, alone, watching new episodes of *Property Brothers*. Seriously, if it wasn't for the prospect of sex, I'd never wear an underwire bra again!"

Brooke laughed and paid for her new purchases. They exited the store and strolled along Commercial Street, which was packed with tourists and still decorated with flags and ticker tape from the Fourth of July.

"Sage!" Eliza exclaimed suddenly. "For your dinner tonight. It's the hottest new restaurant around, all farm-fresh and rustic. The critic at the paper was raving about it."

"Rustic sounds good," Brooke agreed.

"And, more importantly, I've heard the chef's really hot," Eliza added.

Brooke laughed. "I'll scope him out for you," she offered.

"Now who's after a commission?" Eliza teased.

Brooke felt her phone buzz. She checked, and found a text from Riley. *Pick you up at seven? Or we could just order in... ;)*

"It's him, isn't it?" Eliza smirked. "Is it something dirty? You're blushing."

"No!" Brooke exclaimed. "You're the dirty one."

"I know, sorry." Eliza sighed. "My imagination's working overtime these days, that's what a dry spell will do for you."

"No more internet dates?" Brooke asked. Eliza had a whole library of horror stories from life in the dating trenches. She shook her head.

"I'm on strike. Although, does it count as a strike if nobody's asking you out to begin with?"

Brooke winced. "I'm sorry."

"I'm not." Eliza gave a mischievous grin. "I haven't waxed since Memorial Day."

They laughed. Brooke checked her phone again. *Seven is good*, she typed back. *See you then.*

She felt the flutter of anticipation in her stomach just thinking about it.

"Look at you," Eliza teased. "You *like* him."

"Maybe," Brooke admitted. Her phone buzzed again, and her stomach flipped over, but it was only a junk message. She exhaled. "I'm supposed to be grown up," she said, self-conscious. "Why do I still have butterflies like I'm sixteen, heading out on my first ever date?"

"The butterflies are the best part!" Eliza argued. "When you can't stop thinking about him and you can't even eat because your stomach is tied up in knots."

"Since when did you like a guy so much you stopped eating?" Brooke asked with a smile.

Eliza grinned. "OK, so I haven't met a man who could do that just yet, but I live in hope. Riley definitely seems worth a few butterflies," she added with a knowing look.

"He is . . ." Brooke smiled again, thinking of their day on the boat. Sunshine, relaxation, and enough sexual tension to start a small inferno. She couldn't imagine what was in store for her tonight, but if she knew Riley by now, it would be hotter than ever.

"I know you say he's just a player," Eliza mused. "But good butterflies are hard to find. You think it could get serious?"

Brooke blinked. "What? No! We're just having fun."

"For now . . ." Eliza gave her a look.

Brooke laughed. "Trust me, I've had enough romantic drama to last me a lifetime," she vowed. "Riley was the one who said I needed to just relax and enjoy myself, and he's right," she said. "Sometimes things should just be simple. Uncomplicated. And Riley is about as straightforward as they come."

"Dirty." Eliza winked, and Brooke burst out laughing.

"We need to get you a date, and soon."

"Not before I make a visit to the salon," Eliza cracked, and they laughed so loud, a couple of tourists looked over. Brooke held her shopping bags tighter, and thought of the seductive promise they contained. She'd never been the brazen type before, but something about Riley made her want to shock him —in all the right ways.

He didn't know what she had in store for him tonight, and she couldn't wait.

~

RILEY COULDN'T WAIT for seven p.m. He watched the clock all afternoon, running errands and counting down to when he could see Brooke again—see her. Kiss her.

And more.

What was it about this woman that kept him hanging on for just another touch? He was so used to playing it cool, enjoying whatever fun and games came his way, but not going out of his way to chase anything—or anyone. He didn't need to: gorgeous women practically lined up at the bar.

Now look at him: clean-shaven and dressed in a smart button-down shirt, loitering by the florist stand trying to figure out what kind of flowers she would like him to bring.

He had it *bad*.

"Don't go for roses," Mackenzie's voice came from behind him. He turned. She was hoisting a bag of groceries, with a pencil stuck through her bun.

"Are you sure?" Riley asked. "I thought they were supposed to be a classic?"

Mackenzie shook her head. "Classic means unoriginal. You want to show you've put some thought into it. Picked something especially for her."

"Oh." Riley surveyed the display again. "OK."

He reached for something pink. Mac made a dubious noise. "I think Brooke's more a hydrangea girl," she said. "Pretty, but unexpected."

"What makes you think it's Brooke?" Riley tried to sound nonchalant, but Mackenzie just smirked.

"Well, you're looking pretty dressed up for poker night, and we all know Cooper's into poppies."

"Cute." Riley grinned, then he realized what she'd said. "Wait, it's poker night? Damn, I totally forgot." He had a standing monthly appointment with his buddies, a deck of cards, and a few rounds of beer.

Mackenzie arched an eyebrow. "You forgot about your sacred bro time? Wow, guess someone's going to wind up disappointed tonight."

"The guys will understand," Riley said, and grabbed the hydrangea bouquet.

Mackenzie's eyebrows rose even higher. "So that's how it is then?" she said, looking delighted.

"It's not like anything," Riley insisted as he paid for the flowers. "I already made plans. It would be rude to cancel at the last minute."

"Mmmhmm."

He glared at Mac. "Don't you have some place to be?"

"I might take your spot at poker night," she grinned back. "Since it's going spare and all."

"Knock yourself out."

"Good luck with Brooke!" she called after him as he headed back to his car. "Tell her I said hi!"

Riley shut the door on her teasing and started the engine. He couldn't believe he'd forgotten about poker night—and even worse, that he didn't even care. He called in his apologies on the way over to Brooke's place, almost breaking the speed limit with his eagerness to get to her—which is how he found himself knocking on her door fifteen minutes ahead of schedule.

"Hey." Brooke looked surprised when she opened the door. She leaned up and kissed him quickly on the cheek before ducking back. "You're early. I won't be a minute, I can't find my earrings."

She disappeared back into the apartment, and Riley took a cautious step inside. "Sorry to surprise you." He awkwardly held the flowers by his side. "Did you get everything figured out at work?"

"Yes, thanks to you!" Brooke's voice came from the bedroom. "I don't even want to think about what would have happened if that virus wiped us out. I'm making them back up the system every hour now, and you can bet I gave Kevin a piece of my mind about downloading files on the clock!"

There was a pause, and then she re-emerged.

"Wow." Riley blinked. He'd only caught a glimpse of her before, but now he was hit with the full view. And it took his breath away.

Brooke was wearing a light blue silk dress that skimmed over her curves, with tiny spaghetti straps he already wanted to slip from her bare shoulders. Her hair was falling loose in silky blonde waves, for the first time he'd seen, and those sexy sandals crisscrossed up her calves.

"I . . . uh, you look great," he managed to say.

Get a grip, man.

"Thanks." Brooke smiled, then she saw the bouquet in his hand. "You brought flowers! You shouldn't have."

"I figured . . . you might like them." Riley still felt dazzled.

"They're beautiful." Brooke came and took the hydrangeas from him, then whisked to the kitchen to find a vase—leaving a whisper of light, sensual perfume in her wake. Riley barely had time to pull himself together before she was back at his side with a small beaded purse and an expectant smile.

"Ready to go?"

"Sure." Riley followed her out, as Brooke kept up a steady chatter about work and her weekend.

"I thought we could go to Sage?" she said, as they climbed into the car. Riley knew it well—the chef, Dylan, was a buddy of his.

"How did you get a reservation?" he asked. "Those things are like gold dust in season."

"Eliza made some calls for me. Pulled some strings at the newspaper, I think," Brooke admitted. "I figured it was a special occasion."

Riley was feeling like any occasion with Brooke was pretty special, but he managed to give a casual nod. "Sounds good to me."

They drove up the coast towards Provincetown. The restaurant was set a mile outside town down a dead-end back-country road, and it was a testament to Dylan's skills that the parking lot was full, and there was already a hopeful line by the door for bar seating.

"This place is gorgeous," Brooke exclaimed, looking around as they got out of the car. "It feels so old and historical."

"Cooper did the restoration," Riley explained, leading her inside the converted carriage house. "He's a stickler for details in his construction projects."

"Riley, hi." A sultry female voice made him pause.

Damn.

"Hi, Lulu." Riley smiled politely at the hostess at the front desk. She was tall and leggy . . . and a former fling of his from last year. They'd spent a wild couple of weeks together before he'd made his usual excuses, and they parted on good terms. "I thought you were moving back East?"

"I'm back for the summer." She gave a suggestive smile. "How have you been?"

"Fine." Riley glanced at Brooke, who was standing beside him with a smirk on her lips, like she knew exactly what the deal was. "I, we have a table?"

"I didn't see your name down," Lulu cooed. "I know I would have remembered that."

"It's under Delancey," Brooke spoke up politely.

"Oh. Here we are." Lulu beamed. "Come with me."

She showed them to a table in one corner, set with fresh flowers and twinkling tea lights. "Your server will be right with you, but you let me know if you need *anything*." She gave Riley a meaningful look, then sashayed away.

"Friend of yours?" Brooke asked, when they were seated and left alone.

"Something like that." Riley cleared his throat. "Sorry."

"Don't worry, I know you're not exactly a monk," Brooke said, with a teasing smile. "If we have to avoid all your *friends*, we probably wouldn't leave the house."

He knew she meant it good-naturedly, but Riley felt an odd sense of guilt. "I haven't left a string of broken hearts across the Cape," he said, needing to defend himself.

Brooke looked up from the menu, surprised. "Oh, I didn't mean it like that. You were just having fun, right? Like us." She beamed at him and returned to browsing the page. "Ooh, this all looks amazing, I don't know how I'll pick."

"You can't go wrong with Dylan's cooking," Riley agreed, but inside, his heart had sunk.

Fun.

Of course, that's what they'd agreed, wasn't it? The whole reason Brooke had thrown caution to the wind and wound up in his arms. He didn't do serious, and commitment was always the last thing on his mind.

So why was he looking at her across the table, framed there in the candlelight, wondering if maybe it could be different this time?

14

*D*inner was incredible, but Brooke could barely focus on the food. Even the most delicious seafood and fragrant sauces couldn't distract her from the man sitting across the table, his eyes gleaming blue in the candlelight.

"Good?" Riley asked, nodding to her plate.

"Uh huh." Brooke managed a vague murmur in reply, watching as he tore off a piece of bread and dipped it in the bowl of oil. He took a bite, a drop of the sauce lingering on the edge of his mouth until he licked it away.

She shivered.

What was she doing? She thought she'd have it together by now. She'd spent all afternoon feeling bold with anticipation—taking a luxurious shower, dressing in that gorgeous lingerie, just imagining the look on Riley's face when it came time to undress and reveal her surprise—but the moment he arrived on her doorstep, looking better than any man had a right to look, all that confidence seemed to disappear in a whirlwind of fluttering desire.

Focus, Brooke, she told herself. Just because he's all crisp and clean-shaven, he's still the fun-loving guy you know. The one who makes you laugh with all his charming innuendo.

The one who took you to the brink of pleasure—and right over the edge.

She flushed, her body tightening at the memories.

"Everything OK?" Riley looked puzzled. "You've gone quiet."

"Huh? Oh, no, I'm fine," Brooke covered quickly. "I was just . . . thinking about work. This food is so good, do you think your friend would be interested in catering at all?"

"For your big wedding?" Riley replied. "He doesn't normally, but you can always ask. I'll send word back to the kitchen when we're done."

"Great." Brooke took a gulp of her water, trying to cool down. But it was hard. Every time she looked at Riley, she remembered exactly what they'd done the last time they were together. His hands, sliding over her body. His lips, teasing at her skin. And those fingers—

She stopped short before she could finish the thought. *God, those fingers.* Getting this turned on in public was a dangerous thing, and she would just die if anyone knew the steamy thoughts racing through her mind. Luckily, Riley seemed completely oblivious—lounging back in his seat, totally at ease as he cleared his plate.

She took another sip of water and tried to think of something safe to talk about. But every glance at him only made her heart beat faster, watching the gold tone of his skin against his button-down shirt, and the way his cuffs were pushed back over those strong, tanned forearms . . .

"Dessert?"

Brooke jerked her head up. Riley was smiling at her from across the table. "We could have it here, or . . . take some to go."

His smile turned seductive, and Brooke had to remind herself to breathe. "Sure," she managed, holding onto the table to keep from slipping to the floor in a pool of pure desire. "Sounds good to me."

"Perfect." Riley called their server back over, and a few minutes later, they were set with a couple of crisp bakery boxes and the check.

"This is my treat." Brooke stopped him as he reached for his wallet. "I mean it." She gave him a warning look. "It's my way of saying thank you, for all your help at the hotel."

Riley looked reluctant, but he nodded. "There are other ways of thanking me besides picking up the check," he pointed out, with a raffish grin.

Brooke laughed. "Oh, I know." She gave him what she hoped was a flirty smile. "This is just the first part of my gratitude."

Riley met her gaze, and the air between them suddenly grew hot; thick with electricity. "Then let's go," he said, his voice low, and Brooke couldn't scramble out of her seat fast enough. His hand rested on her lower back as they headed for the door, and Brooke could have sworn she felt his touch burning her, even through the silk of her dress.

"What, so I don't even get a thanks for that meal?"

They stopped. A tall, dark-haired man was emerging from the kitchen. Heads turned, and Brooke could see why—with his roguish smile and an arm full of tattoos disappearing under his chef's whites, he was worth a closer look.

"Dylan," Riley greeted him, slapping him on the back. "I didn't want to interrupt the genius at work."

Dylan chuckled. "That's more like it. And this must be Stephanie." He turned to Brooke with a smile.

Riley paused, looking so uncomfortable, Brooke had to laugh.

"Actually, it's Brooke," she said, shaking his hand. "It's great to meet you. Dinner was amazing. The reviews don't do you justice."

"I like her already," Dylan said to Riley.

"That makes two of us."

"I don't suppose you do any private catering?" Brooke asked. "I have a big wedding I'm planning in a couple of weeks, VIP."

"Sorry, love." Dylan shook his head. "Not my scene."

"Money's no object, if that makes a difference," Brooke added hopefully.

He smiled. "Not one bit."

"Well, it was worth a shot," she sighed. The chefs at the hotel would do a great job, instead.

"Great meeting you," Dylan said. "Come back anytime."

They headed outside. "Sorry about that," Riley said, glancing over.

"What for?" Brooke replied. "He seems like a great guy."

"When he's in the right mood," Riley said, unlocking the car. "He's a little . . . eccentric. The whole temperamental artist thing."

She arched an eyebrow. "God help the ladies of Sweetbriar Cove with the two of you out on the town, huh?"

"It's not like that," Riley insisted, but Brooke wasn't fooled. He was trying to be polite, but she'd known from the start what she was getting into here, and she was under no illusions about Riley's history with women.

"Sure it is." She smiled. "Our hostess was drooling over you all night. But I don't blame her," she added. "How could she resist your charms?"

Brooke certainly couldn't. The whole drive back, her anticipation rose again, twisting tighter until she felt almost feverish with nerves.

Was it possible to pass out from pure desire? She'd always thought her mom's romance novels laid it on a little heavy with their swooning heroines, but now she wasn't so sure. She was practically breathless, stealing glances at Riley in the dark of the driver's seat, passing headlights casting shadows over his strong jawline.

"Here we are."

Was it just her imagination, or did Riley sound almost nervous too? There was a gruff note in his voice as they pulled up outside her gate, his Adam's apple bobbing with a swallow.

Brooke got out of the car. She didn't invite him up, but she didn't need to—Riley followed her up the stairs and inside. Brooke flipped the lights to dim and swallowed.

They were alone.

"I'll, umm, put on some coffee?" she suggested. "Or tea, if you want, and I think I have some beers—"

He kissed her. Slow and sensuous, hands at her waist, tugging her into him. Brooke went willingly, melting into the hard planes of his body, and oh, the taste of him, the stroke of his tongue sending shivers down her spine.

She was lightheaded when they came up for air.

"I don't want coffee," Riley murmured, kissing along her jaw.

"Dessert?" Brooke's voice went up as he reached her earlobe, nibbling with a sexy nip.

"No, thank you." His hands slid over her waist, the silk soft against her skin. "There's only one thing I need," he whispered, and the rasp in his voice made her tremble. "You. Naked. Now."

Brooke gulped. Could he get any sexier? She'd only had a glass of wine, but she felt drunk, reeling from the sensations pounding through her body, and the feel of him, stroking a teasing path over the curve of her hips. What had happened to all her bold seduction plans? She'd wanted to take the lead and relish every moment of this night. Instead, she was practically clinging to him on unsteady feet, her mind a haze of lust.

"I, um." She broke away and bolted for the fridge, pulling out a bottle of water and gulping quickly to try to clear her head.

Breathe.

Why was she acting like this was a huge, life-changing moment? This was supposed to be *fun*. No strings, no drama, no hint of emotional turmoil or guilty regrets.

Brooke took another sip of the water, her daze clearing. This was Riley, *her* Riley. He wouldn't have expectations, and he definitely wouldn't be judging her for anything. She knew what she wanted. *Him.* So what reasons did she have holding her back?

No reason at all.

∾

RILEY WAITED, wondering what was going through Brooke's mind. She needed a beat, that much was clear, so he took the dessert box and moved over to the couch, kicking back with his feet up on the coffee table.

She could take all the time she wanted, he'd still be going out of his mind over here, crazy with lust.

"Don't tell Summer, but I think this chocolate cake is even

better than hers," he said conversationally, digging in. To tell the truth, he could use a beat to cool off, too. The drive had almost done him in. he'd nearly pulled off to the side of the road a half-dozen times, just yanked her into his lap right then and there to claim the kiss that had been building between them all night.

But now, in the dim light of her apartment, away from traffic and crowds and any pesky interruptions, their chemistry had a new simmer. Something crackling at the edges, bright and hot and threatening to burn wild, out of control.

Everything else had just been a preview. Kiss by kiss. Inch by inch. And now . . . ?

Now he wanted everything.

Brooke finally put her water down and walked across the room. "You better get over here, before I eat this whole thing," Riley said, glancing up.

The look in her eyes stopped him in his tracks.

"It's all yours," Brooke said, almost casually. She stood there in front of him, in the dim glow of the corner lamp.

Slowly, she slipped one strap off her shoulder.

Riley paused.

A small smile played on the edge of her lips as Brooke pushed the other strap aside. Her dress slipped down over her body in a ripple of silk, pooling at her bare feet on the floor.

Riley stopped breathing.

She was wearing lingerie, something lilac and lacy that barely covered her incredible body, but still begged him to unwrap her all the same. Lace fluttered over the swell of her breasts, and a trail of silk ribbons gathered at her hips, barely keeping her panties in place. But it wasn't just the outfit that struck him dumb. No, it was her expression that made his blood run hot. Sensual and knowing, and just a little determined, too. Because even Brooke, he knew, wouldn't be doing this without a plan.

God, she was magnificent.

Brooke moved closer. "You like it?" she asked playfully, tilting her head.

Riley couldn't speak, so he just nodded.

"I thought you might . . ." She ran one finger down between her breasts, teasing the lace there. "I think I do, too."

"Good." Riley managed a strangled reply. Was this what a heart attack felt like? He could hear it drumming, louder with every step she took.

Brooke's hands kept moving, skimming lower, over her hips.

"The thing about these," she said, holding up the ribbons. "Is all it takes, is one little tug . . ."

She pulled and the bows unraveled. The silk fell away, and then Riley knew for sure it was a heart attack, because he was dead now. Dead, and gone, and up in heaven, watching the most beautiful woman he'd ever seen slowly peel her last scraps of clothing away until she was entirely naked before him.

When he finally was able to lift his gaze back to hers, Brooke was watching him with that smile on her face. "Now you're overdressed," she murmured. "Let me help you with that."

She closed the distance between them as he sat, still paralyzed. He felt the whisper of heat, radiating from her body, and it shocked him out of his stupor.

"Wait." His hands shot out, and took her by the hips. Brooke paused, standing above him.

He slowly ran his palms over her soft, smooth skin. She shivered beneath his touch, and he loved to see her respond so easily—how just a breath against her made her muscles tense. And a kiss . . . ?

He leaned in and pressed his lips to her stomach. Brooke swayed into him. He teased her bellybutton with his tongue, circling the hollow and straying to kiss her hips, and lower still.

Brooke made a noise that was halfway between a moan and a sigh. Riley's body ached to claim her, but he held back. He was just getting started.

He gently ran his hands down over her thighs, and nudged them apart. His eye-line was level with her now, and God, he couldn't resist leaning in for one, slow, forbidden kiss.

Brooke seemed to melt, clutching on to his shoulders as he delved deeper, tasting and teasing until her breath came in tiny pants, and he could feel her body strain against him. It was intoxicating, making her come undone like this, and when he glanced up, he saw her head thrown back and her eyes half-closed, glazed with abandon and desire as she gasped for more.

His ragged self-control snapped.

Riley surged to his feet, grabbing her by the waist and kissing her with a hunger he couldn't disguise anymore. He needed her, every inch, every taste, until the world seemed to melt away and there was nothing but the riot of lust pounding through him, demanding more. They tumbled back towards the bedroom, Brooke tearing at his shirt and belt, and Riley was only too happy to oblige, stripping his clothes away until finally they were falling back onto her bed, skin to skin.

"Riley," she gasped, as he bent his head to lavish kisses on her breasts. "Don't hold back, I need— *Oh*," she moaned loudly as his lips closed around one perfect, taut nipple.

He sucked, slowly, and Brooke seemed to melt beneath him. God, she was too beautiful, too perfect to believe with her hair spilling around her like some kind of tangled halo, and those pink lips parted in a silent plea. His heart was pounding a drumbeat of pure desire as he devoured her. He'd never wanted anyone like this before, and it was all he could do to lose himself in the feel of her body and those sexy little moans she made, twisting and writhing against him as he teased at her breasts, and slipped one hand between her legs to find her slick and clenching for him.

Riley growled.

He couldn't take much more of this, God, he was just about ready to explode.

And then Brooke reached for him.

Riley shuddered at the sensation. She stroked, slow and teasing, as if she knew just how close to the edge she was sending him. He groaned against her, and she answered with a teasing smile. "I want you," Brooke whispered softly, as Riley tried in vain to keep control. "God, I've wanted you for so long."

It was more than he could take. He captured her mouth again, hard and hot, plunging his tongue deep to ravish her as his body ached against her. Brooke broke away, breathless, and reached for the nightstand. Riley gave silent thanks for her efficiency as she rolled a condom onto his hard length and pulled him back to cover her again.

He sank inside her, and lost his mind.

Brooke moaned, wrapping her legs around his waist and urging him on. Deeper. Harder. *God.*

Riley clutched the bed sheets and tried to keep from taking her hard, but this was the best damn thing he'd ever felt in his life before and he didn't know how much more he could take.

With every last ounce of control, he paused, slow, leaning

to drop a ragged kiss on her lips as his body shuddered with tension.

And then Brooke moaned against him. "Don't stop," she whimpered. "God, Riley . . ."

His control severed. He surged deep inside her, and *yes*, he couldn't have held back if he'd tried. It felt like he was possessed with some animal hunger, driving harder with every stroke. Brooke's body clenched and gasped against him, taking him deeper into her sweetness, until he couldn't think, couldn't breathe, couldn't do anything but hold on for dear life as the pleasure pounded through him and the world contracted to just the feel of her body tight around him, and the sound of her moans, driving him on until he felt her shatter against him, and he answered with a strangled groan, exploding into the white-hot pleasure as he fell off the edge of the world and into her arms.

But it wasn't enough.

Even as he lay there, Riley knew somehow. He could never have enough of her.

15

$\mathcal{B}$rooke woke with a strong arm draped over her, and the warmth of a man's body spooned against her from behind.

She smiled, still sleepy, and let out a yawn. Then the memories of last night flared, vivid in her mind, and Brooke's eyes shot open.

She'd seduced him. Bold as day, she'd stripped off her clothes and taken him to bed like she did it all the time.

And God, it felt *good*.

"Morning, sunshine." Riley stretched, a smile on his face. He reached up and lazily pushed her hair from her face. "Sleep well?"

"I did." Brooke realized the sun was already high outside the windows. "What time is it?"

Riley yawned. "Nearly seven, I think."

She brightened at the realization. "That means I got a whole six hours!"

He chuckled. "Good thing I wore you out then."

"A very good thing." Brooke smiled. No wonder she'd slept straight through, she could barely move from all their athletics the night before.

It turned out, the cure for insomnia was a night of great sex.

"C'mere." Riley tugged her gently back into his arms and kissed her, slow and steady, warm as the sun pooling on her bare skin. Brooke sighed against him, melting back into the pillows.

This was definitely the best way to wake up.

Riley's hands slid over her, bringing her body to life in a crackle of heat. The kiss turned deeper, Brooke pressing up against him to—

Her stomach made a growling noise, echoing through the room. Riley smirked. "Hungry?"

"It can wait," Brooke said, tugging him back to her. There were more important things to focus on, like the muscular planes of his shoulders beneath her fingertips, and the way his breath hitched as her touch roamed lower.

Her stomach made another rumble, and Riley laughed. "I can take a hint," he said, hopping out of bed.

Brooke was momentarily distracted by the sight of him: all lean muscle and tanned skin. She'd nicknamed him Adonis before she even knew his name, and she was right. He could have put Rodin's statues to shame.

Riley glanced over and caught her staring. "Like what you see?" he teased, and she laughed, blushing.

"You know I do."

Riley looked at her hotly. "You should put some clothes on, before I ravish you. Breakfast be damned."

It was tempting, but Brooke was running on fumes, and

ravishing would be far more fun with some fuel. "Hold that thought then," she said, and reached for her robe.

She went to the bathroom and started the shower running. "I don't have to be in work until nine," she called. "We could go get breakfast somewhere?"

"Sure, sounds good," Riley's reply came. She stripped off and stepped under the hot water, enjoying the drum against her tired skin.

A moment later, the door opened behind her, and a pair of strong hands slid around her waist. "Room for one more?" Riley murmured in her ear, and Brooke shivered, wet, and naked, and already wanting him all over again.

"Always." She twisted to face him, and taste that gorgeous kiss.

Breakfast could wait.

THE WATER WAS RUNNING cold by the time they finally emerged from the shower, and Brooke had never been so satisfied—or hungry.

"Carbs," she gasped dramatically, as she drove to Sweetbriar. "I need carbs!"

"Aww, poor baby." Riley lifted one hand to his lips. "Remind me to travel with snacks. And a few other supplies." He winked.

Brooke smiled. She wasn't going to argue with that.

"What time do you get off tonight?" she asked, turning off the highway towards the bakery.

"That depends, what time are you coming over?" Riley quipped, giving her a grin, and Brooke laughed.

"I'm meeting with the bride-to-be to go over some of the options, so it's going to be a long day for me."

"That's OK," Riley said. "Call, text, show up naked at the boat whenever you like, I'm not fussy."

Brooke grinned. "So I've got options, then?"

"Absolutely," he said. "I support your choices. Like if you choose to wear more of that lingerie . . ."

She felt a glow of triumph. So, the new set had worked its magic then? She would have to thank Eliza's sister sometime.

They reached the bakery, and Brooke pulled up outside. It was still early, but the place was bustling, and the scent of vanilla and sugar made her mouth water.

"Brooke!" She was greeted the moment she stepped through the door. Poppy, Summer, and Mackenzie were sitting at a table by the window with a spread of delicious-looking pastries and coffee between them.

"I was meaning to call you," Poppy said. "We're having a big Labor Day barbecue, and we'd love you to come."

"That sounds great," Brooke said. "I'll be there."

"Be where?" Riley stepped inside just behind her.

There was a pause. Three sets of eyes looked back and forth between them with delighted smiles.

"Riley." Summer smirked. "You're up early."

"The early bird catches the sticky buns," he said, nonchalant. He rested a hand on the small of Brooke's back, and she flushed. They couldn't have been more obvious if Brooke had run through the Sweetbriar town square yelling, "We had epic sex last night!" but she forced herself to stay cool. She was a grown woman, she could have wild affairs and still show her face in town the next morning.

"Well, you're in the right place," Summer said, getting to her feet. "I'm trying out a new recipe, with hazelnut spread. Why don't you guys join us?"

"Sorry," Brooke said. "I have to get to work."

155

"Another time," Riley agreed. She caught his eye, and he gave her an apologetic smile. Once they were outside again, armed with bags full of pastries, he gave her a kiss.

"Sorry, small town. It's hard to stay under the radar."

"I'm beginning to see that." Brooke checked her watch and sighed. "I really need to get going. Lila's bringing her mother-in-law-to-be, so everything needs to be perfect."

"Lila?" Riley's eyebrows shot up. "Wait, VIP . . . Hollywood . . ." He started joining the dots. "Is it—?"

"Shh!" Brooke clapped her hand over his mouth before he could say another word. "Forget I just said that. You don't know anything!"

Riley laughed, kissing her palm before ducking away.

"You get to your top-secret wedding planning, that absolutely doesn't involve Lila Moore," he winked. "I'll be expecting you later. Clothing optional."

Brooke kissed him one last time before getting in the car. As she drove away, she was already thinking about tonight, and what kind of sexy adventures lay in store. After all, she had that lingerie set in peach, too . . .

She smiled, loving the lightness in her chest, and how her blood seemed to sing with anticipation. It felt good, being with him like this: simple, uncomplicated, and full of pleasure. After all the dark emotion of the past year, it was a relief to just feel happy for once, without the looming specter of guilt and shame.

There was nothing to be ashamed about with Riley. He seemed to know everything she needed—and *exactly* how to give it to her. He was the perfect fling. And maybe even . . .

Nope.

Brooke stopped that thought before it could even form. She shouldn't get carried away on her tide of endorphins. Riley had been clear from the start about what he was looking for, and commitment was nowhere on the list. And, more importantly, she was in no state to open up her heart again. Just the thought of baring herself to someone—trusting them, putting everything on the line again—made her heart clench with fear.

No, she should just enjoy this for what it was:

The perfect rebound.

RILEY STROLLED the long way back to the harbor, feeling pretty damn good about the world. A night in bed with a beautiful woman, and a morning with her in the shower, too. Throw in a couple of fresh pastries, and life couldn't get much better than this.

"And where have you been?"

Riley's good mood disappeared at the sight of the man lounging on the deck of his boat. "Max," he sighed. "To what do I owe this unwelcome visit?"

Max grinned from under his shock of dark hair. "Is that any way to greet your favorite brother?"

"You're my only brother." Riley hopped up onto the deck.

"Exactly."

Riley tossed Max a pastry and took a seat, kicking back on a lawn chair with a view of the harbor. "So, this is where you've been hiding." Max looked around. "Not too shabby."

"It's a quiet life," Riley agreed. "Emphasis on quiet."

"Which is why you didn't come home last night?" Max quirked an eyebrow, and Riley was reminded of growing up with his younger sibling interrogating him at every turn—which was probably how he wound up such an all-star litigator.

"Sorry I wasn't here to meet you." Riley dodged the question. "If you'd given me some warning, I could have rolled out the red carpet for you. Thrown a parade."

"Or pulled up anchor and sailed off into the great blue yonder," Max said, giving him a knowing look.

"That too."

"Well, since you've ignored my emails, calls, and certified mail delivery, I figured I should come bring you these in person." Max reached down and pulled a thick sheaf of documents from his battered leather duffel bag. Riley didn't need to look to know what they were: his settlement with Tate, and the final nail in the whole unfortunate coffin. "If you'll just sign them right now, I can be on my way back to the airport."

Riley groaned. "Come on, man. It's too early for this."

"Actually, it's about six months too late." Max stubbornly held out the settlement papers. Riley stubbornly refused to take them.

Max sighed. "I don't know why you're hanging on to this. Don't you want to just put it all behind you and move on?"

Riley shook his head. "The minute I sign those papers, Tate gets what he wanted."

"He wanted the whole company," Max pointed out. "This only gives him half."

"Which is still a hell of a lot more than he deserves." Riley scowled, hating himself for being so petty—and hating Max for interrupting his good mood.

"So what, you're going to cling on to a dead partnership out of spite?" Max asked.

Riley shrugged. "Maybe."

Max set the file down on the deck. "I don't understand you," he said, shaking his head. "You could sell him your share and be even richer than you are right now. Hell, you've got other companies who are begging to take it off your hands. And instead, you're sitting on it."

Riley allowed himself a smile. "That's the thing about intellectual property," he said. "He can't do a damn thing with our software unless I agree."

"And you can't either," Max pointed out.

"Look around," Riley gestured. "Do I need next-gen streaming apps out here?"

Max sighed. "You always were a stubborn SOB."

"And you always were an irritating brat," Riley said good-naturedly. "Now come on, I need to open the pub. Since you're here, you can make yourself useful and pour a few pints."

"And then you'll tell me about your new girlfriend?" Max asked.

Riley opened his mouth to argue that he didn't have a girlfriend, then stopped.

"I knew it!" Max exclaimed. "Don't tell me you're finally settling down, after all these years. Mom will love this. Maybe she'll finally get off my case. She figured I was the only hope for grandchildren," he added. "Now she can get back to bugging you."

Riley sighed. "I'm not settling down, or having kids. I'm just . . . seeing someone." He finally landed on the words.

"Seeing her naked, exclusively?"

Riley paused. They hadn't said anything about exclusive, but Brooke couldn't be dating anyone else, could she?

He felt a surge of jealousy that took him by surprise. "I don't know," he admitted. "We haven't put a label on anything. It's still early days."

"You better lock that down quick," Max warned him, looking amused. "Before someone else does."

Riley shook his head, "It's not like that. We're just having fun."

"Sure, that goofy look on your face is just fun." Max laughed. "When do I get to meet her?"

"You don't."

"Come on, I'm family," Max argued. "She'll love me. And maybe she can tell you to sign the damn papers."

"You leave Brooke out of this," Riley glared. But Max just grinned wider.

"Brooke, huh? That's a nice name. Mom will be so happy."

Riley groaned. "Please don't say anything to Mom, not just yet."

"That depends . . ." Max kicked the papers closer.

"Anyone ever tell you how damn annoying you are?" Riley grumbled.

Max chuckled. "All the time. Usually right before I send them to jail."

Riley sighed. Something told him he wouldn't be getting his usual relaxing morning coffee today. "I'll just go change. Then you can earn your keep."

"Sure thing." Max rose and grabbed the file. "I'll just bring these along, in case you change your mind."

"Don't hold your breath."

"I missed you too, bro."

Riley shook his head, going below deck to change out of last night's clothes. Max didn't know when to quit nagging, but maybe he had a point about Brooke. Riley wasn't sure she even had time to be seeing anyone else, but even the possibility made him tense. He didn't want to be with anyone else, and he sure as hell didn't want Brooke out on any romantic dates with some other guy.

Talking to him . . . laughing with him . . . *kissing* him.

He scowled. He didn't know where they stood, but he knew he wanted it to be something.

Something real?

He paused. Was he ready for that? Finally trusting someone again. Starting over, and putting his heart on the line. Making room on the bathroom vanity for an extra toothbrush, even.

Riley looked around the cramped cabin, and for the first time, he wondered just how much longer he could keep this up. Hiding out here, pretending like the rest of the world didn't exist. If he was brutally honest, he'd been in limbo ever since the lawsuit, and while Sweetbriar Cove made a damn fine escape, all the festivities and small-town charm in the world couldn't keep real life at bay forever.

Sooner or later, he was going to have to decide what he wanted out of life. And for now, there was only one thing he could think of that might be on the list.

Brooke.

---

16

*B*rooke breezed into work, and found Lila waiting in the lobby with an elegant older woman. "You're late," the woman said in greeting, her lips pursed.

Brooke glanced at the clock. It was 9:01.

"I'm so sorry to keep you waiting," she apologized, coming back down to earth with a bump. It was a long way from soaping up in the shower with Riley to presenting catering plans, but she needed to get her game face on right away.

"You didn't, it's fine." Lila spoke up quickly. "Justin couldn't make it, but this is his mother, Bitsy."

"A pleasure to meet you." Brooke shook Bitsy's hand. The dreaded mother-in-law. She was usually able to keep the peace, but Bitsy looked like a force to be reckoned with in a Chanel tweed suit and pearls. "Shall we go through and get started? I can't wait show you the plans."

Brooke steered them into the salon and ordered tea. "How are you feeling?" she asked Lila. "You must be getting excited, with the big day so close?"

"Excited . . . and nervous," Lila admitted, glancing over at Bitsy. "There's a lot to figure out."

"Just over one week to go," Brooke agreed, and tried not to feel panicked. At least the computer system was up and running, thanks to Riley, and she had a twenty-point plan to see her through the rest of the hectic schedule. "I'm sorry the planning stage will be so rushed. Usually, I have months with a bride to figure out their style and taste, but with you . . ."

"We need to get everything locked down today," Lila finished. "It's fine, really," she said, looking remarkably cheerful for a bride who had to cram her dream wedding into just a few sessions. "I trust your instincts, so whatever you pick out is great with me."

"Wow," Brooke laughed. "That should make this easy."

She pulled out the folder she'd assembled for the big day. She still felt scattered, wrapped in the morning afterglow of everything that happened the night before, but she tried to pull it together. This wedding was her opportunity to prove herself and get her career back on track after this unplanned detour out to Cape Cod.

"I've narrowed things down to a few options," she began. "I know you wanted classic and beachy, so I'm thinking white, with some pink and gold accents."

"Pink?" Bitsy snorted. "That's far too gaudy," she said. "This is a Cartwright wedding, after all."

"Oh no, it's a blush pink," Brooke explained, showing them the swatches. "With pale gold. Very classic and understated."

"That looks great." Lila smiled.

Bitsy pursed her lips, but didn't complain again, so Brooke moved on. "For music, I know you had some ideas. A jazz trio, and a DJ—"

"There will be a string quartet," Bitsy announced. "Playing traditional classical music. Some Vivaldi, and Brahms."

Brooke paused. "Lila?" she shot her a questioning look.

"Sure, why not?" Lila gave a polite smile.

"Okay . . ." Brooke made a note. "Our chefs are preparing the menu options as we speak for you to sample, and you're using your own photographer—"

"Henry Miller," Bitsy interrupted. "He does all the Cartwright occasions."

"Right. So let's talk about—"

"Is the hotel unionized?" Bitsy spoke over her again.

Brooke stopped. "Excuse me?"

"The hotel staff. Servers, janitors, etcetera," Bitsy looked around, assessing. "Are they part of the local chapters?"

"Umm, yes, they are." Brooke frowned.

"And there have been no issues here? Disputes, complaints, scandal?" Bitsy continued.

"No, not that I know of." Brooke was still confused. "I've only been working here a few months, but the place has an excellent reputation. You don't need to worry about anything disrupting the big day."

"Hmmm." Bitsy made a note in her little leather notebook.

Brooke was unsettled. "Let's go see about those catering options," she said, getting to her feet. She took them through to the private dining room, and soon they were sampling smoked salmon sandwiches and an array of hors d'oeuvres.

"These are all delicious," Lila said, reached for another sandwich.

Bitsy cleared her throat. "Is that wise? You'll want to fit into your dress."

Lila paused. "No, I'm good." She took a deliberate bite, and smiled at Bitsy.

Uh-oh. Brooke sensed tension in the air, so she quickly moved onto the drinks, but Bitsy—predictably—had more questions.

"The seafood is all local?"

"That's right." Brooke tried not to sound impatient. "We keep in-season as much as possible."

Bitsy peered at the crab cakes. "It's very important this all be Massachusetts crab," she said sternly. "None of that Maine stuff."

Brooke blinked. Most bridal parties cared about flowers and wedding favors, not the provenance of the shellfish and whether or not the hotel staff were part of a union. Nobody would notice those details unless—

Oh. Brooke put two and two together.

"So the rumors are true," she said, finally understanding. "Justin *is* going into politics."

Lila snorted with laughter. "No way," she said. "I'm the performer. He's happy out of the spotlight. He'd never go for that."

"Oh, my mistake," Brooke said. "I just thought, you know, with the requests. Local, unions . . . Isn't there a Congressional seat opening up in the district?"

"Nope," Lila said. "Over my dead body . . ." She trailed off, a strange look suddenly coming over her face. "He's not . . ."

She frowned, looking at Bitsy. "Is he?"

"That's a conversation for another day." Bitsy stood there, looking smug. "Now, about the cake . . ."

But Lila didn't move.

"A Cape Cod wedding," she said slowly. "I wondered why you all were so set on it being here in Massachusetts. We could have eloped, or done it in California, but no, it had to be here."

"Lila." Bitsy sounded stern. "This is neither the time nor the place."

Lila shook her head stubbornly. "We talked about it. He promised."

"Well, plans change," Bitsy said brightly. "Now, about the dessert?"

Brooke saw Lila's stormy expression and quickly stepped between them. "You know, I think we're all done here. Lila, there's a great florist nearby, I'd love to take you to see their arrangements."

Bitsy scowled. "But we've already decided."

"No, *you* decided," Lila spoke up, stronger. "I'd love to see my options."

"Great." Brooke steered her out of the room. "Let's go now. Lovely to meet you, Bitsy!"

WHEN THEY WERE DRIVING a safe distance from the hotel, Brooke looked over at Lila. "I'm so sorry, I put my foot in my mouth back there."

Lila slowly shook her head. "It's not your fault. You weren't to know. God, I can't believe I didn't put the pieces together before now." She looked upset, toying with the sleeves of her casual sweatshirt. "We talked about it, I asked him point-blank, did he want a career in politics, and he swore the answer was no."

Brooke didn't know what to say. Had she just sent this whole wedding into a tailspin? "Maybe he's just trying to placate his mom," she suggested. "I mean, with that kind of legacy, there's always going to be pressure."

"But he hates all that," Lila said. "It's one of the things that brought us together. Dealing with fame, all the paparazzi and attention . . ." Her voice caught. "I thought he understood I don't want any of that, not when it comes to my personal life."

Brooke felt terrible. "You just need to talk it out. I'm sure it's just a misunderstanding, you guys can clear it up."

Lila nodded, but she didn't look convinced.

"I read you were starring in a new version of *Sense and Sensibility*," Brooke desperately changed the subject. "I love that book."

"Me too." Lila seemed to brighten. "Everyone always talks about *Pride and Prejudice*, but I'm a sucker for all the unrequited pining, it's so emotional."

"Are you playing Marianne?"

Lila shook her head. "Elinor," she said, and started chatting about Dash Everett, the hot British director they had signing on, and scouting for locations. She looked a hundred times happier than when she was discussing her wedding plans, but Brooke would take whatever she could get. By the time they arrived in Sweetbriar Cove, Bitsy's bombshell was almost a distant memory.

"What do you think?" Brooke asked, leading Lila to the floral shop. It was a cute, lush corner filled with fragrant blooms. "Did you want to keep it simple, or go for something bright and exotic?"

"I don't know why we're looking," Lila sighed, looking listlessly around. "Bitsy's already decided on white roses."

"Didn't you want lilacs?" Brooke asked, remembering their first appointment.

"Bitsy says lilacs look cheap." Lila toyed with the ribbon on the bouquet. "Which, in Bitsy-speak means I'm a common slut unworthy of her darling son."

"Well, she's not the one marrying him," Brooke declared. She never usually stirred the pot; her job was all about compromise, but after a morning of Bitsy running roughshod over the whole event, she figured Lila needed someone in her corner. "It's your day, you should have whatever you want."

"No, it's fine." Lila sighed. "I don't want to cause problems."

Brooke watched her browsing listlessly. It was strange; she had such a reputation as being a diva on all her movies, but looking at her now, she seemed almost meek.

"You know, you're not how I imagined you," Brooke couldn't help saying.

Lila arched an eyebrow. "You mean, a spoiled Hollywood drama queen? Don't believe everything you read."

Brooke blushed. "Sorry."

"No, I get it. Drama sells magazines." She shrugged, pushing her blonde hair back.

"I can't imagine," Brooke said. "I get tongue-tied just making a presentation. I could never get up in front of a camera like you do."

Lila gave her a smile. "It's all an act, in the end. I hate the spotlight, especially when it comes to my personal life. I just thought . . ." She swallowed. "I thought Justin was the same. He promised we would get away from it all."

"You will," Brooke insisted, but Lila didn't look so sure.

"Not if he follows his family into politics. Even this wedding isn't what we wanted. He said it would keep Bitsy happy, but . . . Well, she's not exactly sunshine and roses." Lila gave a rueful look.

"Here's an idea," Brooke said, hating how defeated her bride-to-be looked. "How about we let Bitsy worry about Bitsy, and focus on giving you a dream wedding?"

Lila smiled. "You're sweet."

"I mean it," Brooke insisted. "This is your day. You're only going to do this once, right?"

"Here's hoping."

"So, forget about Bitsy and the Cartwright way and Massachusetts crab," Brooke grinned. "What do *you* want?"

"To be on a beach in the Caribbean with nobody else around?"

"OK, second choice," Brooke said.

Lila paused a moment. "I did love the lilacs," she said slowly. "And the peach cake, and all those gorgeous antique books you suggested."

"Done," Brooke declared.

"Really?" Lila bit her lip. "Bitsy won't be happy."

"Bitsy doesn't have to know." Brooke grinned. "This is about you and Justin, and I promise, you're going to have the wedding of your dreams."

Lila smiled, for the first time all day. "Thank you. For everything. Seriously, I don't know what I'd do without you. Justin said he'd be here for all the appointments, but he's busy, and there's no time, and my team are already freaking out in LA—"

"It's my pleasure," Brooke cut her off. "You worry about saying 'I do,' I'll take care of everything else. Now, want to try out another round of appetizers?"

Lila shook her head. "You know, I think I need to take a walk and clear my head. I can make my own way home."

"Are you sure?" Brooke didn't want to strand her without a ride.

"Yes, I'm fine." Lila smiled again, but it didn't quite reach her eyes. "Thanks for everything. I'll talk soon."

She exited the florist shop and started walking across the town square. Brooke watched her go, feeling a lurch of apprehension in her stomach. She was used to skittish brides getting cold feet—but never with just a week to go before the big day.

Note to self: keep Bitsy far, far away from any future wedding plan sessions.

If there was even a wedding left to plan.

"Shall I put in the order?" the florist assistant asked.

"What? Oh, yes, please." Brooke filled out the invoice. Luckily for her, the Cartwright deposits were non-refundable, so even if this whole thing fell apart, the hotel would be covered.

Her career, however? That might be a whole other thing.

Brooke finished up at the florist, then stepped back out into the Sweetbriar town square. She'd blocked off the whole morning for Lila, so she had some time before she needed to be back at the hotel, and even before she could think about it, she found herself strolling towards the pub on the corner. She could drop by and say hi to Riley—and maybe even get another kiss, or two, or three, to last her for the rest of her day.

Brooke smiled. One night together, and she was already craving her next fix. Whatever that man did, he did it well.

But when she stepped into the pub, she found another man behind the bar. "Hi," Brooke said, approaching. "I'm looking for Riley?"

"Why settle for him when you can talk to me instead?" the man replied with a teasing blue-eyed smile. There was something familiar about him, and Brooke wondered if she'd seen him around town.

"I'm not sure about that," she said. "Is he around?"

"Just on a call," the guy replied. "He'll be back in a second. By which time I'll have charmed you so much, you'll barely remember his name."

Brooke laughed. "We'll see about that." She took a seat on a barstool to wait. It was quiet in the pub, just a few locals enjoying their lunch, and the new bartender leaning back against the counter, watching her with an assessing look.

"Drink?" he asked.

"Sure, just a lemonade, thanks," Brooke replied.

"Coming right up." The man poured and slid it over. "I'm Max."

"Brooke."

His eyebrows shot up. "Ah, the famous Brooke. It's a pleasure."

She paused. "Famous?"

"Riley may have mentioned you," Max said.

Brooke sipped her drink, not sure what to say—or what Riley had said about her.

"Don't worry." Max must have seen her hesitance. "He hasn't said a thing. In fact, he's been uncharacteristically tight-lipped. Care to fill me in on all the salacious details? Since I'm family and all."

"Oh, you're his brother," Brooke realized. The familiar blue eyes, the cocky flirting . . . Now it made sense. "You know, I can see the resemblance," she added. "You're both too charming for your own good."

"I'll take that as a compliment." Max grinned. "So, is my big brother behaving himself?"

"Does he ever?" Brooke asked.

He laughed. "Touché."

"What brings you out here?" Brooke asked, relaxing. She was curious now, getting a window on Riley and the rest of his life. "You live on the West Coast, right?"

"He's here to annoy me," Riley interrupted, entering through the back door. He gave Brooke a questioning smile. "This is a surprise."

"A good one?" Brooke asked.

"Always." Riley leaned over the bar and kissed her, the kind of slow, lazy kiss that sent shivers down her spine and made Brooke forget for a moment they had company.

Then Max cleared his throat loudly. "Let's keep things PG-13, people."

Brooke pulled back, flushing, but Riley just chuckled. "See what I mean about annoying?"

"Aw, he likes having me around, really," Max said. "So, what are we doing tonight? We should all grab dinner and get to know each other."

"Nope," Riley answered, at the same time as Brooke said, "I'd love to."

"Great." Max grinned. "Meet around seven?"

"I'm working," Riley reminded him, looking irritated.

"That's OK," Max said. "Brooke and I can spend some time together. Isn't that right?" He smiled at her, and Riley's scowl deepened.

"I'll get someone to cover."

Brooke looked back and forth between them, interested to see their sibling dynamic. It was obvious they were used to bickering like this, but despite the barbed words, the affection between them was clear. But the show was interrupted as Max's phone buzzed. "I've got to take this, but I'll be seeing you later." He winked and strolled away.

Riley let out a sigh.

"Don't worry." Brooke patted his arm gently. "It'll be fun."

"You don't know Max," he said darkly, and Brooke had to laugh.

"Let me guess, he's a smooth-talking, charismatic player?" she grinned. "I guess he learned that from you."

Riley didn't look any happier, so she leaned over and kissed his cheek. "Relax. You're still my favorite Ford brother."

"Want to blow off dinner and show me just how much?" Riley suggested, his smile returning.

Brooke laughed. "Dinner first, fun later."

Riley gave her a smoldering look. "I'll be holding you to that."

---

*R*iley had always liked his brother. Sure, he could be annoying sometimes, and just loved getting under Riley's skin, but at the end of the day, they'd always had each other's backs, played wingmen, and offered whatever help and advice the other needed—especially when it came to women.

So why was Max keeping him stuck in a crowded bar listening to stories he'd heard a dozen times before when Riley could have been alone with Brooke somewhere?

Naked.

". . . and then the wife started whaling on him, right there in the courtroom. Grabbed my briefing papers and whacked him around the head," Max said, halfway through the tale of his favorite case. They were sitting at a corner table down by the harbor, with a spread of fried seafood and beer.

"No!" Brooke gasped, looking rapt. "What did you do?"

"Put her in an armlock and called for a continuance," Riley finished for him.

Max gave him a look. "Way to ruin the good part."

"I thought about becoming a lawyer," Brooke said, with a wistful look. "I even took the LSATs in college."

Riley paused. "I didn't know that."

"There's a lot you don't know." Brooke gave him a teasing grin.

"You had a lucky miss," Max told her, peeling some shrimp. "I clocked fourteen-hour days at the firm starting out, and now that I'm partner, it's not much better."

"Talk to me when you've got three weddings in one weekend on back-to-back shifts," Brooke retorted. Max raised his glass to hers in a toast.

"Here's to the workaholics."

He looked to Riley then back to Brooke, and gave a curious smile.

"Uh-oh," Brooke said, taking a gulp of beer. "Do I want to know what that look's about?"

"Nothing," Max said. "Just . . . You're not his usual type, that's all."

"Max." Riley gave him a warning glare.

"What?" Max protested. "That's a good thing. It's a compliment," he reassured Brooke. "It's about time my brother wised up and found someone who could give him a run for his money."

Brooke arched an eyebrow. "Sounds like there are some stories there."

"I wouldn't know," Max said. "You're the first one I've met in a long while."

"You live across the country," Riley interrupted, uncomfortable now. "And since when did this become a debate about my love life?"

"You're right," Brooke said, patting his shoulder. "If we start now, we'll never stop. We can't go anywhere without running into one of his old flings," she said to Max. "Women practically line the sidewalks, swooning over him."

"No wonder his ego is getting so big," Max laughed.

"Come on," Riley protested. "That's not true."

"Isn't it?" Brooke grinned. "Our waitress the other night nearly lay down in the middle of the restaurant. I'm surprised she didn't try and slip you her number," she added. "Oh, wait, she already has it, doesn't she?"

He coughed. "Maybe."

Brooke laughed out loud. "I bet you five bucks she texts, inviting you to a little rendezvous."

Riley busied himself with his beer. The truth was, Lulu had already sent a flirty message inviting him to get together, but he hadn't replied. He still got messages all the time from his old hookups, just checking in, or suggesting a late-night rendezvous. He used to think of it as a good sign—that they all stayed friendly, no hard feelings—but now he wasn't so sure. Did they all just think he was available for a good time, no questions asked?

"I have to say, I'm impressed." Max sat back, regarding Brooke. "You're taking this all in stride. Most women would be jealously checking his messages by now."

Brooke shrugged, eating another fry. "Riley's a free man," she said. "He can do whatever he wants, with whoever he likes." She smiled at him, looking relaxed, but Riley felt a strange twist in his gut.

He *wanted* her to be jealous. Or at least not so fine with the idea he could pick up and date some other girl anytime he chose.

Didn't she care about them at all?

"That's . . . wow. Mature." Even Max looked surprised by her casual reply. "Hey, good for you. I wish my dates could be so relaxed about things. It's like we have one dinner, and suddenly, they want me to pick out end tables and meet their parents."

"You just have to be upfront about things, like Riley is." Brooke smiled at him, then bobbed up. "I'll be right back," she said. Riley watched her weave through the crowd towards the bathrooms.

"Don't screw this up."

He looked back at Max. "Seriously," Max said. "She's awesome. And doesn't seem to mind your long, long list of conquests."

"Will you stop talking like that?" Riley scowled. "You've done nothing all night but make me look like a total man-whore."

"Aren't you?" Max shot back, then he laughed. "Come on, relax. Brooke doesn't care."

"But I do." Riley still felt unsettled. He and Max ribbed on each other all the time, but for some reason, it was hitting close to home. "I'm trying to impress the girl, not make her think I'll never settle down."

Max's eyebrows shot up. "So it *is* serious. Hey, sorry man, I didn't realize. You said it was just some fun."

"It is. *Was*," Riley corrected himself. He sighed. "I don't know." He took another drink of beer. "It's complicated."

"Message received," Max said. "Want me to start playing up your respectability? I can tell her about all that babysitting you did for our cousins, back home."

"Little Elliot fell down the stairs and broke his leg," Riley said, remembering.

"So I'll leave out that part." Max grinned. "Come on, you're great. Annoyingly successful, and almost as handsome as me. She'd be lucky to have you."

Riley shrugged off the praise, but watching as Brooke made her way back towards them, he couldn't help noticing the way heads turned to watch her, every guy in the bar tracking the sway of those hips, and how her blonde hair was falling temptingly out of that bun . . .

He was the lucky one. He knew how her sweet lips tasted, and the way her body moved, the little gasping moans she made when he touched her, just right, and the look in her eyes as she came apart, begging for more.

He'd craved her from the start, but he was only just realizing how much more there was to want. Mornings with her, just laughing in bed. Late-night phone calls, and those texts that brought a smile whenever he saw her on the screen.

His name on her lips as she came undone.

"What did I miss?" Brooke was smiling when she reached their table.

Riley shot to his feet. He needed to get her alone, and fast. "Max has to call it a night. Jet lag, you know how it is."

Brooke frowned. "Isn't that going the other way?"

Riley gave his brother a look. Max obliged with a yawn. "I'm beat. All that travel."

"We'll let him get his beauty sleep." Riley took her arm, already needing her so badly he couldn't think straight. "You can take the boat," he said to Max. "Don't sink it."

"It was great meeting you—"

Riley dragged Brooke away before she could finish. "Hey," she protested. "What's the rush?"

Riley leaned in, still propelling her through the crowd. "In five seconds, I'm going to kiss you. I can do it right here, wherever you want, but I'm guessing you'll want us to be alone."

Brooke looked at him, and she must have seen the desire in

his eyes, because her cheeks flushed. "Alone," she repeated, looking breathless. "OK."

He pushed open the back door and slammed it shut behind them, propelling her into a blissfully deserted alleyway. Even if there had been another hundred people back there, it wouldn't have stopped him.

He needed her. Now.

Riley pushed Brooke back against the wall and claimed the mouth that had been teasing him all night. Her lips were soft, parting to let him deeper, and just like that Riley lost control. He kissed her hard and fast, demanding everything she had—and more—and *God*, Brooke was right there with him, her hands up around his neck, pulling him closer, and her body melting against him, all heat and curves and dangerously sensual surrender.

He tore away from her mouth, already needing more. The curve of her neck, the delicate hollow of her collarbone—he trailed a blazing row of kisses, feeling her gasp and leap to his touch. His hands slid possessively over her waist, roving to feel every inch of her, even through her sundress. He palmed her breast in his hand and felt her shudder, her breath coming faster as he teased through the fabric, peaking her nipple in a stiff nub that he rolled between his thumb and fingertip, teasing harder until Brooke was writhing against him.

Dear God, this woman was intoxicating.

Riley felt like a man possessed. Every thought, every instinct, it was all drowning in *her*. Capturing her lips again for another fevered kiss, he grabbed her wrists, pinning her in place against the wall as he bent his head and turned his attention to her other breast, licking over the gorgeous swell and pushing the fabric lower to kiss and suck at the stiff peak of her nipple until Brooke's gasps became a moan.

"Riley . . ."

The sound of her voice was dizzying, a breath of need, and it took everything Riley had not to shove her skirt up and take her right there, driving deep inside the way his body was demanding. But this wasn't about him. It was her, only her, and dammit if he didn't need her coming apart for him, crying out his name, and cresting on a pleasure so sweet she couldn't walk away from him if she tried.

He needed to show her he was the only one who could make her feel this way.

He kissed her again, deliberate this time. His blood ran hot, heart pounding in his ears, but he forced himself to slow, easing her lips open and stroking his tongue deep into her mouth. Brooke shuddered in his arms, still pinned in place, and Riley kept her there, up against the hard brick, as he took one hand and slowly, teasingly, trailed it over her breast and down, down past her hips to rest there at the apex of her thighs.

Brooke tensed. Even through her dress, Riley could feel her, hot and trembling to his touch. He pressed lightly, stroking through the cotton, and Brooke's whole body seemed to sway closer.

"That's right, sweetheart," he murmured in her ear. "You need me."

He pressed again, deeper, and Brooke sucked in a breath.

"We can't . . ." she whispered faintly. "Not here. People . . ."

Riley stroked again and her words died on her lips, replaced with a melting, "*Ohhh.*"

It was all the invitation he needed. He hitched her skirt higher, hidden between their bodies, and stroked up her bare thigh, finding her wet and trembling and God, everything he wanted in the world.

Brooke's head fell back, her eyes shut in ecstasy as Riley teased and caressed her, sliding one finger deep as his palm kept up the pressure right where he knew she loved it most, a soft rhythm that had them both panting, low in the dark of the empty alleyway.

This was where he'd kissed her for the first time, Riley realized through the haze of red-hot desire. Right here in the darkness, with the noise of the street beyond. Back then, he'd been the one in control, surprised by the passion of her kisses and the electric heat that surged between complete strangers. But now?

Now, God, he was the one at her mercy, recklessly coaxing every moan from her lips, strung out on a mix of pride and pleasure and pure, desperate need.

Did she know what she was doing to him?

Did she understand the inferno pushing him on?

Brooke whimpered softly, straining to his touch. She was close, so close, and God, he didn't think he could hold it together much longer. His body roared to take her, and every muscle wound taut as he slid another finger deeper and pulsed, again, over and over until he felt her stiffen and clench around him, and then he kissed her hard to swallow her cry, feeling her body rise and shake as her climax swept over them both.

She gasped for air, slowly coming back down to earth. "I can't believe you just did that," she said at last.

Her cheeks were flushed, and she tried to wriggle free, but Riley kept her there a moment longer, loving the liquid pleasure in her eyes.

He smoothed her skirt down and gently tugged her bodice back into place.

Let her try to forget about him now.

~

BROOKE WOKE in darkness in a strange room. It took her a moment to realize they were back at Riley's apartment over the bar. The pale light of dawn was just creeping over the horizon, but his bed was still bathed in shadows, Riley sprawled across the covers by her side.

She watched him for a moment, her skin still electric from his touch. The things he did . . . She could hardly believe it—or the person she was when she was with him. Panting his name louder, begging for more, urging him on no matter where they were, or who could see . . .

She flushed. It was wild and reckless, but it felt too good to ever turn him down. Even in the alleyway last night, she'd taken leave of her senses and surrendered to the pleasure, despite the risk, and how out of character it seemed.

Returning to the scene of the crime.

She smiled, running her fingertips lightly over Riley's naked back. She couldn't believe it was just a few short weeks since that first night in the bar. She owed Doug her thanks—if her disastrous blind date hadn't gone in an unexpected direction, she would never have met Riley, or unleashed this new, sensual side of herself.

She could get used to this . . .

Brooke's phone suddenly buzzed with a new message, and she leaned over to scoop it from her purse before it could wake Riley. She yawned, clicking through to the text.

I miss you.

She froze.

Brooke clutched her phone, and in a heartbeat, her blood ran cold. She didn't recognize the number, but the sick lurch in her stomach told her it could only be one person.

One person texting her in the middle of the night, with no introduction, like she should know exactly who it was.

One person who could steal her good mood and send her heart crashing to solid ground.

Archer.

The man in bed beside her stretched and let out a yawn. Brooke quickly shoved her phone away and slid back under the covers with him. Riley tugged her closer, still half-asleep, nuzzling a kiss to her forehead before he drifted off again, but Brooke couldn't relax. She lay there, wired, her whole body pounding with panicked adrenaline, until she couldn't take it anymore. She slipped out of bed and fumbled in the dim light to find her clothes, dressing quickly, trying to stay quiet. But she knocked against a chair, and the noise made Riley stir.

"Brooke?" Riley murmured, sleepy.

"Shh," she whispered, leaning over to kiss him on the cheek. "Its OK, I'm just heading home."

Riley sat up, awake now. "Creeping out in the middle of the night? Should I be worried?" His voice was teasing, but she saw the question in his eyes.

"Sorry," she said, guilty. "I can't sleep. I figured I'd go home, get some work done."

Riley looked concerned. "Is it your insomnia again?"

"Yup," Brooke lied. "Don't worry, I'll be fine. I need to prep for work, anyway. Go back to sleep."

Riley drew her closer, kissing her shoulder. "Stay. We can *not* sleep together."

Brooke slipped out of his embrace. "Really, it's fine. I'm used to it now. You relax, and I'll call you tomorrow. I mean, today." She grabbed her purse and headed for the door, feeling like a traitor. What was she doing?

Brooke paused a moment in the doorway, wishing she

could just tumble back in bed and blot the past from her mind with Riley's lips, and hands, and incredible body, but that wouldn't be fair to him. Not with thoughts of another man heavy in her mind, pulling her back to the past. "Thanks, for a lovely evening," she blurted, then hurried out.

SHE DROVE home along the dark roads, the message still burning a hole in her phone. Back at the apartment, she put the lights on and music up, filling the space with as much life as she could manage even at four in the morning, but still, there was no escaping it.

Archer was back.

Back in her messages, at least. Her mind. Her memories. It had been five months now since she'd fled Chicago, leaving all his lies behind, and for some reason, she'd figured that would be enough—that putting a thousand miles between her and that heartbreak would somehow wipe it from the face of the earth.

But of course, she was wrong.

Brooke took a long, hot shower, trying to scrub it all away even as she was flooded with memories of the relationship she'd tried so hard to forget. Just like that, the past months of sunshine and happiness fell away, and it felt like she was back in the middle of it again, her wounds still fresh and aching. All those nights together, those lazy weekend days. Trips, and holidays, and special dinners out for no special reason at all . . . God, it would be so much easier if she could just forget the good times—if learning the truth could have somehow erased them from her mind—but that wasn't how it worked, was it? She was doomed to remember, in all its excruciating hope and excitement, how it felt to be falling in love with the man of her dreams.

A man who, it turned out, had never existed at all.

Brooke shut off the water and stood there a moment, dripping wet. Her heart clenched with shame and regret, and a desperate, angry ache, as if it were yesterday.

What right did he have to miss her, when she was finally moving on?

Brooke flung the shower door open and grabbed a towel, angrily striding out to find her phone again.

I miss you.

The message was still sitting there, causally, like a time bomb ready to detonate at any moment. But she didn't have room for it in her life, not anymore. Before she could stop herself, Brooke found herself texting back.

Tell that to your wife. Don't EVER contact me again.

She hit send with an angry stab of her thumb, then blocked the number and deleted the message, too.

It was gone.

She exhaled. She should feel better now, having banished him back to the past where he belonged, but still, she felt that uneasy twist in her stomach.

Archer didn't quit that easily. When he wanted something . . . *someone* . . . he didn't give up.

Brooke shook her head and put her phone away. Whatever he said or did, it wouldn't make a difference now. You couldn't take back that kind of lying, and all the four a.m. texts in the world wouldn't fix the damage after breaking her trust—and her heart—so thoroughly.

She should have known from the start. She should have seen what kind of man he truly was. But she wasn't a fool anymore, and that old saying circled in her mind like a protective mantra:

When someone shows you who they are, believe them.

That was why things were working with Riley now—she didn't have any illusions about their relationship, or what kind of future they had in store. And no matter how much she wondered if maybe they could be more than just a delicious rebound fling, she already knew the answer to that question—and she wouldn't make the same mistake again.

When someone shows you who they are, believe them.

She grabbed her laptop and tried to focus on work.

It was going to be a long night.

18

*B*rooke threw herself into work that week, trying to distract herself from Archer's text. She didn't have to try too hard—with the big Hollywood wedding just days away, she had no time to spare for memories. There were last-minute guest requests arriving daily, travel arrangements to book, and the entire production of the wedding day to schedule, so smoothly the happy couple wouldn't even notice the labor behind the scenes. By the time Labor Day rolled around, she was elbow deep in wedding favors, and barely had time to eat and sleep, let alone dwell on the ruins of her past relationships.

Her phone buzzed.

Brooke froze, feeling the same sick lurch she'd suffered ever since getting that message from Archer. She should have changed her number by now, instead of having to brace herself whenever she heard the alert, wondering if it was him again. She fished her phone out from under a stack of purchase orders, almost afraid to read the name on the message ID.

Riley.

Brooke exhaled, and clicked through.

What time do you want to meet for the party?

Brooke paused. She'd forgotten about the Sweetbriar get-together, but looking at her list of things to do, she'd be lucky if she was out of here by midnight.

"Brooke?" One of her assistant managers appeared in her office doorway, weighed down with a stack of boxes. "Where do you want the moisturizer?"

"The what?" Brooke put her phone away without replying. She was trying to coordinate the car services to collect everyone from Boston International Airport—a hundred VIP guests arriving over two days all expecting their own luxury sedan to whisk them out to the Cape.

"I think it's moisturizer?" Jenny nudged a box open with her nose. "Or is it face cream? Anyway, a whole crate of the stuff just arrived out front. The delivery guy says it shipped from California."

"I have no idea." Brooke felt frazzled. "Just leave it here, and I'll try to figure it out."

Moisturizer? She opened a bottle, and took a sniff. Orange-blossom. Maybe it was for the welcome gifts for the guests, but Brooke couldn't imagine Bitsy planning something like that, not when there was already a tasteful collection of chocolates, vintage wine, and cigars—just for the gentlemen, of course.

Her phone rang, and she answered, still sniffing the tube. "Hello?"

"Brooke, good." Meredith's crisp tone was on the other end. "Where are we on the airport transfers?"

"I have every car service in a hundred miles booked." Brooke returned to her schedule. "They're all scheduled to each guest's arrival, and will be waiting for them in Arrivals."

"And security?"

"Will be increased here at the hotel. I've already hired extra staff for the duration, and talked with the local police force. They know to expect extra activity, and will be on call to help with any crowd control or paparazzi—if word gets out."

"Which it will, of course," Meredith sighed. "You can't have two hundred of Hollywood and DC's biggest stars descending on one town without drawing attention."

"*Two* hundred." Brooke's heart stopped.

"Yes, didn't you get the revised guest list?" Meredith sounded surprised. "I sent it to you ages ago."

Brooke frantically clicked through her inbox. Sure enough, there was a new message from Meredith titled "tiny change," sent all of . . . seven minutes ago.

"Double the wedding guests? But . . . we don't have the rooms." Brooke gulped.

"Oh, that's fine. They're staying in private homes nearby. The Cartwrights have a compound down in Hyannis Port. These are just additional names for the ceremony."

"Uh huh." Brooke murmured weakly, already mentally doubling the catering, drinks, favors, seating . . . "Wait, did you guys send face cream?"

"It's a facial masque," Meredith explained. "The rest of the supplies will be arriving today. Lila has a sponsorship contract, so we'll need the toiletries in the hotel all traded out, you understand."

"Sure." Brooke added it to her very long list. "Why not?"

"I'll let you get back to it."

"One thing," she remembered, before Meredith could ring off. "I haven't heard from Lila."

Meredith paused. "What do you mean?"

"I've left her several messages, but she isn't replying."

Brooke paused, remembering their last conversation. "I really need her to sign off on a couple of things before the ceremony, and the last time we spoke . . . Did she mention what happened with Bitsy?"

"I'll do all the signing off you need." Meredith was firm—and didn't answer the question. "You don't need to bug her with these details. The less thinking she does right now, the better."

"I'd really like her feedback on a couple of these changes," Brooke pushed. "It's her wedding, after all."

"She doesn't care about the details," Meredith stated crisply. "Trust me, she just wants all this to be over with."

"OK . . ."

Brooke hung up, still feeling uneasy. It didn't sound like a recipe for a perfect wedding, but what did she know? To someone like Lila, it was probably just another big event, like all the red-carpet premieres she attended, just with a different colored dress.

She had bigger things to focus on. Like making sure every guest got to enjoy the benefits of an ultra-hydrating retinol mask. It was going to be another long day.

~

RILEY CHECKED his phone for what felt like the hundredth time. Still no response from Brooke. He'd texted hours ago, and it was no big deal, but it smarted to see the message sitting there: delivered but unanswered.

He wondered if he should send another message. No, that would look desperate. Or would it?

Riley sighed. Was this what his former flings had felt like

when he didn't text them back? If so, karma was having a field day with him right now.

And yes, it was a bitch.

He looked around the bar, restless. Like every holiday, they were packed out with happy tourists, pink-eared from the beach. He should be happy to see the business thriving, but for some reason, he remembered Cooper's questions—and his brother's annoying teasing during his visit.

Was this all he wanted out of life?

Most guys would kill for the set-up he had going here: great job, great friends, and a great woman happy to keep things low-stress and drama-free. He'd cut all the cords and skimmed through life, as easy as his boat bobbing on the evening tide. But for some reason, he felt an odd itch in his veins. Wondering if maybe there was something he was missing out on, if sailing on by meant he was leaving something better on dry land.

"Riley."

He turned, glad for a distraction from the pesky existential questions buzzing around in his mind, and found his favorite potter, looking frazzled in cut-offs and a tank top.

"Mackenzie, hi," Riley grinned. "What can I get you?"

Mackenzie fanned herself. "Two crates of beer and a dozen bottles of wine, please."

Riley gave her a fake stern look. "Do we need to talk about your drinking problem?"

Mac grinned. "You mean the fact I invited half the town to this party, and forgot that meant we had to feed them?"

"You need some help?" Riley offered.

"Don't tempt me," Mackenzie groaned.

"I mean it," Riley said, glad to be useful. "Neil can cover for me here, and when it comes to shifting beer crates, I've got the goods." He flexed his biceps, and Mackenzie laughed.

"Who am I to stand in the way of a man offering help?"

"Smart woman," Riley grinned. He threw down his dish-cloth. "I'll go grab the booze. Do you have your car, or do you want me to use the jeep?"

Mac batted her eyelashes. "What do you think?"

"I think you're lucky to have me."

Riley headed in back, loading up his trunk with enough booze to keep the people of Sweetbriar merry for at least a few hours. "You're a lifesaver," Mackenzie said, hopping up into the jeep with him. "Poppy and Coop bought out the wholesaler with steak and hamburgers, Summer's got dessert locked down, but I totally forgot about my share."

"Working on something new?" Riley asked, driving towards the beach.

Mackenzie nodded. "One of my weird projects," she said vaguely, and Riley remembered how protective she was of her personal art. She was happy to churn out cute sailboat ceramics all day long, but when it came to anything else, he'd never even seen a glimpse.

"Are you ever going to show your personal stuff?" Riley asked. "I feel like you've kept it under wraps for years."

Mackenzie looked awkward. "You're not missing anything," she said. "So, how's Brooke?"

Riley snorted. "Way to change the subject."

"Come on," Mackenzie said, protesting. "Don't hold out on me. She's great, isn't she?"

"Sure." Riley tried to sound casual, but he couldn't stop the smile spreading at the thought of her.

"I knew it!" Mackenzie whacked him in the arm. "I knew

this day would come! You're in *lo-ove*," she said, sing-song, like the annoying little sister he'd never had.

"Mac," he tried to stop her, warning, but she kept on, excited.

"When are you guys making it official? You know, moving in, settling down, setting a date."

"Whoa, hold up!" he interrupted her stream of excited chatter. "That's moving way too fast. We're not even officially dating just yet."

"Why the hell not?" Mackenzie frowned. "What are you waiting for?"

"Nothing," Riley said evasively. "It's just . . . not the right time."

"Seriously?" Mackenzie fixed him with a stare. "That's your play?"

He sighed. "C'mon . . ."

"I don't get you guys sometimes." She shook her head. "You know, I always figured you'd drop this playboy thing when the right woman came along, but here you are, with her standing right in front of you, and you still can't bring yourself to get real. What are you so scared of?"

Riley blinked. "I'm not scared," he protested, but Mackenzie just snorted.

"Sure."

"I'm not," he said again, less forceful this time.

"So you don't want to be with her?" Mackenzie asked. "My bad."

Riley scowled. Of course he wanted to be with Brooke, but is wasn't as simple as that.

Was it?

"Hey, I'm sorry, I shouldn't be giving you a hard time." Mackenzie reached out and patted his arm. "It's none of my business. If you're happy, and she's happy, then it's your business. Don't listen to me. I mean, I'm hardly the authority on relationships, am I?"

Riley couldn't argue. As long as he'd known her, Mackenzie hadn't dated anyone—at least, not seriously. So either she was somehow carrying on torrid affairs out of the eye of Sweetbriar gossip, or she'd been single all this time. Which didn't seem right for someone as warm and beautiful as her.

"No guys on the scene with you?" he asked, changing the subject.

Mackenzie snorted. "Not the last time I checked. If you see them lining up in the wrong place, let me know."

She was kidding, but Riley thought he heard a wistful note in her voice. Still, he didn't press her. It wasn't his place, and Lord knew he wasn't the man for a heart-to-heart about true love—not when he couldn't even give her a straight answer about what was keeping him from having a real relationship. Instead, he pulled up outside Poppy's and Cooper's beach house: the location for the big barbecue that night. There was already festive ticker tape wound around the front porch railings, and the door was open, so Riley set about hoisting the crates of booze out of the truck, while Mackenzie went on ahead.

"Hello?" he called, stepping into the cool hallway.

"We're in back!" the answer came.

He headed through the house to the back deck, where it looked like the entire contents of the local discount warehouse were stacked by the grill.

"We went a little overboard," Poppy greeted him with a hug. "But Cooper swears you'll all eat your body weight in hamburgers."

"It's true." Riley set the crate down in a shady spot and

looked around. They had a gorgeous property that Cooper had restored himself, right on the beach with a full panoramic view that almost rivaled his boat. Almost. "Mayor Keller underestimated the crowd at his Fourth of July bash last year," he added, teasing. "There was a riot when they ran out of hotdogs. You know, we haven't seen his German Shepard since . . ."

Poppy laughed. "Don't even joke about it! It's my first time hosting a town event," she added with a bashful smile. "I just want it to go smoothly."

"Everything looks great here," he reassured her. Mackenzie was setting up folding picnic tables down on the sand, and he could see Cooper prepping for a bonfire, too. "Besides, this is Sweetbriar Cove. As long as you have beer and burgers, you can't fail."

As the sun set over the ocean, Riley's prediction was right: practically the whole town came out for the barbecue. Music echoed across the sand, kids ran riot, smeared with ice cream, and everyone was having a great time . . . except Riley.

Brooke still hadn't shown.

He tried to shake it off and enjoy himself, but he couldn't stop watching for her arrival. She said she was working late, but it was almost nine, and there was still no sign—

"Hey." A pair of hands suddenly covered his eyes, and he caught a breath of lavender, faint but unmistakably sweet. A familiar voice murmured in his ear. "Guess who?"

Riley was already smiling. He would have known Brooke just from the feel of her, sending his blood surging. "Hmm, let me think about this one . . ." he teased, relishing her touch. "Angelina Jolie?"

"Nope."

"Debra from the farmer's market?" he said, naming a pensioner in town who was pushing eighty years old, and spry as ever.

Brooke laughed. "Try again."

"I know. It's Poppy. You've finally left Cooper behind for a real man."

"Sorry to disappoint." Brooke dropped her hands, and he caught her around the waist, spinning her to face him.

"You could never be a disappointment," he said, leaning in to kiss her. His tension melted away, and he relished the soft caress of her lips on his. "Did you finish up at the hotel?" he asked, finally drawing back. Brooke looked tired, still wearing her smart work outfit of a crisp navy dress. "I can't believe you have to work the holiday. What's the point of being boss if you can't get your underlings to cover for you?"

She gave a weary smile. "It's all hands on deck with the wedding. I've been running around all day dealing with last-minute disasters. Did you know organic and bio-dynamic flour are two very different things?"

"I'm sorry." Riley touched his hand to her cheek. "Hey, at least it'll all be over soon."

Brooke nodded. "To tell the truth, I wonder if it's even going ahead at all. I just get this vibe from Lila, like she doesn't want any of this . . ." She shook her head. "Ignore me, I've been obsessing over this stuff too long."

"What can I do?" Riley asked, and Brooke gave him a smile, brighter this time.

"A kiss would help."

He obliged, cupping her cheek and gently brushing his lips against hers. Brooke gave a little sigh. "Now, if you could just put a burger in my hand, I'd be set."

He chuckled. "Coming right up."

Riley took her hand and led her towards the grill. It felt so natural, intertwining his fingers with hers, and for a moment he let himself imagine what it would be like if he did take the next step, and make this something real. Waking up with Brooke in the morning, falling asleep with her there in his arms at night. No tentative texts and casual, "maybe" plans, but someone he could depend on.

Opening up, and really letting himself trust again.

Part of him shrank away from the thought, the same way it had ever since his business went down in flames. He'd joked about it feeling like a divorce, but in a way, it was true. He'd invested everything in that company, and been left bitter and burned out at the end. It was why he'd escaped out here and built a new life, with zero attachments tying him down.

If he didn't care too much about anything, he wouldn't get hurt again.

But what if he wanted to care?

Riley swallowed. For the first time, he wished he hadn't been so brazenly casual with Brooke. Strolling around town, swearing he was only looking for a good time seemed like the most honest, upfront approach at the time, but now that he was thinking about more, he suddenly realized his plan had backfired.

What if she believed him? And, worse still, what if that was all she wanted from him, too?

"Brooke?" he found himself asking.

She turned, her hair flaring gold in the firelight, and Riley's voice caught in his throat. She was beautiful—and his, for the night at least. Things were just fine the way they were. Did he really want to ruin a good thing while he had it?

"What is it?"

"Nothing," he said, exhaling. "It can wait."

19

*B*rooke spent the rest of the evening learning to unwind, Sweetbriar-style. There was food, and cocktails, a local band playing music, and people dancing right on the sand. Summer had even set up a s'mores station, where you could build the perfect skewers with candy and chocolate before toasting them in the open bonfire.

"I'm a purist," Summer said, snuggled up to her boyfriend, Grayson, as they all watched their marshmallows melt in the flickering firelight. "Plain chocolate and graham crackers all the way."

"You've got to mix it up," Mackenzie argued, wrapped now in a big blue blanket. "Live life on the edge."

Brooke smiled. She was tucked in the crook of Riley's arm, feeling more relaxed than she had in a long while. "Is it ready?" she asked him.

"Let's see." Riley pulled their branches out, and expertly slid the gooey toasted marshmallows onto their waiting crackers.

"I haven't had one since I was a kid," Brooke said, nibbling the edge. The taste of chocolate and sugar took her back. "We used to go to my grandpa's cabin, eat nothing but s'mores and hot dogs all summer long."

"Sounds like fun." Riley smiled at her, his eyes bright in the firelight.

She nodded. "It was. I always thought . . ." Brooke caught herself in time. She'd always thought she'd like to do that with her kids one day, let them run wild in the woods and by the lakeshore the way she had. But of course, that wasn't the kind of thing she should be saying to Riley. Any talk of kids and the future, and he'd probably bolt before their s'mores got cold.

"You were saying?" he nudged her gently.

Brooke shook her head. "Nothing. You know, it's getting kind of cold. I'm going to grab my sweater from the car."

"I can go," he offered.

"No, you stay here. Toast me another." Brooke kissed him on the cheek and headed back to the house. People greeted her as she passed, now-familiar faces she'd seen at other events, and as she made her way out to her car, Brooke felt a quiet sense of satisfaction. She was finally settling in: making friends and putting down roots. She may have wound up in Sweetbriar Cove by accident, but perhaps it was exactly where she was supposed to be.

She unlocked the car and grabbed her sweater, but couldn't stop herself from reaching for her phone, too. She'd stashed it in the glove compartment to put Archer out of her mind for the night, but after what had happened at the hotel last time she went no-contact, she couldn't resist checking it, just in case.

No SOS text messages from the hotel. She exhaled in relief, then saw the little icon flashing. A voicemail was waiting.

Brooke clicked through, and then she heard it. Archer's voice, clear as the day before she'd left him.

"It's me."

She froze. In an instant, he was right there with her. Flashing that apologetic smile, his dark eyes full of charming remorse.

"I can't stop thinking about you," the voicemail continued. "I know I screwed up, I should have told you about her sooner, but baby, you have to understand, I was always going to choose you. You're the one I want, our life together, and I know you want it too. Please, just give me a chance to explain. Don't throw away the rest of our life together because I made one stupid mistake. I love you, baby. I'll do anything to make this right."

The message ended. Brooke slowly lowered the phone. She felt sick to her stomach, as if she'd just stepped off a roller coaster, solid ground not so solid anymore.

What the hell was he playing at?

But she knew that answer already. He thought he could turn back the clock, charm her into loving him again and conveniently forgetting just what a liar he'd been. Archer was used to getting his way, and now, he was turning all that charm and smooth focus on her.

She gulped for air.

Running away from him had been a mistake, she could see it now. If she'd told him to his face it was over, then maybe he wouldn't be chasing after her like this. They would have fought, and screamed, and yelled; she would have told him he was a liar, and a cheater, and she never wanted to lay eyes on him again.

It would be done.

But instead, she'd let shame and guilt drive her out of town, trying to forget her own foolishness by pretending it had never happened at all. As if paying penance by planning a dozen perfect weddings could ever erase the marriage she'd helped tear apart.

This is what denial got you: skulking in the shadows outside a party, feeling like one rogue voicemail was blowing all that hard-won resolve apart.

She wasn't ready for this. She didn't have space in her heart to deal with him, not with the biggest event of her life in just two days, and Riley waiting down on the beach, and a million other things to juggle—that didn't include raking up the biggest betrayal of her life.

Brooke could hear the music and laughter from the party, but she couldn't imagine going back in there and faking a smile. Not now.

She got behind the wheel, and typed out a quick text for Riley.

Sorry, not feeling great – heading home.

She already felt guilty hitting send, but she didn't know what else to do. Tell Riley that even a message from her ex sent her spinning? She was supposed to be over him now. Immune. And she would be, one day.

But this wasn't that day.

SHE DROVE HOME, feeling terrible for leaving the party behind. She could hear her phone chirping with new messages, but she didn't pick it up; she didn't want to have to answer Riley's concerned questions, not when she was bailing on him like this. Back home, she changed into sweatpants and put some tea on the stove, then stood there in the middle of her empty apartment, feeling lost.

This wasn't just about Archer anymore. It was everything.

Wondering if she was making the same mistake all over again, opening up to a man who should be off-limits. Setting herself up for heartbreak when love should be the last thing on her mind.

When you don't see the truth that's right in front of you, how can you ever trust yourself—or anyone else—again?

Brooke didn't even hear the tea kettle whistle until there was a knock at the door, breaking her reverie.

"Just a second!" she called, hurrying to take it off the flame before opening up.

Riley was standing outside. He looked too good in the darkness, in those jeans and a T-shirt, soft enough to touch, and Brooke's heart twisted to see him there.

"Oh. Hey." She gulped. "Sorry I left in a hurry like that. I, umm, had a headache coming on."

Riley didn't look convinced. "Are you sure everything's OK? What's going on?"

He looked so tender and concerned, Brooke hated telling these half-truths. But what could she say?

She'd been wrong before. So wrong. And now, that mistake was lingering in the back of everything she did, making her question her instincts, and carefully second-guess each new choice.

She shook her head. "Like I said, I'm not feeling so great. Stress, and work . . ." She shrugged. "I didn't want to ruin your fun."

"Poor baby." Riley pulled her closer and gently cradled her in his arms. "It's OK if you're not up to a crowd. I'd rather be here with you, any day."

Brooke relaxed in his arms. She shouldn't let herself get used to it, but he felt too good to resist. Solid, and stable, holding her against him. Riley stroked her cheek. "How about I take care of you?" he said, with a smile that took her breath away. "I'm guessing you don't let anyone else do it."

"What gave me away?" Brooke managed a faint smile, and he chuckled.

"Lucky for you, I came equipped." Riley picked up a bag from beside the doorway, and held it up. "I stopped for supplies. Aspirin, vitamin C, and Summer's famous peach cake."

"You covered all the bases," she said, feeling a wave of affection.

"Yes, ma'am."

Brooke stood aside and let him in. He set the bag down and looked around. "Now, you get to bed," Riley told her, "and let me take care of the rest."

Brooke did as she was told. After running around all week, it was a relief to go sink into her fresh sheets and listen to him pottering around outside. Soon, Riley appeared in her bedroom doorway with a tray. He set it down on the night-stand, and she scooched over, making room for him beside her on the bed.

"There," he said, setting a plate of cake between them on the covers. "All the best parts of the party, without the chaos."

Brooke relaxed back against her pillows. "You're sweet."

"Shh." Riley winked. "Let's keep that between us. You'll ruin my reputation."

She laughed. "Don't tell me the smooth-guy routine is just a front, and you're really itching to settle down with two kids and a dog?"

"Right." Riley laughed along, but there was a look on his face she couldn't decipher, and it reminded her of when she and Max had been teasing him the other night.

"Hey, you know I'm only kidding." Brooke nudged him

gently. "I think it's great you're so honest about who you are and what you want. I'm guessing you save everyone a lot of heartache this way."

Riley nodded slowly. He looked like he wanted to say something, but he closed his mouth instead.

"I wish everyone could be so upfront," she added, feeling a pang. "Just say, 'this is a fling,' instead of pretending it ever meant more."

"Like your ex?" Riley asked slowly.

She sighed. "He wants to talk," Brooke admitted. "He's texting, and calling. I wish I could just make him disappear, but it's not so simple."

Riley seemed to tense. "Do you still love him?"

"No," Brooke answered honestly. "But it still hurts to think about. That's how it works, right?" she said ruefully. "Breakups take time. You can wish someone was covered in honey, stranded in a pit of killer ants, but that doesn't mean you don't still feel the pain at everything you went through."

"That's a pretty specific revenge fantasy," Riley said, with a glimmer of a smile.

She grinned. "I had a lot of time on the road between Chicago and the Cape. Believe me, killer ants are only the start of it."

He chuckled, pulling her closer. "I'd say you're doing pretty well getting over him."

"Thanks to you." Brooke tilted her head up to face him. "Seriously. You were right from the start. This is exactly what I needed. No strings, no drama. Just fun." She kissed him, glad he was with her, and after a moment, Riley kissed her back.

Brooke sank into the moment: the sweetness of his embrace, and the low heat that sparked between them, every time. He eased her lips wider, and stroked his tongue into her mouth, and she shivered at the intimacy, the feel of his body, hot and taut against her.

Riley shifted, scooping her into his lap to straddle him. Now, Brooke had free rein to cup his face in her hands and press closer, loving the feel of him, hard against every inch. His hands slipped over her back, her hips, straying to her chest to gently stroke and tease her through her tank. Brooke gasped against his mouth, and she felt his lips curl in a smile.

"If you're getting sick, you shouldn't exert yourself," Riley said, drawing back to give her a wicked smile. He brushed hair out of her eyes, and Brooke melted at his touch.

"No?" she asked.

He shook his head, teasing. "You need to conserve your energy."

In one swift movement, he rolled them to the side, tipping her under him so he was braced above her. He kissed her again, lazy and hot. "You should be relaxing . . ."

Brooke felt his hands slide over her again, purposeful this time. Her pulse kicked. There wasn't anything relaxing about the desire snaking through her, already tight and craving for more. Riley lavished her with kisses, slowly peeling her clothes away until she was naked on the bed. His touch was incredible, but she needed to feel everything, so she tugged at his shirt.

"Play fair," she whispered. He grinned, and stripped off his own clothes so fast, she had to laugh. He quirked an eyebrow, and she shook her head. "Nothing."

"Really?" Riley teased, gently caressing over the swell of her breast. "This is doing *nothing* for you?"

Brooke bit her lip. "I didn't say that," she breathed, as he toyed with her nipple, sending tiny shockwaves of pleasure ricocheting through her body.

"No?" Riley dipped his head, licking over her skin.

She shuddered. "What do you think?"

He closed his mouth around her, and she moaned.

"I think we can do better than that."

Riley sucked softly, and then there was no time for teasing words, not with his mouth hot against her, and his tongue doing wicked things, and his hands—*oh, his hands*—sliding over her stomach and easing her thighs apart. Brooke moaned in pleasure, loving the feel of him, how he knew just the way to touch her to bring her closer to the brink. She reached for him, stroking until he groaned against her, and he pinned her wrists to the bed, holding her back as he panted for air. Brooke shuddered, her body electric beneath him, needing more. But Riley made her wait, teasing her with kisses, watching her come apart. His eyes were dark in the dim light, and Brooke could have lost herself right then and there, but there was still a hunger burning in her bloodstream, and only one thing would take over the edge.

He slowly entered her, and everything fell away.

Brooke gasped, feeling him move inside of her. Thick, sweet pleasure, rocking higher, filling her up. It was incredible, how he could do this to her, the way their bodies fit so perfectly, every inch driving her closer to the brink. She surged against him and felt Riley tense, every muscle in his body rigid under her hands. He rocked into her again, and Brooke whimpered, clutching hold of him for dear life as the pleasure blossomed and bloomed, an inferno crying out for release.

It had never been like this before, not with anyone, and even as Brooke tried to cling hold of her reason and keep from falling into Riley's steady gaze, remember that this was just fun and games and nothing she could hold onto, she couldn't help it. She surrendered to the moment, lost herself in him, over and over, until there was no holding back, no hiding from the pleasure and the deep, aching connection that seemed to surge between them, her heart laid wide open and bared for him to see.

"Riley," she gasped, overwhelmed, and he thrust inside her again.

"I'm here, baby," he groaned against her. "I've got you. I'm not letting go."

He plunged deep, so deep, just right, and Brooke wanted to believe. For that moment, in that pure, sweet rush, he was hers.

She came apart, crying out his name, and held him through the rush. And when it was over, her blood thick with a hazy glow, she held him, and never wanted to let go. There, in the darkness, tangled up in each other's arms, it felt right. It felt perfect, even though she knew it wasn't real.

It was sex. Fun. Pheromones seducing her with a glimpse of forever when she already knew forever wasn't on the menu at all.

But for tonight, just maybe, she could believe.

20

$\mathcal{T}$he day of the Cartwright wedding dawned cloudy and overcast, with dark grey clouds looming over the water and rain already spluttering from the sky.

"It's a disaster." Bitsy was waiting when Brooke arrived, at seven a.m. sharp. "I mean, just look at it! Someone leaked to the press, those vultures are lined up outside, and this weather!"

"Good morning," Brooke managed, shaking off her jacket. "Ready for the big day?"

"It's raining!" Bitsy squawked. "The hair will be ruined! Did nobody check the weather reports?"

"Three times," Brooke reassured her. "Which is why I know it will clear by lunchtime. And if it doesn't, I have a canopy and tents on standby. Everyone's hair will be beautiful."

She headed for the lobby, but Bitsy trotted alongside. "Tents aren't good enough. I heard there was a hurricane warning!"

"We have plenty of time." Brooke tried to keep her voice

even. "The ceremony's not until two. That's seven hours for the storm to pass. Have you had breakfast?" she swiftly changed the subject. "There's a wonderful buffet being laid out in the main dining room. You should go have something. It's a long day ahead!"

She nudged Bitsy towards the dining hall and quickly changed direction, joining the rest of her staff, who were waiting in the conference room. "OK, listen up." She clapped her hands, and all eyes turned to her. "We've got a lot going on today, but I don't want anyone to worry. This is just another wedding, and we've done a dozen already this year."

She could tell from the dubious faces they weren't buying it —and she didn't blame them. Most of their events didn't come with trained security details and a who's who of Hollywood's A-list stars.

"Who am I kidding? This is the big one. But I believe in you guys. If we stay calm and professional, and all do our jobs, this will be the best day of Lila Moore's life. OK?"

They nodded.

"Let's get to it!"

"Umm, Brooke?" Neil caught her as the room emptied. "Richie called in sick. And Brent too. They were at some rock show last night in Boston, they say they won't make it back."

Her bartenders. Brooke took a deep breath. "OK, thanks, I've got this."

She tried calling a few back-up options, but they wouldn't be free until the evening, so she dialed the first person in her phone. "Save me," she said to Riley.

"Always," he chuckled. "What dragon do you need slaying this time?"

"She's in pink Chanel, but I can handle her," Brooke said, thinking of Bitsy. "I need your expertise."

"Really?" Riley drawled, so suggestive that Brooke blushed.

"Your bartending expertise," she explained quickly. "Both my guys are slacking off sick. Any chance you can come tend bar for a few hours from noon until the cavalry arrive? I'll pay."

"No need," Riley assured her. "I'll be there in twenty. To tell you the truth, I'm curious about this whole party. It's not every day we get Hollywood royalty descending on this part of the world."

"You're a lifesaver." Brooke breathed a sigh of relief. "What would I do without you?"

"Pray, nightly, to meet a man like me," Riley joked, and she laughed.

"Easy there. OK, I better get back to it. Wish me luck!"

She hung up and turned her attention back to the well-orchestrated circus currently taking over the hotel. She ferried guest requests, kept the press at bay, and deftly kept champagne flowing in the dining hall, until the entire building was decked out in fresh lilacs and silk streamers, a picture of cool elegance. By the time Lila and Justin emerged from their wedding brunch and another round of photographs, the storm had passed, and the clouds were parting to reveal another warm, sunny day.

"Everything looks so beautiful," Lila said, looking around. "Thank you. I can't imagine what you went through to get all this done last-minute."

"Of course she got it done," Bitsy sniffed beside her. "We're paying them enough."

"Mother!" Justin looked mortified.

Brooke cleared her throat. "I'm glad you like it," she said. "Now, let me get you ladies settled in the salon to get dressed for the main event. Justin, you and your groomsmen are in the library."

"That's great." Justin gave Lila a kiss. "See you at the ceremony, sweetheart. I'll be the one with a tux, at the end of the aisle."

"I'll try not to miss you." Lila smiled, but Brooke thought she detected a flicker of apprehension in her eyes.

Uh-oh.

"This way!" She quickly led Lila and her bridal party to the salon, now transformed into a confection of white, lilac, and pale blush pink. Tiny tables were set with delicate finger sandwiches and cakes, and there was even more champagne waiting. The group cooed and immediately started snapping photographs. "Your makeup artist and stylists are en route, they'll be here any minute, and if you need anything at all, just let me know."

Bitsy peered at a fork. "Has this been polished? I see smudges."

Brooke whisked it out of her hand. "I'll send fresh ones immediately."

She closed the double doors behind her and let out a breath.

"Demanding, much?"

She turned. Meredith was standing with a phone in one hand, a clipboard in the other, and a Bluetooth headset fixed to one ear.

"Oh no, it's fine," Brooke said quickly. "Lila's actually great. Really relaxed."

"I wasn't talking about the bride," Meredith said, and Brooke allowed herself a grin.

"She's certainly . . . challenging."

"And I thought I had to deal with divas all day in Hollywood." Meredith intercepted a passing waiter, snagged a glass of champagne, and downed it in one.

Meredith and Brooke stood for a moment, watching the hustle of activity out on the lawn. "You ever think you put so much energy into planning everyone else's life so you don't have to focus on your own?" Meredith asked suddenly.

Brooke sighed. "All the time."

They were silent, until Meredith's phone began buzzing angrily. She lifted it, not even pausing to answer before snapping, "No, I told you, the contracts were for six percent."

She stalked away, and Brooke went back to her schedule. Soon, it was almost time for the vows, and they began ushering guests outside to take their place in front of the gorgeous oceanfront wedding arch.

"Brooke? There's a guy in the lobby to see you," one of her clerks said, looking about as harried as Brooke felt. She headed over to see what the latest demand was, making a note to do something special for the staff when all this was over, to thank them for all the late nights and overtime. Spa vouchers, maybe, or a big dinner out somewhere, off the clock—

"Hey baby," a male voice cut through her thoughts. "Surprise."

Brooke froze. For a moment, she couldn't look; just the sound of his voice sliced clean through her, baring her wounds again, raw and bloody as the day he'd broken it in two.

Archer.

She couldn't believe it, but there he was, standing in the middle of the lobby like he had any right at all. "What . . . ?" she stammered, her heart racing. "What are you doing here?"

"You wouldn't answer my messages, so I had to come talk to you face-to-face." Archer strolled closer, clean-shaven and smartly-dressed in a button-down and pants that perfectly fit his tall, limber frame. He fixed her with a melting smile. "You look great, baby. God, I've missed you."

He reached out, and Brooke flinched back at the touch. How many nights had he reached for her, just like that?

How long was it the only thing she wanted in the world?

She finally found her voice: stern. "You can't be here."

"Look, I know we've had our . . . misunderstandings, but you can't stay mad at me forever." Archer looked at her from under his shock of dark hair, those eyes full of affection and regret. "Let's just talk, it's all I'm asking. Hear me out, baby. Please."

"No. I mean, you *can't* be here," Brooke repeated, trying her best to keep it together. "Everyone coming in and out of the hotel needs a security clearance. How did you even get past the doors?"

"I have my ways," Archer grinned. "You think I was going to let a couple of rent-a-cops keep me away from you?" He reached for her again, and Brooke had to slap his hand away.

Hurt flashed across his face. "Hey, look, I know you're mad, but I came all this way to see you. The least you could do is give me a chance to explain."

Brooke stared at him in disbelief, but she shouldn't have been surprised. Somehow Archer always managed to glide his way through any situation; flip things around so neatly, you couldn't resist the full force of his charm. Brooke had admired him for it, once. He'd handled VIPs and janitors with the same deft charm. But she knew the dark side to that silver tongue now, and he wasn't ever "handling" her again.

"I'm busy. I'm working. Please leave. Now." Brooke drew herself up to her full height and glared at him, right in those dark, soulful eyes she'd adored. "Don't make me call security."

"Baby." Archer looked wounded, and she had to grit her teeth.

"Don't call me that," she snapped, doing her best to keep her voice down. Wedding guests were meandering through the lobby, heading outside; she could see Meredith and Bitsy arguing about something in the corner. They were twenty minutes away from the wedding ceremony—it was the worst possible moment to be faced with the ghosts of heartbreak past, but somehow, Brooke was going to get through it. "I'm not your baby, and I never was. Go tell it to your *wife*."

She turned on her heel to walk away, but Archer caught her arm, pulling her back. "Look, I don't know what she told you, but you can't believe her," he implored Brooke. "She's crazy, vindictive, and bitter. She's trying to break us apart, and you're letting her!"

Brooke tore away. This was supposed to be a good day—a *perfect* day—for Lila and her family. One more wedding to help even the scales, one more happy couple launched into their life of matrimonial bliss, to make up for the damage Brooke had unwittingly done.

"Julia," she said, feeling sick inside. "Your wife has a name."

"*Ex*-wife," Archer insisted.

"Oh yeah?" Brooke stared back. "Show me the papers. Better yet, don't. Because you're too late. It couldn't be more over."

She made to leave again, but Archer blocked her path. "You have to listen," he said, his façade crumbling. "Please, you're all I have left. Brooke—"

"Hey!"

A loud voice came from across the lobby. Before Brooke even had time to react, Riley came storming over and hit Archer with a solid left hook, sending him tumbling to the ground.

21

*R*iley saw red.

"Is this him?" he demanded, standing over the sniveling figure, crumpled on the floor. "The guy from Chicago, your ex. Not such a big man now, are we?"

This bastard. He'd seen it on Brooke's face the minute he walked in, the hurt and heartache in her eyes. It tore him up that anyone could make her feel that way. She didn't deserve it, not for a second.

With a growl, the man hurled himself at Riley, sending him stumbling back into a table. There was a smash as a vase of flowers shattered on the ground behind him, but he barely noticed as they tussled and swung. The asshole got in a lucky blow to the face, and then Riley buried his fist into the man's stomach, sending him reeling to the floor again.

"Riley," Brooke hissed, tugging at his arm, but he barely noticed. Every muscle was tense and ready for action, focused on the man with a bloody nose on the floor.

"Get up," he growled at the guy. Hell, he didn't even know

his name, but that wouldn't stop him. He was just getting started. "Get the hell up so I can hit you again."

"Just try!" Brooke's ex staggered to his feet, blood dripping down his chin. "That was a sucker punch! I could take you in a fair fight, any day!"

"Like hell you could!" Riley lunged, but something dragged him back.

"Stop it!" Brooke moved in front of him, and shoved him back, hard. "For God's sake, calm down. You too, Archer." she whirled around, stabbing a finger at the bastard. "Are you trying to ruin my entire career?"

Riley paused. For the first time, he realized they were in the middle of the polished marble lobby, with people all around.

People staring at them in horror and disgrace.

He came to his senses. What had he just done?

"Brooke—" he started, but she cut him off.

"Come with me," Brooke ground out. "Both of you." She stalked off down a hallway without a backwards glance. Riley shot a look at Archer, who scowled back, but they both wound up shuffling into her office after her.

"I can't deal with this right now." Brooke glared at them. "In case you haven't noticed, I've got the wedding of the year out there!"

"You're right," the asshole, Archer, quickly spoke up. "I'm sorry this brute made a scene."

"Says the cheating scumbag," Riley shot back, still furious. What the hell was he doing there? Did Brooke invite him? Did she *want* to see him again?

The thought of losing her hit harder than any right hook. He hadn't had a chance yet, to tell her how he felt.

"Who the hell are you anyway?" Archer got up in his face, sneering. "This has nothing to do with you."

"Both of you, stop it!" Brooke yelled. "Please, just stop. I have to get back out there and apologize for that scene, and then do a million other things so Lila can walk down the aisle without worrying someone's going to throw another punch. So either you kill each other here, quietly, or you get the hell out of this hotel—I really don't care."

She slammed the door behind her. Riley took a breath, chastened, then lunged for it at the same time as Archer, but he got there first.

"Brooke—" he called after her.

"No!" She spun around, and Riley realized to his horror that she had tears in her eyes. "I can't talk to you right now. I can't believe you just did that, in front of everyone!"

Riley swallowed. "But he was hurting you."

"I'm a big girl, Riley," Brooke said. "I can tell him to get lost all on my own. I don't need you to come rushing in and humiliate me—" Her voice broke, and Riley realized for the first time it wasn't Archer she was mad at, and feeling betrayed by.

It was him.

Guilt slammed through him, and he opened his mouth to apologize, but she was already looking past him, wiping frantically at her eyes. "Meredith, hi!" she exclaimed, her voice loud and false. "Look, I'm sorry about what just happened. I can explain—"

"Save it." A brisk-looking woman hurried over. "We've got more important things to deal with. The bride is gone."

"WHAT DO YOU MEAN, GONE?" Brooke stared. She'd thought this day couldn't get any worse, but clearly, she was wrong.

"I mean, she's missing!"

Brooke tried to process the news. She was still scattered, reeling from Archer's sudden reappearance and Riley's wild punch. Everything was crashing down on her at once, but she couldn't fall apart.

Focus, Brooke. One thing at a time.

A couple of guests passed by, heading out to take their place for the ceremony, and Meredith plastered on a smile. "Isn't it lovely?" she cooed. "Be right out!"

The moment they were outside, Meredith grabbed Brooke's arm and dragged her around the corner. "I've looked everywhere," Meredith said.

Brooke gulped. "You think she left?"

"No, security are stationed at every exit, and they haven't seen her. The paparazzi is camped out front, and you'd think a Hollywood star in a big white dress would make an impression!"

"OK, so she's still on the property somewhere." Brooke thought fast. "Maybe she just needed a moment. It can all be overwhelming."

"The Oscars are overwhelming!" Meredith exclaimed, her voice rising. "Having your naked photos leak to the press is overwhelming. Getting married is a freaking walk in the park to her!"

"You need to calm down," Brooke said, wishing she could take her own advice. "There are two hundred people out there expecting a blushing bride, and we don't want them to know anything's wrong right now, not until we figure this out. I'll look for Lila, you keep the crowd distracted, OK?"

"OK." Meredith grabbed a bottle of champagne from the closest table and gulped. "Good luck!"

Brooke took off at the fastest walk she could manage

without turning any heads. The salon, the dining hall, the honeymoon suite upstairs . . . ?

Nothing. No sign of Lila.

As she searched, her mind kept going back to what had just happened. She couldn't believe Riley had laid into Archer like that. Any other time, maybe she could have enjoyed the look on Archer's face, just a little, but today, it felt like even more proof she was screwing up beyond repair. A public brawl in the middle of the wedding? She could just imagine what Bitsy would have to say about that—if she wasn't already on speed-dial to Brooke's boss, demanding her head on a (perfectly polished) platter.

Brooke's stomach twisted with shame. First she'd ruined everything back in Chicago, now her mistakes were haunting her all the way across the country. She couldn't even keep her personal life from blowing up and ruining someone else's big day.

She'd been right from the start: she was dating kryptonite, and she had no business following her heart, not while it was still radioactive enough to level a small city. Or, in this case, a whole wedding.

She detoured past the lobby, her panic rising. Riley was waiting in the corner with a remorseful expression. "Brooke," he started.

"Not now!" Brooke couldn't wait around, not with this wedding hanging by a thread. She'd made Lila a promise, the day of her dreams, and she'd already jeopardized it enough with her own romantic drama. She wasn't about to let the whole event go down in flames.

She charged onwards, leaving him behind. She must have checked every supply closet and office on the staff level, before finally, a waiter waved her over.

"I think I've found your missing package," he said meaningfully, nodding towards the kitchen.

Brooke stepped inside. It was a bustle of activity—chefs working, the burners on full, but in the back, she found Lila sitting on a stool, her gorgeous dress bunched around her as she dug into the five-tier wedding cake.

Brooke could have cheered in relief.

"Lila!" She hurried over. "There you are! Everyone's looking for you. Come on, the ceremony is about to begin."

Lila didn't get up. "I found his campaign slogan," she said sadly. "On his laptop. The slogan, the campaign pitch, the whole thing. He's running for Congress."

Brooke exhaled in a whoosh.

The fiancé, and his future plans. "Maybe it was just a proposal?" she said hopefully.

Lila shook her head. "He'd made notes. Edited the speeches. They're going to announce next month."

"I'm so sorry." Brooke gulped. There were two hundred people waiting upstairs, the string quartet poised to begin the wedding march, and her bride was hiding out here, with frosting smeared all over her face.

As wedding emergencies went, this was DEFCON 1.

"He promised me," Lila said, digging her fork deep into another layer of pristine cake. "He promised, so many times. And all along, he knew."

"Did you talk to him about it?"

Lila shook her head. "What can he say? He lied."

"But maybe there's an explanation!"

"Like what?" Lila asked. "Whoops, forgot to mention, I'm signing us up for life in the spotlight, I know it's the opposite of everything I promised you, but hey, it's only four years. And then the governor's race. And then a presidential run. No time at all."

Brooke opened her mouth to argue, then stopped. Who was she kidding? This was the Cartwrights. Justin had President written all over his handsome face.

She took a seat beside Lila and reached for another fork instead. If the wedding was about to go down in flames, she needed a sugar hit to get through it. "This is really good cake," she said, through a mouthful. Summer had outdone herself.

Lila nodded. "It's beautiful. At least, it was. The whole wedding is gorgeous. You did a great job."

"Thank you."

They ate in silence for a moment.

"I really thought he was different," Lila said quietly. "He's so smart, and funny, and sweet. I wasn't even looking for a relationship, but he came along, and I just . . . couldn't help falling for him, you know?"

Brooke nodded. She knew. She'd never meant to fall for Riley, but she'd gone head over heels for him all the same.

And look how that had turned out.

"When you get him away from his family, it's like he's another person," Lila continued. "I thought that's all it would take. Us starting out on our own, doing things our way."

"Maybe you still can." Brooke saw the heartache in her eyes, and wished she could spare the other woman, somehow. "Do you love him?"

Lila nodded sadly.

"Then maybe that's enough."

"Is love ever enough?" Lila asked, her voice quiet, and Brooke's heart clenched.

No.

It wasn't. You had to have honesty, too. Trust, and loyalty;

you had to be willing to open up and put your heart on the line, and make something together, no holding back. Love alone only left you heartbroken and betrayed.

"I can't tell you what to do," she said softly. "They're all waiting for you. But if you want to get out of here . . ."

Lila shook her head. "I'm not running away. The press would eat me alive for this."

She slid down from the stool, and arranged her skirts around her. "Lipstick?" she asked, and Brooke found a napkin to blot at her face.

"Perfect."

"The show must go on, right?" Lila gave her an empty smile, put her shoulders back, and then glided out of the kitchen like she was walking a runway.

Brooke followed behind. She should be relieved, her once-in-a-lifetime wedding event was going ahead as planned, and aside from a minor scuffle in the lobby, everything was running like clockwork. The photos would be beautiful, and they would be booked solid for years with brides all wanting the Hollywood touch. But as she trailed Lila down the hallway and out to the lobby, she didn't feel any pride or sense of accomplishment.

She just felt empty, watching as if it were a crash in slow motion.

Meredith was waiting by the doors, and cheered to see them. She gestured outside, and then a moment later, the sound of the wedding march began. Lila's bridesmaids descended, fluttering around to adjust her gown and veil, and then they set off, marching out to the altar with their bouquets and bright smiles. Lila took a breath, and then she followed, stepping out, alone, to the crowd.

Brooke lingered in the doorway, watching her walk down

the aisle. Justin was waiting with his best man, and his face lit up at the sight of Lila, just like they always did. Brooke never got tired of seeing that smile, but today, knowing everything she did, it felt hollow.

"Dearly beloved . . ." the priest began. "We're gathered here today to celebrate the union of two people embarking on a lifetime together."

"Wait."

Lila's voice was so soft, Brooke almost didn't catch it.

"Vows are not to be entered into lightly," the priest continued, and then the voice came again, louder.

"Please, stop."

There were gasps.

Brooke held her breath, watching as Lila stepped back. "I'm sorry," she said to Justin. "But . . . I can't do this. You want me to play the perfect politician's wife, but that's not me. It never was. I thought you knew that!"

Justin shot a desperate look at Bitsy.

"Babe—" he started. "You really want to talk about this now?"

"No. It's too late for that." Lila held her head high. "Those vows mean everything to me, and I'm only going to say them once."

She turned on her heel, and started walking back up the aisle, away from him.

"Babe!" Justin called after her, but Lila just picked up speed, breaking into a run by the time she reached Brooke.

"Is that getaway offer still open?" she asked, hurrying inside. There was bedlam behind her—Justin hurling the ring down in anger, guests waving their cellphone cameras, and Bitsy looking like she was about to pass out.

"Come with me." Brooke hustled her through the lobby, and

back to the staff exit. "Neil!" She grabbed her clerk on the way through. "Can you get her out of here?"

His eyes widened. "The press . . ."

"Take the delivery van. She can hide in the back." Brooke grabbed the keys from the office and thrust them into his hands. "Good luck."

She shoved them out the door. Lila picked up the skirts of her ten-thousand-dollar gown and sprinted to the van, and then they were speeding out the back gate, past a pack of photographers, out to the main road.

Brooke watched her go, silently wishing Lila luck. She was going to need it. Brooke had learned the hard way you couldn't just run out on your problems—even if it seemed like the easy way out. She hadn't been able to escape her own mistakes, and she didn't have every tabloid magazine in the country lined up at the gates for an exclusive scoop.

With a sigh, she returned to the patio to face the music.

"You!" Bitsy accosted her the moment she stepped outside. "This is all your fault! I knew from the moment we stepped foot in this place it would be a disaster. You'll be hearing from my lawyers!"

"Where is she?" Meredith shoved Bitsy aside. "Where did you take her? I've got her agents on one line and the studio on the other. We need damage control, now!"

Brooke looked around numbly. Guests were talking in huddles, already scrolling through their phones; a fight had broken out between the groomsman, and somewhere, a helicopter was buzzing overhead.

It was a scandal. It was a disaster.

And it was all her fault.

---

22

*B*rooke spent the rest of the day cleaning up the mess Hollywood left behind. The guests departed, the throngs of paparazzi melted away, and soon they were left with nothing but limply hanging streamers and a hotel full of heart-shaped cookies.

"What do you want us to do with all the food?" one of her waitstaff asked, toting a tray of elaborate hors d'oeuvres.

Brooke pushed back her hair and tried to focus through her pounding headache. "I don't know. Is there a shelter or food bank on the cape? If not, tell everyone they can take whatever they like."

The waiter rushed off to stake his claim on some prime suckling pig, and Brooke turned her attention back to dismantling the gorgeous wedding arch. The bridesmaids had all abandoned their bouquets, and now roses and lilacs were trampled underfoot, wilted petals scattered all around the patio.

She felt like crying.

"And I thought we did some damage inside."

Brooke looked up. Riley was hovering nearby, a bashful expression on his face. "What do you want?" she asked tiredly. She could have laid down and slept for a hundred years, but there was still so much to do to wipe the memory of this disastrous day from the hotel.

"I want to talk," Riley said, moving closer.

Brooke glanced up at him. God, the man even looked good with his shirt askew and the purple shadow of a black eye forming, but she fought to stay strong. This was how she wound up in this mess in the first place—letting a rising heart rate and that slow, delicious flip in her stomach overpower all her logic and reason.

"You want some help with that?" he asked, then reached up and lifted down the frame she'd been straining for.

"Thanks." Brooke swallowed. The drama of the day had faded, leaving nothing but a dull ache behind. "Where's Archer?"

"He left. A while ago. Said something about getting a red-eye out."

She nodded. That was one thing less to deal with. Maybe, this time, he'd gotten the message that it was over.

"You didn't say he was in town." Riley stacked a couple of chairs.

"I didn't know," Brooke said. "He showed up about five minutes before you did."

Riley nodded slowly. "And if I hadn't interrupted you . . . ?"

"What, you think I would have fallen into his arms again?" Brooke paused, a flicker of irritation sparking to life. "I told you what happened with him, how he lied to me. I was handling it, I didn't need you muscling in and humiliating me in front of everyone."

"He deserved it," Riley protested.

"And what did I deserve?" she challenged him. "You guys brawling in the middle of my biggest event? Don't pretend you did any of that on my behalf. I don't know what macho guy thing you were trying to prove, but it had nothing to do with me."

"I'm sorry," Riley said, looking chastened. "It got out of hand. I just couldn't stand to see him standing there, after everything he put you through."

"Put *me* through," Brooke repeated. "What happened with Archer has nothing to do with you! You knew how much this wedding meant to me, how much time and work I put into making everything perfect. Did you stop for a second to think about that? About my reputation, and career? No," she answered for him, emotions storming inside. "You just went in swinging. Because you have no idea what it means to work like this, put everything into a project so you can be proud."

Riley's eyes flashed. "Yeah, I think I do."

"Since when?" Brooke shot back. "You've been here two years now, pouring beer, and partying late, and screwing everything that moves!"

The moment the words were out, she regretted them, but it was too late. Riley's expression hardened.

"So it took me some time to figure out what I wanted," he replied. "But I'm here now, trying to make it happen. You're the one still running. You know there's something real between us, but you're still so scared of being hurt again that you don't trust your heart at all."

"What are you saying?" Brooke asked, confused. "You've been telling me from the start all you wanted is fun."

He looked away. "I was wrong. I want more, Brooke." He

met her eyes again. "I was going to tell you tonight, that I want us to be exclusive. For us to do this, for real."

Brooke stared at him in disbelief. He was saying exactly what she'd been hoping he'd say, but it was all wrong. How was she supposed to believe him now?

She shook her head. She couldn't handle this, not after everything. "I can't."

"Why not?"

"Look around!" she exclaimed, tears stinging in the back of her throat. "Everything's a mess. I'm not ready. I trusted Archer. I trusted you! And then you turn around and pull a stunt like this!"

"I'm sorry, I screwed up." Riley's expression slipped. "But you and me, we're great together. I know you feel it too."

He reached for her, but she pulled back. She knew that if she touched him, held him, it would be too much. She couldn't resist the chemistry between them, but she knew now she had to.

"This was a mistake from the start," she said, her heart raw and aching. "I'm not ready."

"You are," Riley insisted. "You're just scared, and I get that, but I'm not like him. You're the first thing I've been sure about in so long. I promise, I won't let you down again—"

"You're not listening to me!" Brooke interrupted. "I can't do this again. I can't. You've spent the past month telling me all you want is a good time. No drama, no strings, remember?" she quoted his own casual promise back at him, and saw Riley flinch at the reminder. "Now you're standing here, promising me . . . what? A date on Friday night? Commitment? A future together?" Brooke gulped back the tears. "Until you change your mind again. You don't even know what you want, Riley, but I do. I want you to leave me alone."

He shook his head. "You don't mean that. I know you. I know you deserve someone who really loves you—"

"Stop," Brooke said again, feeling her last thread fray. "Please, just stop. I have work to do here, and a million calls to make, and . . ."

And if he kept talking any longer, she might just give in. Let him wrap her up in his strong embrace and promise that everything between them was going to be fine. And maybe it would, for a little while. But Brooke knew herself now, better than she had a few months ago, and jumping straight into a new relationship was the last thing she needed—especially with a man who prided himself on staying unattached.

How long would it be until she was just another tether holding him back? How long until Riley pulled up anchor and sailed away, and Brooke was left with a heart that hadn't even begun to start healing?

"It's finished," she said finally, even though it felt the furthest thing from over. "It was fun while it lasted, Riley, but we were never going to be anything real. Good luck with everything, OK?"

She turned and hurried inside, before she could see the hurt in his eyes.

Before he could see the stitches on her beat up, broken heart rip open all over again.

23

1 month later . . .

*R*iley stared at the doors, willing them to open. He'd never believed in all that "positive thinking, manifest your destiny" nonsense, but maybe if he focused hard enough, Brooke would come breezing into the bar like all of this had never happened, flashing him a teasing smile, and strolling over to—

"Riley?"

Someone snapped their fingers right in front of him, and he blinked out of his daydream. Mackenzie was standing by the bar.

"Oh. Hey," Riley sighed. "I didn't see you there."

"I've been calling your name for like the past five minutes." Mackenzie frowned. "Still moping?"

"Real men don't mope." Riley flashed a smile. "We brood. In a manly, strong fashion."

"Uh huh." Mac didn't look convinced by his nonchalant routine. "Same difference. Still no word from Brooke?"

Riley shook his head and busied himself wiping down the bar. "It's probably for the best," he lied. "We both know me plus commitment would have been a recipe for disaster. Plus, think of the damage to the Sweetbriar tourist industry. Hot girls would have been canceling their trips in droves."

Mackenzie softened. "You don't have to pull that routine with me. It's OK if you miss her."

"What's to miss?" Riley shot back. "I barely knew the woman."

He moved off to clear some dirty glasses—and avoid Mackenzie's sympathetic smile. They both knew he was putting on an act, but these days, it was second nature to him. It had been a month now since that day at the wedding, when he'd screwed everything up with Brooke. He'd cycled through the usual stages of post-breakup grief—drinking, wallowing, and more drinking—but still, he didn't feel like he was any closer to moving on. He could tell himself it was her loss, and that some things weren't meant to be, but deep down, her words lingered.

You don't even know what you want.

Riley's jaw clenched. He'd straight-up told her what he wanted: the two of them, together. He'd put his heart on the line, and she'd thrown it back in his face. She was the confused one, not him. He had nothing to regret.

Except his timing could have been better, a small voice reminded him. Brawling through the middle of her big event didn't exactly scream "trust and commitment." And who could blame her for not believing him, when he'd bragged about his easy, no-strings life for so long?

Riley stifled a sigh. He'd been over it all, a hundred times, but it still didn't change the ending. Him, alone, the same as always—except this time, he knew just what he was missing.

"There you are," a female voice cooed. He looked up as Lulu came sashaying across the bar. "I haven't heard from you since our dinner. Have you been avoiding me?"

Her smile was flirty, but Riley's heart still sank. He'd been on one ill-advised date with Lulu, back during his whole "drinking and wallowing" phase. He wasn't even halfway through his appetizer before realizing what a mistake it was; he'd given her some excuse about an emergency at the bar and made a quick escape, but Lulu didn't seem to mind his disappearing act. She'd been messaging him all month with invitations to get together, and clearly, she figured it was time to hunt him down in person.

"I've been busy," Riley said, and cleared his throat.

"How about tonight?" Lulu asked. "You could come over after you're done here and have a little fun. Unwind." She grinned, and Riley knew exactly the kind of unwinding she was talking about, but even the prospect of wild, no-strings sex with this gorgeous woman couldn't shake his mood.

Damn, he really was in a bad way.

"Sorry," he said, flashing a rueful smile. "I'm not in the market for that kind of fun anymore."

Lulu looked surprised. "The great Riley Ford? Say it isn't so."

"I'm as surprised as anyone," he agreed. "But you take care, OK?"

"Oh, I will." Lulu reached up and gave him a kiss on the cheek. "Say, is your new bartender single?"

He laughed. "Jamie? Sure he is. Go tell him your drink's on me."

Riley watched Lulu head over to the bar—and slay poor

Jamie with a single smile. She was a great girl: gorgeous, laid back, and fun-loving, but somehow, after Brooke, he couldn't find it in his heart to want anyone else.

Brooke, with her smart mouth and endless ambition.

Brooke, who could render him speechless with a single, blissful smile.

Brooke—

"Earth to Riley." Mackenzie snapped her fingers again. "Lord, if you're going to wallow—I'm sorry, *brood* much longer, I should get a whistle or something."

Riley shook his head, annoyed at himself as much as Mac. "Are you still here?"

"I figured we could walk over to the bookstore together," she said, unbothered by his grumpy tone. "It's boys versus girls at poker night. Which means Poppy's going to wipe the floor with us all. And before you bail again, I'm not taking no for an answer." Mackenzie fixed him with her sternest stare, and Riley knew he didn't have a choice.

"Fine. Let's go."

He grabbed his jacket and held the door for her on their way out. The brisk October winds whipped around them, and Mackenzie shivered, pausing to bundle up in her brightly-knitted scarf and cap. "I think it's going to snow soon," she said, looking up at the cloudy night's sky. "I can always taste it in the air."

"I hate the cold," Riley said, starting to walk across the town square. "I lived too long in California. I've half a mind to head back there and spend Christmas on the beach."

"You don't mean that!" Mackenzie protested. "Fall is my favorite time of year on the Cape. And Christmas, too. Hot apple cider, and the leaves turning, and sleigh rides at the Starbright Festival . . ."

"What are you, the official Sweetbriar tourist board now?" Riley teased.

"You better watch out," Mackenzie warned him. "You're turning into a regular Scrooge. If you're not careful—"

She stopped, and the strangest expression crossed her face.

Riley turned. "What is it? You look like you've seen a ghost."

"I . . ." Mackenzie blinked. "Nothing. I thought I saw someone, that's all."

"An ex?" Riley asked, amused to see her so ruffled.

"No." Mackenzie's voice went quiet. "No, forget I said anything. So do you think Grayson's going to pop the question to Summer yet? Soon we'll be the only single ones left in the group." She changed the subject without even pausing for breath, and then chattered the rest of the way about town gossip and her new line of snowfall ceramics until they reached Grayson's bookstore.

"Hey!" Poppy greeted them the minute they stepped inside the snug store. The card table was already set out in the main room, and Grayson, Cooper, and Summer were seated, drinking beer and passing around a pizza box. "Are you guys ready for battle?"

"I should just empty my wallet and call it a night," Riley said ruefully. Poppy's poker skills were legendary around town.

"Aww, I'll go easy on you, I promise." She grinned.

They took their seats, and the game began—punctuated with teasing, and gossip, and their usual smack-talk. It was the perfect Friday night in Sweetbriar Cove, but looking around the table at his friends, Riley knew something was missing. Some*one*.

Brooke.

It was amazing how fast she'd found a place here in the community, but she seemed to fit, just right. She would have a plan to beat Poppy, of course, be trading jokes with Mackenzie and Coop, and suggesting new dishes for Summer to try at the bakery. She belonged here.

With him.

"Your turn," Grayson prompted him, and Riley swallowed back his empty pang. He tried to get Brooke out of his mind and just focus on the game, but he couldn't shake the regret that was lodged, cold and hollow, behind his ribcage.

He'd pushed her too fast.

Brooke was right. She wasn't ready—but he hadn't listened to her, not really. He'd been so swept up in his own feelings, finally wanting to commit, that he didn't stop to think about her past heartbreak, and how she was still rebounding from Archer's betrayal.

If he'd slowed down a beat . . . If he'd given her time to move on . . . They could have built a relationship moment by moment, adding up to something real. Instead, he'd barreled ahead, ignoring everything she'd told him, and assumed that just because he was finally ready to take that risk and open up with someone, she would be too.

He was wrong.

"You think he'd notice if I peeked at his cards?"

"Nah, I already know what he's holding. His poker face is the worst."

Riley came back to reality and found the rest of the table staring at him. He was missing his turn all over again. "Sorry," he said, glancing half-heartedly at the cards in his hand. "Uh, fold."

"You're no fun," Poppy complained, with a heap of M&M winnings already piled in front of her. "You used to be my only rival."

"Gee, thanks," Mackenzie piped up, munching on a slice of pizza.

"Please. You have zero game face," Poppy laughed. "All your emotions are written all over your face."

"I'll have you know, I'm a woman of mystery," Mackenzie declared—with pizza sauce smeared over her chin.

They all laughed, but Riley's thoughts were a million miles away. Or, to be precise, fifteen miles up the coast. He wondered if Brooke was still up—or if she'd kicked her insomnia for good. He'd almost driven over there a dozen times to apologize and beg for her back, or better yet, seduce her until she couldn't resist him anymore. Sometimes he made it out the door, into the car, halfway up that dark coastal road. One night, he even sat outside her apartment with the engine running, talking himself out of storming up those stairs. But every time, he managed to turn back around and come home, alone.

She wasn't ready.

She needed time.

He hadn't listened before, but he wasn't going to make that mistake again, no matter how much he wanted to.

He pushed back his chair. Distraction wasn't working when it came to forgetting her. Maybe drinking would.

"Anyone want another beer?" he asked, then headed in the back to the tiny kitchenette. He remembered the days when Grayson's refrigerator had been empty, save a six pack and some questionable takeout remains, but now it was packed with Tupperware from Summer's bakery: neat stacks of brownies and quiches and other snacks.

He paused to read the messages, scribbled on bright post-it notes.

Sweets for my sweet.

Can't wait to see you tonight.

XO.

It hit him in the gut, the casual affection in every note. They had each other, in a way he could only imagine.

"Want to pass those brownies?"

He turned. Grayson was in the doorway, dressed casually—for the Englishman, at least—in a button-down and corduroy pants. Riley retrieved the container.

"How are things with you these days?" Grayson asked, arching an eyebrow. "We haven't seen you at the harvest festival events."

"Not in the mood," Riley said, opening another beer.

"No?"

He caught the look on Grayson's face and sighed. "Is this where you give me a pep talk about love and risk and following my heart?"

"You mean, the way you've done with the rest of us?" Grayson looked amused.

"Yeah, well maybe I should have kept my mouth shut," Riley sighed. That was the thing about being a bartender: you wound up giving everyone a heart-to-heart sooner or later. But just because he'd dispensed his share of motivational speeches, it didn't mean he wanted them coming back to haunt him.

Luckily, Grayson could take a hint. He just munched on a brownie and gave a thoughtful nod.

"What's cooking?" Summer appeared behind them and wrapped her arms around Grayson's waist. "Save some of those for the rest of us."

"Like you don't already have another batch of dough stashed at home," Grayson grinned, tipping his head down to smile at her. They shared a private look, and Riley felt that blow again, watching something intimate from the outside, a glimpse of the one thing he wanted more than anything, but was far out of reach.

"Come on, time for another hand," Poppy called from the next room. "Double or nothing. The M&Ms will be mine!"

THE BAR WAS CLOSED by the time Riley made it back. He unlocked the side door and headed to his apartment upstairs. He'd moved in off the boat after the first cold snap that fall. For all his love of that tiny cabin, he loved central heating more, but that night he found himself wishing he was back out in the harbor—frost and all. At least on his boat, there wasn't any room for someone else. Here, he couldn't help wishing there was someone curled beside him in front of the fire, or tucked up in his king-sized bed, stealing the blankets and taking up space.

He put the tea kettle on the stove and flipped through the stack of mail on the counter, pausing when he found a post-card from his brother.

412 DAYS, he'd scrawled in big black letters.

Riley winced. Max had stopped bugging him to sign the settlement papers—and started sending these weekly reminders instead, marking off just how long Riley had been dragging his feet on the paperwork. Over a year now. Any other case, and his opponent would have run screaming to the judge long ago, or blown up the settlement and started from scratch. But Tate wouldn't risk it. Not with the kind of money on the line he had coming. He clearly had decided to wait Riley out, however long it took for him to move on.

And Riley had nothing but time.

Literally.

Riley paused a moment, thinking over that simple phrase. What did he have going on? The bar ran itself these days; he just needed to call in orders and check that his bar staff weren't drinking all the profits. He'd been restless for months now, but he'd chalked it up to things with Brooke, and wanting something he couldn't have.

Now he wondered, why the hell was he stuck there, just killing time?

He turned the postcard over in his hand. The deal gave him a stake in Tate's new company. He didn't have to hold onto it— he could sell at any time. He'd always planned to keep it, though—keep that control hanging over his former partner's head, as payback for everything he'd done.

But Riley wanted to just be done with it all. The settlement, Tate, every reminder of the whole damn mess. He'd been pretending like it didn't exist, but that hadn't changed anything. They were all still waiting for him to make his move. And him?

He was sitting in an empty apartment above an old bar that barely paid rent.

Who the hell was he kidding anymore?

Riley went to the desk in the corner and dug out the paperwork. Fifty-plus pages of dense legal writing they'd fought and bickered over, and spent months hammering out. Years of his time and effort, and love, too, poured into that company. He'd wanted to keep hold of it for as long as possible, but who was he hurting here?

Not Tate. He'd already moved on to another flashy, high-paying gig, living it up as a king in Silicon Valley. Riley was the one stuck in limbo, waiting for Brooke to move on from her own past, when he couldn't even put pen to paper on his own.

What could he do if this was already over?

Riley seized a pen from the cabinet and scribbled his name on the first page before he could take it back. There were a dozen sticky tabs dotted throughout the document, and he tore through them all—signing over and over, until he reached the last page, and it was done.

He took a breath. He'd expected to feel different, somehow, but instead, he just felt foolish. He'd let this drag on long enough.

It was time to start something new.

24

"...Now, visualize a place you feel safe. Happy. Hold that feeling with you, and come back to the room."

Brooke blinked awake to find herself sitting in the middle of the yoga studio, surrounded by the rest of the motley assortment of lunchtime meditators.

"Great session, everyone!" their teacher—ahem, spiritual guide – clapped her hands. "Enjoy the rest of your day."

Brooke folded her mat and slipped her shoes back on, retrieving her phone from the basket out front. Eliza called just as she was getting in the car, and Brooke switched her to speaker, turning onto the highway back to the hotel.

"How's life on the higher plane?"

Brooke laughed. "Pretty peaceful, and this plane seems quiet, too. So far."

"I can't believe you've stuck it out." Eliza sounded admiring. "I took one look at those healing crystals and knew I couldn't keep a straight face."

"Aww, it's not so bad. The teachers are kind of kooky, but it's a great group. And it's important to take some time out from the hotel, just for me."

"Brooke Delancey, poster child for work-life balance, who would have thought?"

Brooke grinned. "Not me."

She'd had her doubts about the place when she'd started, but after a month of lunchtime sessions, she could already feel the difference. A moment to zone out and collect her thoughts let her juggle everything at work with a clear head—and she was finally sleeping through the night, too.

"How's Boston?" she asked. Eliza was back in the city working at the newspaper, but from her sigh, it wasn't going well.

"The subway broke down this morning. I spent forty-five minutes pressed up against some guy's sweaty armpit."

"Was he at least cute?" Brooke asked hopefully.

"Would I be complaining to you if he was?" Eliza countered. "Anyway, I have this killer deadline looming, I think I'm going to drive down to the cape tomorrow and hole up at my parent's house. Ooh, we should go out!"

"Sounds great, but what about your deadline?" Brooke smiled.

"I need inspiration," Eliza declared. "I think a bottle of wine and some clam chowder ought to do it."

"Sounds like a plan," Brooke said, turning up the hotel driveway. "Give me a call when you get here."

She rang off, and turned up the collar on her coat to make the dash inside. The weather had turned to brisk fall winds, but even without their summer tourist trade, the hotel was booked solid all the way through the New Year. Inside, they were decorated in the warm autumn hues, with pumpkin centerpieces, and a roaring fire in every fireplace, inviting guests to linger with blankets and a book.

Today, she found Ash Callahan waiting on one of the couches, scrolling through his phone. "Ash," she exclaimed, hurrying over. "I'm sorry, I thought we were meeting at three. I was just at an appointment," she added, fumbling to explain. "It was my lunch break, and—"

"Please." Ash waved away her apology. "I know the importance of taking some time out. Although, with a newborn, it usually means a nap."

"How's Noelle doing?" Brooke asked, taking a seat.

"Tired. But we're loving it. And I'm loving the fact you have everything under control here." He looked around, smiling. "I feel like I should be doing something, but you're running this place all on your own."

"I have a great team," Brooke corrected him, not wanting to take all the praise. "And to be honest, I don't need to do anything to get the bookings these days. The phone is still ringing off the hook with calls from all over the world, and we have a waiting list a mile long. I even got an email from a woman in China today, offering to hold her wedding on any free day we had for the next two years!"

Ash chuckled. "I wonder how her fiancé feels about that."

"It turns out, Lila didn't even need to say 'I do' for it to be the most famous wedding of the year," Brooke noted. "We probably got more press from the disaster than if she'd actually gone through with it."

"Did you ever hear from her?" Ash asked, looking curious. "My brother is an actor, Blake, and he says she's disappeared from Hollywood. Nobody knows where she went."

Brooke shook her head. "I've read the rumors, same as everyone. Someone said she was off in the Caribbean somewhere, or having plastic surgery in Brazil. I hope she's OK, wherever she is."

"The Cartwrights certainly don't."

They exchanged a look. As predicted, Bitsy had caused a fuss, threatening lawsuits and all kinds of retribution, but then suddenly, the angry calls had melted away. Last Brooke knew, Justin was gearing up for that political bid of his—with a new blonde girlfriend at his side.

"Well, whatever you've been doing here, keep it up," Ash said with a smile. "And let's talk in the New Year about your future plans. I wouldn't be surprised if you've already had headhunters sniffing around from the big luxury chains."

"Well . . ." Brooke said, flushing. As soon as the dust settled after the wedding, they'd started calling—everyone from the head of events at the biggest chain hotel on the planet to the most exclusive wedding planning agencies. She couldn't start to think about making another big change in her life, so had politely turned them down, but she had to admit it was nice to be asked.

Ash saw her bashful expression and laughed. "Don't worry, they'd be fools not to. But I'd love to keep you. Here, or at one of my other properties. You can have your pick."

Brooke paused, flattered. "Thank you. I haven't thought about leaving, we've been so busy here."

"Why don't you think about it, and we'll talk?" Ash got to his feet. "Now, do you think I can convince the chef to rustle me up a steak? We've been living off frozen casseroles at home."

"I'm sure the boss can persuade him." Brooke waved him off. A promotion to one of his other, bigger properties? Brooke should have been excited at the idea, but as she looked around the familiar lobby, she felt settled, and at home. She'd been building a life here on the Cape, with a routine, friends, and even—gasp—hobbies. It felt like she was finally back on solid ground, after a year of the ground shifting beneath her feet. It had taken time, and work, but she finally felt like herself again, the way she'd glimpsed when she was with—

But no, she wasn't thinking about him. Brooke busied herself with upcoming wedding event plans for the rest of the day, then drove the short distance home. She changed quickly into running gear and a warm vest, and then took off along the beach path, letting the crisp afternoon air chill her lungs and set her heart pounding.

She ran every other day now, slowly increasing her pace. Maybe she'd try for a half-marathon one of these days, or maybe she'd just keep enjoying the way it felt to tumble into her bed at the end of a day and fall into deep, uninterrupted sleep. And for those few miles, her footsteps pounding on the worn dirt path, she finally allowed herself to think about Riley.

She missed him.

It was such a simple thing, that little ache she felt every time she thought of him, but it lingered, no matter how much she tried to put him out of her mind. She wanted to pick up the phone, just to talk late into the night the way they'd done in the beginning, or to curl up in her courtyard with a cup of tea, sharing stories in the dark. And his kisses . . .

Brooke flushed, running faster as she remembered the nights with him, that tangle of pleasure, and how free she'd felt, letting go completely in his arms. She hadn't tried dating since him, she hadn't even wanted to try. But every time Eliza gently broached the subject, Brooke just thought of the way she'd felt with him and knew, somehow, that it would never be the same. She could try and find some other man, but Riley was one of a kind.

The one-of-a-kind man who had come to her, wanting a real relationship, and she'd turned him down flat. Even now, Brooke wondered if she'd done the right thing. Taking the time to get over her breakup was one thing, but late at night, alone, she found herself craving him, thinking maybe it didn't matter if she was still figuring out her life, not if she got to have him back again . . .

Brooke looped around and headed back for home. She'd made the right decision, she knew that in her bones, but she also knew that didn't make the regrets just disappear. And now that her life made sense again, those regrets had a way of whispering louder.

She'd told him she wasn't ready.

But when would that be?

Brooke was sweating hard by the time she let herself back into the courtyard. She'd done three miles. Maybe next time, she could try four.

"Hi."

Brooke startled at the voice, almost tripping on the stairs.

"Sorry, I didn't mean to scare you," her visitor continued. "I should have called, but . . . I wasn't sure if you'd even want to talk."

Brooke stared at the woman waiting outside her apartment —a face she'd never expected to see again.

It was Julia—Archer's wife.

"How . . . How did you find me?" Brooke asked, her heart still racing from the run.

"My lawyer tracked you down." Julia stood there, in a crisp winter coat and bright-red scarf. She looked better than when

Brooke had seen her last, standing tall and confident. "Would you mind talking for a moment? I won't stay long."

"I . . . sure." Brooke's heart sank as she climbed the stairs and unlocked the door. What did Julia want with her? In an instant, all her old shame and guilt came rushing back. How could she have so easily forgotten what she'd done to the other woman? Brooke's heart had been broken, but she'd torn Julia's whole life apart.

Julia followed her into the apartment and looked around. "It's a nice place," she said, and Brooke swallowed.

"Thanks." She'd decorated, piece by piece, until it was a warm, bright space filled with art and textiles, an old record player in the corner, and plant pots spilling greenery down the window ledge. "Can I get you something to drink?" she offered, still uneasy. "I have tea, or coffee . . ."

"Bourbon?" Julia noticed a bottle on the shelf, and Brooke blinked.

"Why not?"

She fetched the bottle down and poured two glasses. She sat opposite Julia at her small dining table, and took a gulp.

"You're probably wondering why I'm here," Julia started, turning her tumbler around in her hands. "Don't worry, it's not to blame you for the collapse of my marriage."

"You have to know how sorry I am," Brooke said anxiously.

Julia nodded. "I know," she sighed. "The truth is, I did hate you, for a little while. It was easier to be angry at you than at Archer. You know, after I confronted him with everything, he broke down, begging me to stay. He swore you were an evil temptress who'd set out to seduce him."

Brooke's jaw dropped open.

"I didn't believe him," Julia added quickly. "Although, a part of me wanted to. To just put all the blame on you, and move on. But, I know my husband. Soon to be ex-husband," she added. "And I could tell you had no idea what was going on."

"I didn't," Brooke said quietly. "I wish I had, that it had been different, but . . ."

"Shit happens." Julia took a long gulp of bourbon. "Anyway, I'm divorcing him. I filed papers a few months ago."

"I figured," Brooke said, putting two and two together. "He showed up here, begging for me to come back. I told him where to go," she added.

Julia shook her head. "He can't bear it, being alone. He always needs someone to adore him. It would be sad if he wasn't such a bastard."

"Agreed." Brooke lifted her glass, and Julia clinked it in a rueful toast.

"He wants a no-fault divorce, but I've decided to take him for everything he has," Julia announced, looking more cheerful. "Would you mind if I named you in the proceedings? You'd only need to give a statement, explaining how he lied, how long the affair went on. I know you probably don't want to go digging through it all again, but my lawyer says it would help."

"Of course," Brooke agreed. "Anything you need. I'm just so sorry it all turned out this way. Really, I feel terrible."

"Don't." Julia reached across the table and patted her hand. "I've been down that road—the guilt, and the blame, and all the wondering if I should have seen the signs. It nearly drove me crazy."

"So what changed?" Brooke asked. "You seem so . . . calm."

"Well, I had a lot of therapy." Julia cracked a smile. "And yes, I'll be billing him for that, too. But I realized I have my life back now. All the things I sacrificed to support his goals, his career, I have a chance to do it on my own. So, I'm going to Europe for a while, taking the trip I always wanted. And then . . . who knows?" Julia shrugged. "But this time around, it will be what I want."

"That's great," Brooke said, feeling a little envious. Julia seemed to have emerged from the wreckage with more freedom and poise than she could have imagined. "You deserve it."

"And so do you." Julia got to her feet. "I mean it. I know you loved him, and it must have hurt like hell to find out that was a lie, but don't let him hold you back, either."

"I want to move on," Brooke admitted. "I just can't get over what a fool I was, believing in him."

Julia gave her a sad smile. "We both did. But that's on him, not us. For what it's worth, I forgive you."

"Thank you."

Brooke showed her out, and wished her luck with her travels, closing the door behind her. Julia seemed to have found exactly what she needed to move on, but Brooke still felt those treacherous chords from the past, tugging her back when she wanted nothing more than to sever them for good.

What would it take to move on? More time? More building a life she could be proud of? Brooke had thought she was getting there, but deep down, she still didn't quite trust herself. Trust her heart to make the right call next time, and know that the way she felt wasn't just in vain.

Maybe it wasn't Julia's forgiveness over Archer she needed.

Maybe it was time to finally forgive herself for loving him.

25

*B*rooke was still thinking about Julia's parting words the next day, when Eliza picked her up for dinner.

"She just showed up?" Eliza blinked when Brooke told her about the unexpected visit. "That's ballsy."

"She seemed . . . happy. Or at least, determined," Brooke said, remembering the glint in Julia's eyes. "I'm glad. I hope she wins out in the divorce."

"Finally, that douche-nozzle gets his payback," Eliza agreed.

Brooke snorted with laughter. "Douche-nozzle? What are you, six?"

"It's fitting," Eliza grinned. "Anyway, I'm glad you two squared everything away. That has to be a weight off your mind, right?"

Brooke nodded. "I'm going to try not to feel guilty anymore," she confided. "I feel like I've been dragging around all these regrets, but it's time to let them go."

"Atta girl."

"Wait a minute." Brooke saw a familiar sign fly by out the

windows. "I thought we were going to Provincetown. You know, wine and chowder like usual."

Eliza looked evasive. "Actually, there's a movie on. They're showing *The Thin Man*, I figured it could be fun."

"I love that movie," Brooke exclaimed. "Where is it playing?"

"Well, about that . . ."

Eliza turned off the highway, and Brooke saw the Sweetbriar Cove sign up ahead. "Eliza!" she exclaimed.

"You've been avoiding this place long enough," Eliza argued. "Come on. We had to skip Sunday pastries at the bakery because you were so worried about running into Riley, and karaoke at the pub, and the best lobster rolls—"

"OK, OK," Brooke sighed, but still, she felt a twist of nerves at the thought of being on his turf again.

"It'll be fine," Eliza reassured her, pulling up to park just off the square. "He won't even be there. I mean, classic movies at the town hall? That's not really his scene."

"No, it's not." Brooke tried very hard not to think about Riley's scene—probably charming some gorgeous woman's pants off on that boat of his. "You're right. I can't stay away forever."

They got out of the car and headed inside. The main hall was already busy with locals, and had been set up with a massive projector screen and rows of mismatched chairs and comfy beanbags. "Ooh, they have snacks." Eliza brightened, making a beeline for the trestle table along one wall, practically groaning under the weight of homemade goods. A handwritten sign explained that donations were welcome and all proceeds would be donated to the Sweetbriar Nog-Off Prize Fund.

"Do I even want to know?" A familiar voice beside Brooke

made her turn. It was Poppy, looking at the sign with a bemused expression.

"Don't ask me," Brooke agreed. "I'm guessing it's some town tradition."

"A grand one," Mackenzie announced, joining them. She had two brightly colored cushions under her arms, and deposited a couple of bags of chips on the table. "The big town eggnog competition, at the Christmas festival. People work on their recipes all year round. Debra usually has it locked down," she added, nodding to the older woman who was pouring something from her flask into a mug of coffee. "But Summer's a wild card now. My money's on an upset victory."

"The drama never ends," Eliza laughed. "Maybe I should write an article, eggnog at dawn."

"Don't even joke about it," Mackenzie said darkly. "We're still reeling from the dairy-free incident of '09."

"I won't ask." Eliza nudged Brooke. "I'll go grab us some seats."

"I'll get the popcorn."

"So, I haven't seen you around," Poppy said to Brooke, as she filled a bowl with snacks. "How have you been?"

"Good," Brooke said slowly, wondering how much of what happened with Riley made it back to the gossip mill. "Busy. Things are hectic at the hotel."

"Summer said!" Poppy exclaimed. "She's baking around the clock, you have so many weddings."

"Or maybe I'm just telling her that, and eating all the cakes myself," Brooke cracked.

They all laughed, and then Mackenzie paused and gave her an appraising look. "You know, we should all get together, when you have a break. Girls' night, or something like that."

"I'm in," Poppy agreed.

"Sure," Brooke said, touched. "That sounds nice. If you're sure," she added, thinking of Riley again. She didn't want to make it weird, hanging out with his friends, but everyone had been so welcoming, she'd love to get to know them better.

"Positive." Mackenzie nodded. "Oh, look, I think they're starting the movie."

Everyone moved to take their seats, but no sooner had Brooke delivered her armful of snacks to Eliza than she realized her glasses were in the car. "Be right back," she whispered, and ducked out as the lights started to dim. She turned down the hallway—and almost smacked straight into someone just entering the room.

"Easy there."

Brooke sucked in a breath. She knew the strong arms holding her steady, even before she looked up into Riley's blue eyes.

"Brooke."

He said her name softly, and her mind went blank. Suddenly, her pulse was racing, and the few inches of space between them seemed at once too close—and not nearly close enough. In an instant, it all came flooding back. Every hot, reckless kiss.

Every blissful moment of pleasure.

"Riley, hi." Brooke reeled back. "Sorry, I was just . . ." She gestured vaguely, her brain still trying to catch up.

"No problem."

There was a pause, and she felt his gaze on her, burning through her defenses.

"How are you?" Riley asked slowly. "You look good."

"Thanks." Brooke gulped. "So do you."

He did. Riley was clean-shaven, and wearing a pale blue pullover that looked soft enough to touch, but there was something else about him too, some new energy crackling in the air around him.

"How are things with the bar?" she asked, still feeling tongue-tied.

"Fine." He shrugged. "You know it pretty much runs itself. I'm actually working on something else these days," he added, looking bashful. "Consulting for some tech start-ups, you know, kids just starting out."

"That's great!" Brooke exclaimed.

He nodded. "I like it, pointing them in the right direction, showing them the mistakes to avoid."

"Does this mean you finally figured everything out with your old business partner?" she asked.

"No." Riley gave her a rueful look. "But I decided I wasn't going to waste any more time on the past. Some things you just can't change."

Brooke's heart clenched. Did he mean them, too?

"I should . . ." She backed away.

"Right. I won't keep you." Riley looked into her eyes and gave a quiet smile. "It was good seeing you, Brooke. Take care."

"You too." She ducked back into the main hall and made her way blindly to sit beside Eliza. The opening scene was playing, but the movie was a blur to her, her heart still pounding with a reckless drum.

What just happened?

She knew it was inevitable that she'd see him again. In a community this small, she was surprised it hadn't been sooner. But nothing had prepared her for how it felt, up close and personal after all these weeks apart.

It was like no time had passed at all.

His smile still made her heart skip. His eyes still seemed to pierce beneath the surface. And she still craved to touch him, to fold herself into the strong and steady warmth of his embrace.

She sat through the movie in a daze, replaying every moment of their awkward encounter, searching for clues about how Riley really felt. He'd talked about leaving the past behind, but did he mean more than just his old business? Had he moved right along, the way Brooke was afraid of—to some other girl, another fling, replacing her as if she'd meant nothing at all?

She burned with jealousy just thinking about it, even though she knew she had no right. She was the one who pushed him away.

And there she was now, wanting nothing more than to pull him close again.

By the time the final credits rolled, and the lights came on, Brooke felt more confused than ever. She'd thought that time would give her clarity, and that somehow, if she just waited long enough, all her conflict would melt away, and she'd know for certain what she wanted. And it had been working. Every day, she felt more focused, more like herself again, the person she'd been before Archer made her second-guess everything.

But seeing Riley had thrown all that into chaos. She wanted him so badly, every cell in her body ached to turn back the clock. All her good intentions were clouded with memories of them together, and just how good it felt to be with him.

But it was too late. She'd made her choice, and it was done.

"Ready to go?" Eliza asked, shrugging on her coat.

Brooke swallowed back the regret and forced a smile. She wasn't ready, nowhere close, but sometimes, you just had to move on. "Sure, let's go."

Eliza dropped her off at the apartment, and Brooke

fumbled for her keys, but just as she reached to unlock the gate, it swung open of its own accord.

Brooke paused.

"Hello?" She pushed it wider. Her landlord was usually a stickler for security, but maybe she'd forgotten to shut it properly on her way out. Still, she kept her keys in her hand, sharp edges facing out, and took another few steps inside—

She stopped, amazed. The small courtyard had been transformed. Tiny lights were strung over her balcony, glittering between the shrubs and trees. Music was playing, and dozens of candles flickered on tabletops and in every corner. It was magical—and she had no idea what was going on.

"Is somebody there?" Brooke looked around, and then Riley stepped out of the shadows and she forgot how to breathe.

26

"*H*ey," Riley said, taking a cautious step closer.

"Hi," Brooke echoed, feeling dizzy. He stood there in a duffel coat and scarf, with that gorgeous smile, and she couldn't believe it.

What was happening right now?

"I've thought a lot about what you said," Riley started. He looked almost nervous, with his hands jammed in his pockets, and she itched to push his hair out of his eyes. "You were right. I didn't listen to you. You weren't ready for something serious, you told me over and over again, but I was so caught up in the way I felt, I didn't want to slow things down. I'm sorry. For what happened at the wedding, and . . . everything. I never meant to hurt you, or screw things up with your job."

Brooke had to reach out and steady herself. She couldn't believe what he was saying—or that he'd gone through this effort, transforming her little courtyard.

"And you were right about the other stuff, too," Riley

continued, with a rueful smile. "I didn't know what I wanted. I was stuck in limbo, I didn't want to let go of the past, or put myself out there again. It took me a while, but I finally realized I want more than that. I want new challenges, and to care about something again. And Brooke," he took a step closer, meeting her eyes with that gorgeous stare.

"I want you."

His words shivered there between them, full of promise.

"Not now," Riley added quickly. "I know, you're still figuring everything out, and that's OK. I'm not putting any pressure on you, or saying I expect anything to happen. I just want you to know, I'm in love with you. And I'll wait as long as it takes for you to be ready to take that chance again."

He stopped. "That's . . . all I wanted to say." Riley cleared his throat. "And that I want to be your friend. Just know you can call me, any time you like. To talk, or hang out, or . . ." He stopped. "Whatever you want from me."

Brooke was frozen in place. She felt like this was a dream, but no—her breath left a puff of steam in the chilly air, and her nose was running, and still, the electricity between them was brighter than anything she'd ever felt before.

Riley gave her a soft smile. "I won't keep you up," he said, and turned to go. "Sweet dreams."

She watched him walk towards the gate, and something inside her snapped.

She couldn't walk away from him again.

"Wait!" Brooke called after him, her heart pounding so hard it could have burst right out of her chest. She was on the edge of something here, and she could fall, hard, and hit the ground.

Or she could fly.

Riley paused, and slowly turned back to her.

"I don't want you to wait," Brooke said, looking at him. This man, God, this man. She'd met him at the worst possible time, and still, somehow he'd turned it into the best.

"I don't need more time, or to move on, or anything like that. It's you, Riley," she said, her voice cracking with emotion. "I'm falling in love with you too, and I don't want to wait anymore. There's never going to be a perfect moment, when I'm suddenly healed enough to do this again. But I think . . . I think any moment with you is going to be the right one."

She caught her breath, suddenly feeling naked and exposed. What if she'd gone too far? What if, after everything, he still wanted the chase?

Then Riley's expression changed, and that smile broke over his features, bright as the purest summer's day. He closed the distance between them in a few short strides and swept her into his arms, and his kiss told her everything she needed to know.

Hot and sweet, slow and impossibly tender. It was a kiss that promised a thousand days—and nights—to come.

Brooke surrendered to it willingly. She'd step off the edge, take the fall, because she knew with every instinct in her body, that he was the only man for her.

She'd trust her heart, because she trusted *him*.

Riley drew back, cradling her face in his hands. "You love me?" he repeated, grinning widely.

She smiled. "For my sins."

Riley laughed. "Oh, we can work on those . . ." His hands slid over her body, drawing her closer, but instead of a hot, fevered embrace, he just held her to him, like he was savoring every breath.

"I missed you," he murmured softly.

She melted into him, holding tightly. "I missed you too."

This was where she belonged, right here. And maybe it had taken her some tears and heartache to get there, but she'd made it. They both had.

And she couldn't wait to see what happened next.

27

"Where do you want the chair?" Riley called, hauling it through the door into Brooke's apartment. Or rather, *their* apartment. After all, as Brooke said, it didn't make sense for him to keep all his stuff above the bar when he spent most of his time over there anyway.

Brooke emerged from the bedroom, looking sweaty from hauling boxes—but still more beautiful than anyone he'd seen. It still took his breath away, waking up beside her in the morning, and knowing he got to be the one to fall back in bed with her at night. After the months apart, Riley would never take that for granted again.

"How about in the corner?" Brooke suggested, and he maneuvered it into place. "Perfect," she grinned. "Now where's the rest of it?"

"This is it."

She blinked. "You travel light."

"Not anymore," Riley grinned, tugging her into his arms. He dropped a kiss on her collarbone, hands roving lower. "I'm thinking about getting something very heavy and permanent. What would you think about a grand piano?"

She laughed. "Do you play?"

"I could learn." Riley kissed her, taking his time. He meant it, too: for the first time in a long while, he had no intention of leaving. His new clients out in California were begging him to relocate, but they would just have to live with Skype. This was his home now, right here, with Brooke.

"Ahem," a teasing voice came from the doorway. "Sorry, are we early?"

He looked around. It was Mackenzie, with a package in her arms, and behind her, he could see Cooper and Poppy on the landing. They were all decked out in Halloween costumes— ready for the big party in town later that evening.

"No, come on in!" Brooke skipped away, and went to usher them inside. "You're late, actually. Turns out, Riley doesn't have anything else left to unpack!"

"My favorite kind of moving party," Mackenzie grinned. "All that's left is helping with the housewarming celebration." She was dressed in a black catsuit, while Cooper and Poppy were in 1920s clothes, right down to their slicked-back hair and bootlegger shoes.

Riley got the glasses out and poured everyone a drink. Mackenzie had brought some of her new pottery as a gift, and they all admired the sailboat scene. "Is that . . . us on the boat?" Brooke peered at the tiny details. "Oh my God, it is. Look, she's got my blonde hair! I love it, thank you!"

"Any time." Mackenzie smiled. There was another knock, and Grayson and Summer arrived. Brooke went to welcome them inside, and Mackenzie gave Riley a thoughtful look.

"What?" he asked, grabbing some snacks.

"Nothing. Just, look at you," Mackenzie teased, munching

on a chip. "Putting down roots on dry land, a steady relationship . . . I'd hardly know you."

Riley laughed. "You're the one who saw it coming, remember? You said you'd be here with popcorn." He tossed a kernel at her and she caught it in her mouth.

"I did, didn't I? Damn, I'm good."

"Just wait, you'll be next."

"I don't think so." Mackenzie gave a wry smile, her painted whiskers crinkling. "I'm all set. The Spinster of Sweetbriar Cove," she quipped, but Riley wasn't convinced.

"You'll find someone. How could they resist you?"

"You're getting soft on me," Mackenzie teased. "All this coupling up, you're losing your edge."

"Ha," Riley snorted good-naturedly. "My edge is still razor-sharp, baby."

The others joined them, and Brooke raised her glass in a toast. "To moving on," she said, giving Riley a secret smile. "And moving in."

"I'll drink to that."

Riley looked around, and felt a satisfaction he'd never known before. Gliding over the water was fun enough, but putting down roots was something else. They would grow into something solid and beautiful, a life where he belonged—with the woman who'd shown him he was ready for the next chapter of his life.

After all, they had nothing but time.

The End.

The Sweetbriar Cove Series:
1. Meant to Be
2. All for You
3. The Only One (August 2017)
4. I'm Yours (November 2017)
5. Holiday Kisses (A Christmas Story) (Dec 2017)
6. No Ordinary Love (Feb 2018)

The Beachwood Bay Series:
1. Untouched
2. Unbroken
3. Untamed Hearts
4. Unafraid
5. Unwrapped
6. Unconditional
7. Unrequited
8. Uninhibited
9. Unstoppable
10. Unexpectedly Yours
11. Unwritten
12. Unmasked
13. Unforgettable

The Oak Harbor Series:
1. Heartbeats
2. Heartbreaker
3. Reckless Hearts

The Dirty Dancing Series

The Promise

ABOUT THE AUTHOR

Melody Grace grew up in a small town in the English country-side, and after spending her life reading, she decided it was time to write one for herself. She published her first book at twenty-two, and is now the New York Times bestselling author of the Beachwood Bay series, which has over three million downloads to date.

She lives in Los Angeles, writing books and screenplays full-time with the help of her two cats.

Connect with me online:

www.melodygracebooks.com

melody@melodygracebooks.com

Made in the USA
Middletown, DE
28 July 2020